She awoke next morning feeling much worse. Much worse. Thirst as she had never known it plagued her. She went into the bathroom and picked up a beaker. She filled it from the tap. She raised it to her lips and was confronted by a reflected face of horror. She could not swallow. Just that . . . Iron bands were upon her windpipe, tightening and strangling her to death. She swayed, the beaker splashed away. Her lungs were bursting as if she were trapped under water and the bathroom reeled about her in a whirling submarine dance of death . . . She saw in a vast and lucid close-up the corgi licking her face where John had struck her. She saw the glazed look in its eyes as it had tried to bite her. In that fatal cut and in that look she knew her death sentence was confirmed. She knew what she had always known. Asp had had rabies. Now she had it too . . .

David Anne

Day of the Mad Dogs

CORGI BOOKS
A DIVISION OF TRANSWORLD PUBLISHERS LTD

DAY OF THE MAD DOGS

A CORGI BOOK 0 552 10631 3
Originally published in Great Britain by W. H. Allen
& Co. Ltd.

PRINTING HISTORY
Corgi edition published 1978
Copyright © David Anne and Anthony Fowles, 1977

This book is set in Intertype Baskerville

Corgi Books are published by
Transworld Publishers Ltd,
Century House, 61–63 Uxbridge Road,
Ealing, London W5 5SA
Made and printed in Great Britain by
Cox & Wyman Ltd, London, Reading and Fakenham

AUTHOR'S ACKNOWLEDGEMENTS

I should like to express gratitude to Tim Fitzgeorge-Parker, from whom I received so much encouragement and help, even before a single word had been put to paper. I am also indebted to Alastair Fraser, M.V.O., Ph.D., M.R.C.V.S., Peter Batt, M.R.C.V.S., Roger Edmonds, M.D., and Jim Scudamore of the Ministry of Agriculture at Itchen Abbas for their invaluable technical advice.

'*For my Nici*'

Part One

CHAPTER ONE

George's death hung like a shadow over the whole holiday. Following their footsteps like a ghost that any moment they might see, |the memory of it stayed with them, projecting its ill luck on all they tried to do. A sense of waste, irreparably final, clung about. Everything was set on edge and turned sour.

On the long drive southwards down Route Nationale Sept, the BMW, impeccably behaved during its first six months throughout the length and breadth of the UK, blew its two rear tyres within less than an hour. Sweating and cursing in the late summer sun John changed the first, while local drivers blatted past with loud derisive bursts from their horns.

'They wouldn't do that to each other,' Paula said. 'The sods can see our number plate.'

John hissed agreement. The sweat was trickling down the side of his nose. His hands were ingrained with oily dirt. The left was smarting painfully from where he'd skinned his knuckles.

Unable to assist, his wife was lounging, slim and dark and elegant, against the dust-streaked off-side wing.

'Christ,' she said, 'what happened to all those trees we kept on passing? It's like an oven in the car and like a frying pan outside.'

She settled back more heavily, began to light a cigarette.

'Careful!' John snapped. 'You'll have it off the jack.'

'And serve it right! Cheap German junk!'

'You're joking,' John said feelingly. 'O.K. That should get us there!'

When the brand new spare went on them, he was lost for all such small-talk. Via the autoroute they limped on

3

to a garage. The humming and hawing that ensued, while in increasingly more broken French they urged the bored, uncaring men to go off down the road and fetch the replacement tyres, made it certain they would never reach their destination in one hop. They could thus have, as John remarked, the pleasure of paying for two domiciles in France that night – the rented villa they were heading for and the shabby 'routiers' pull-up just outside Dijon that, too fatigued to be fastidious, they settled for that evening. Even with the exchange rate of the falling pound to the French franc so punitive, the food was exceptionally good value for their money. But chatter from the drivers downstairs and the thunder of their comrades hurtling their juggernauts past outside gave John and Paula little sleep until the small hours. As for the brown and dusty room, the iron-framed bed – both, said Paula acidly, were vintage Jean Gabin. They put her right off sex. . . .

The Dennings reached their villa, just outside Cassis, late the next afternoon. It was too late to do anything about the gas that would not work. It took some seven phone calls and waiting in three-quarters of the following day before a man could find the time to fix it. Surliness became the keynote of all such person-to-person dealings. Towards the end of another long hot season, the French were at their blasé, take-it-or-leave-it worst. Waiters and barmen tried to overcharge and short-change John with a blatancy inspired by boredom. Their contempt seemed open for this English couple and for the first time in his life John began to take against the French. And against the sun, their ally.

Try as they might, the Dennings could never match their programme to the sun's. On days they went for drives, it blazed down through the windscreen beyond the power of any cold air fan to counter. On days they made for the beach at Cassis or Les Lecques the sun allowed itself to be effaced by towering columns of white cloud and the wind blew cold.

Despite his whole intention of cossetting Paula and seeing that her mind be taken off George's death, John found himself uptight and snapping at her. He went for her one day as she lit yet another cigarette.

'For goodness' sake!' he said. 'How many's that a day you're up to?'

'So what!' she snapped right back. 'You get them free. If it's bad for me, it's good for the company and what's good for them is good for you! Besides, I've got a stomach ache.'

'Something you've eaten?'

'Oh, don't be so obtuse.'

So he had apologised. John and Paula Denning were both thirty-six. They had been married for ten years but to their frequently voiced mutual regret were still childless. And likely now to be so always. That was why the accident to George had loomed so disproportionately large and the idea of a compensating holiday so immediately attractive.

Yet as the holiday wore on, John realised his good intentions had misfired. Paula was still brooding. And he, having mortgaged some of next year's holiday from the company on grounds of 'compassionate leave', knew at the back of his mind that he could ill afford this time away from his desk upon the eve of such a vital launch. God knew what Petersen would be attempting by way of ensuring that his absence was extended permanently.

Or ill afford the holiday! The second holiday. Yes, they were well enough off, quite comfortable, it was true. They didn't have that running financial sore of kids – damn it – but all the same... He was finding himself counting his cartridges now. Leaning upon his Diners Club and American Express cards whenever opportunity allowed. He might, you never knew, be able to get something fiddled back from HM Revenue. ... Ah, Scotland! He thought back with a keen nostalgia to the vast quantities of salmon and sea trout that he and Paula, Allan and Maggie Jamison, had landed from the running estuary. That was more like it! That was what holidays were all about, not this strenuous pretence that everything in the French garden was just lovely and you were having the time of your life. ...

5

The day they went to Aix-en-Provence the mocking ghost of what had happened played its most spiteful trick. John had known Aix one halcyon schoolboy summer twenty years before, and revelled in its gracious, royal air. But now the Cours Mirabeau, the Fontains des Quatre Dauphins were hemmed in by graceless high-rise blocks that took him straight back to Southampton. He did not want to spoil his former memories. After a token coffee at Les Deux Garcons he said to Paula that they might as well push off.

They nearly had to literally. The BMW had suddenly opted for vapour lock. It was as he tried to improvise some sort of plunger that he heard Paula shriek aloud. He raised his head. Around the corner of a little square, his owner just behind, strolled George. It wasn't, of course. It couldn't be. But this was George's twin and later he was to wonder if he'd ever seen two dogs such absolute dead ringers. For the moment, though, Paula was all his concern. He rushed around to her. She was weeping uncontrollably. Awkwardly, trying not to touch her Simpson blouse with greasy hands, he helped her from the car and held her. Passers-by stared at the sobbing woman in fiercely vague annoyance that no visible accident had occurred to entertain them.

'George . . . oh, George!' Paula moaned. She was weeping less now, beginning to dab at her reddened eyes.

'All my fault,' she sniffled. 'If I live forever I'll never forgive myself, I swear. Never.'

'You must,' John said. 'Hush. It wasn't "all your fault" as you know very well.'

In saying that he was gallantly lying. If George's death was not Paula's fault it was hard to see at whose door it could be laid. George had been John's gun dog and (to the detriment of his retrieving) Paula's besotted darling. One scorching July morning the labrador had found his water bowl bone-dry. Paula who was hurrying to finish off some weeding while the bed was still in shade had most untypically forgotten to replenish it. The phone, as she was later to explain, had rung. Paula had gone in to answer it and found herself the victim of an endless burst of terrified hysteria from Pamela Forsyth whose husband after fifteen years of marriage and three boys had just announced that he was leaving her for good. Paula had made the regulation noises. George meanwhile had wandered over to the flower bed and there found ample means to slake his thirst. Paula had left a cool inviting liquid in an open bucket: Paraquat.

The vet had predicted that the cream labrador would know a few more 'normal' days but Paula's own hysterics made only one course possible. He had done the cruellest yet kindest thing, and taking the beautiful and happy dog away had put him down the same evening. An immediate replacement might have been the answer for some people, but for John and Paula at that stage it was quite unthinkable. Hence the holiday. And hence, beyond the comprehension of the passers-by the cause of an attractive English-woman's tears on an overcast morning in Aix-en-Provence.

'Has my eye-shadow run?' she asked at last.

'Yes,' John said. 'But no matter. Here, I'll wipe it off.' He did and then he kissed her.

At last the car condescended to start. They drove almost in total silence back to Cassis.

'You O.K. now, my love?' John asked as they drew up outside the garish modern villa.

'Yes, thanks,' Paula said. She exhaled smoke. 'Sorry about back there.'

'Oh . . . Really was uncanny – the resemblance.'

'Yes. Look, you go on to the village and get the shopping. I'll nip in and put the kettle on. If the gas works today.'

'Sure?'

'Sure.'

'O.K. Back in ten minutes.'

Peppering the hydrangeas with a shower of gravel, John shot away. Paula let herself in and went straight to the kitchen. The tea-pot still had tea-bags in from breakfast. She opened the back door to empty them straight in the dustbin. Confronting her was total anarchy and fatal charm. Surrounded by the strewn contents of the bins a kind of dog sat regarding her with a droll dolefulness.

As well it might. If all dogs bear resemblance to their

owners, this one had strayed from Don Quixote's side. Its ribs stuck through its matted coat as the visible witness of seven years' bad luck. To anyone at all fond of animals, the effect was bordering on the horrific and Paula's indignant heart winced at the sight. And yet, even in this extremity, there was a lugubrious kind of muttish cheerfulness about the stray that took the edge off total nightmare. The sprawling frame in its emaciation was pure Disney. The square scaled-up terrier muzzle, the lank floppy spaniel ears enhanced the leaning towards comedy. The black and close-curled coat showed here and there pink patches of skin, and suggested Merino ram lay in its ancestry. Or would do, Paula thought, if only the poor beast had flesh upon those bones.

She went straight to the fridge and took out a plastic milk bottle and a cooked chicken. Crumbling some bread, she mixed it with a good part of the chicken in a bowl and topped it up with milk. She went to the back door. The dog had not so much as moved its tail. It still directed at her its limpid, unblinking stare. Paula put down the bowl. Quite slowly, without haste and also without fear the animal got up. It was quite large. With wobbly dignity it moved toward the bowl. It sniffed. Then, in moments, it had wolfed the lot. The eyes and a pathetically quivering tail pleaded for more. The promise, in return, was of lifelong friendship. Paula's heart, wincing no more, was won. In a short time the entire chicken, a half kilo of stewing steak, all of the bread and nearly a litre of milk were gone. And at last the animal seemed satisfied. It wagged its tail. It yawned. Still without fear, offering no threat, it ambled up to Paula as she sat upon the step. She felt her hand being licked in rough but formal thanks.

In that simple instant she felt a weight lift from her. It seemed a sign that she had been forgiven. Once more the tears ran down her face but this time they were tears of happiness. She stroked the dog, one benefactress to another. The feathery tail wagged back appreciation.

'Good bloody grief! What the hell is that!'

Quite out of mind while he was out of sight, the long overdue John had crept up on the new friends unheard.

8

'Who does he belong to?' he went on.

'He's not a he but a she,' Paula replied. 'Aren't you beautifuls? That's one. Second, she's just turned up. And third she's all woofly and adorable.'

'Adorable! She looks like a demented sheep that's been dragged backwards through a hedge!'

'Oh the wicked man! Don't you listen to him, then!'

John put some odds and ends on the kitchen table.

'Is he – she – quite safe? She looks half-starved.'

'Safe as houses. Gentle as a lamb. As to half-starved. Hardly.'

'Oh no!'

'I'm afraid if we're to eat tonight it's another touch of *chez-le-boucher*.'

'Oh Christ! What's the French for overdraft?'

As if on cue, in mitigation, the bitch again rose upon her spindly legs. She came to John. Snuffling softly she began to lick his hand. As flattery it was so gross and obvious John could only smile. Now recognising that he owed this walking wreck a vote of thanks for snapping Paula out of her pale mood of melancholy, he was patting the thin, elongated neck.

'Anyway,' Paula said, getting to her own feet, 'you took your time. Was she that good?'

'Ah yes,' said John, 'I'm glad you asked me that. You see, while you were indulging yourself with this *femme fatale* here, I was doing much the same.'

'John! You—'

'I kept thinking of Scotland these past few days so, to cut a long story sideways, I went out and hired this.'

From off the kitchen table John raised up the three disjointed lengths of a cheap fishing rod.

'Oh, John!'

'I know it's a joke in a village pond as dirty as the Med but I'm just dying to take this for a little spin. No pun intended. Come on. The beach will do you good. We'll hit the grocers for another big run on the pound on the way back.'

'What about her?'

9

'Forget her. She'll sheer straight back home the moment that we've gone.'

They got a few things and walked out to the car. As Paula swivelled herself into her seat she saw the bitch had mooched around to the front of the villa. John let out the clutch. Looking through the window Paula half expected to see a grey shape bounding hard upon their tail. But no such thing. Yawning, a lion couchant now, the bitch was settling down in the warm sun.

The beach and sea were fun. John, a fly fisherman of some finesse in Scottish streams and along the Hampshire chalk streams, met only with continuing ill-luck in these polluted, unfamiliar waters. Tiny crabs made off expertly with all his bait long before more worthy quarry could appear to show an interest. Spinning, which he next tried, had always been anathema to him.

'No connection with real fishing,' he disgruntedly protested. 'Nothing more than chucking a lump of bloody ironmongery into the water. Where's the skill in that?'

Paula laughed as he kept up his purposely exaggerated running commentary. Somehow ill-fortune was suddenly quite unimportant or irrelevant. They had each other and happiness had sneaked up on them just when they'd given up their hopes of finding it. Later, in seas of perfect temperature, they swam. With Paula all but naked in a lawn bikini, John had chance again to see the marvellous inward curving to her waist, the flatness of her lean and sinewed flanks. No surplus flesh bulged uglily around the narrow strip of her bikini pants. His thoughts as, having shopped again, they once more approached the villa were far from dwelling on stray dogs. But there she was. Forepaws still crossed, she hadn't budged an inch since their departure. Now, recognising the car, twice as large as life, three times as grotesque, the bitch was on her feet gambolling up to meet them. Tail swishing from side to side, she made the perfect picture of a family dog in minor ecstasy at seeing the return of its beloved owners.

'God, I'd forgotten our supreme champion,' John said as he braked.

'I hadn't,' Paula said. She reached down deep into her beach bag. From it she extracted two large cans.

'While you were in the baker's, I nipped over to that mini-market,' she confessed. '*Voila deux* tins of your food *de chien.*'

'*Chienne,*' John put in automatically. 'You didn't think to ask while you were there if anyone had lost this masterpiece of nature?'

Paula's answer came without a pause.

'Yes. I did. Actually. Apparently no one will own up to owning her.'

'And I'm not bloody surprised!'

Paula was out of the car by now. The subject of their chat was frisking and cavorting at her side.

'Looks like we're stuck with her,' Paula said.

Husband and wife exchanged a look a little less than loving.

Paula had purchased more than dog food. It was only later that evening after John had downed a good three-quarters of the richly bodied bottle of dark Hermitage that she ceased to hold her fire and circled back to what was soon a fully frontal attack.

'Oh look at her,' she said. 'She's quite divine.'

Well-fed a second time, their acquisition was stretched full length on a rug. She pricked her ears a moment, turned her head. Seeing all was well she relapsed into peaceful reverie.

'We absolutely have to keep her, darling,' Paula went on. 'Now don't say "no". In your heart you know as well as I do it's just what Fate has settled on for us.'

John had a moment's difficulty in framing his reply. It was somewhat understandable. Paula had slipped on to his lap. She had taken his right hand and guided it, without resistance, inside her blouse and over her left breast. John was aware, most feelingly, that some time in the evening she'd found a moment to discard her bra.

'Well, as to that,' he said at last, 'let's see what happens this next day or two. If she's still here then – well, we'll see about it.'

Paula kissed him at some length and depth. He began to wonder when he had last felt her nipple so erect. His hand moved to a lower button. This time her own was there forestalling him.

'She has to have a name,' Paula said. 'An English name. You're always good on names. What shall we call her?'

John snorted.

'Asp,' he said derisively.

'Asp?'

'All Spare Parts.'

'Oh! Not very regal, poor dear. Rather venomous in fact. Snakes in the grass and all that. What about Cleo? Short for Cleopatra of Cassis.'

'She may be made of an infinite variety but I never in my life saw anything that less looked like a Cleopatra. Asp or—'

'Or we can't keep her? So we can keep her! Oh John! I do love you.'

She kissed her husband like a lover.

'Well,' he finally was able to get out, 'if no-one comes.'

'I will,' she said. 'And you. I promise.'

This time her own hand sought the buttons. And shortly, as for the first time on that trip she let her husband have her, Paula fulfilled her own side of the bargain at extended length. Asp looked on with calm, unruffled equanimity.

No owner did turn up. For the next three days Asp was to the Dennings what her little lamb had been to Mary. She went everywhere with them – to the beach and shops, in the car, on to the foot of their bed at night. By that time familiarity had bred inevitability.

'O.K.,' John said, as they prepared to pack, 'you've won. We'll take her back. God knows, though, what your father will say if I show up with her in the shooting field. He'll probably have a fit. And I shall no doubt have one when I get the kennel bill from the old quarantine dooflip. For what that'll run up to, you could go out and buy a pedigree dog of champion class. You're sure you wouldn't rather—'

'Oh bugger the quarantine!' Paula said with sudden fierceness. 'We'll smuggle her back home. The Parkers did with theirs. And the Gregsons. Tons of people do.'

She saw John looking at her with a hardening, concerned expression.

'Oh, John,' she hurried on. 'I really don't see why a bunch of little jumped-up jacks-in-office should have the right to make those interfering regulations just to part people from their pets. It's all a racket, really. Look what it costs nowadays to go on holiday and leave a dog behind. I really think we—'

'Before you've talked me into a cell,' John said, 'let me just make one point. I know you can't resist a dog in distress. I know there's nothing you like more than lifting two stiff fingers to bureaucracy. All the same, England's quarantine regulations really make quite good sense. We happen to live on an island and we might as well enjoy the advantages. We have a moat. A barrier of water. Look at the foot and mouth and swine fever on the Continent.'

'Oh don't be such a bloody prig. Honestly – you get so pompous holding forth on topics that you know sod all about. Foot and mouth! What foot and mouth has Asp? Just look at her. She's absolutely healthy. She's gaining weight hand over fist. I haven't even found a single flea on her, the worst that you can say is that she's got a nasty scar or two – haven't you, my boofuls, but don't you worry then. Look, I swear she's taken in every last word we've said.'

That could almost have been true. From where she lay curled up on the bed's end, Asp's eyes were following the conversation like a spectator at a tennis match. John preferred though, to be unconvinced.

'She's a French dog,' he said. 'All she hears is noise.'

'We don't know that,' Paula guessed wildly. 'She could very well be English. Left behind or lost when—'

'Oh come on,' said John. 'Let's not lose all perspective. It's been a running item in the papers all this summer. We both know it. "Rabies Nears Channel".'

'Rabies! Oh, John, for Heaven's sake.'

'The authorities haven't been pussy-footing about. They've been doing Spaniards and Dutchmen and the like

13

three, four hundred smackers a time – just for bringing the old family pet in for a day or two.'

'That is exactly because of the papers and all their scaremongering. The magistrates have to put up some sort of a show. But it's only the odd token case. The one in a hundred. The ones who get caught – the idiots who have their poodle sitting up and begging to be noticed on the front seat of their car.'

'Paula—'

'And even then it is so bloody unfair. Everyone knows there is absolutely nothing wrong with the dog in the first place. They're family pets for Christ's sake. If you ask me, it's just a nasty way of trying to narrow our balance of payment gap.'

'Maybe it is the way things have been played up in the papers lately, but I wouldn't be surprised if, being English, it'd be jail we ended up with. Not just your swingeing fine.'

'If we get caught.'

'Or both. And God knows what in legal fees.'

'If we get caught. Not if we're part of the ninety-nine. The nine hundred and ninety-nine. Oh, darling, let me say one thing. We both know if we're absolutely honest that this trip started out quite dreadfully. And carried on like that. I know we both pretended to each other that we were having a good time but, really, we weren't. Everything was wrong. George . . . dying like that was depressing both of us. And then, well, all at once it changed. And why it changed and how it changed was Asp. Dear lovely Asp. It's just as if after punishing us – me – for George, Fate decided to take pity on us and give us both another, lovely chance. I know that all sounds soft and silly but, well, I can tell you feel a bit of all that too.'

'She's a big girl,' John said. 'Not like with the Parkers – dope it half dead with aspirin and smuggle it back in under a load of clobber in the back of a VW camper. I am not trying to bluff my way through the green check point with that stuffed in my boot.'

Paula smiled a tiny smile. From her husband's shift she knew that, as so often, she had won the day. She was again possessor of the field. She looked at John. He looked at her.

'You're thinking just what I'm thinking,' she said.

John's head came questioningly up.

'He said he would,' she said.

'That was just a joke,' he said. 'A giggle. And he was talking about booze.'

'So buy some booze and throw in [Asp as a last-minute afterthought. Go on – call him up and call his bluff.'

'You know damn well that's the sure way to have him come. The playboy in him wouldn't dare risk losing Peter his freebooter reputation.'

'Will you phone or will I?'

'I will,' John said with a quick stiffening of tone. The idea of his best friend being summoned to a rendezvous by his wife was just the sort of thing that, even after all the years and good times, brought out the doubting John Thomas in him. He went into the room next door. Paula continued smiling to herself. She turned again to Asp.

'See what trouble we'll go through for extra special lovable woofly dogs,' she said. She was forcing herself not to listen to John's muted mumbling at the distant telephone. A dashing Peter would come through. He had the best of reasons to, God alone knew.

John came back into the bedroom. Infuriatingly his face was absolutely straight.

'Well?' Paula asked. She suddenly knew how much this meant to her.

John nodded. Paula squealed her joy.

'Quite an audio adventure,' John said, 'but in the end, he said "Yes". I played it like you said – hinted at demon drink. He said he couldn't wait to see us. Claimed he's always thought of himself as an old rum-runner manqué. We'll toss in the Hound of the Baskervilles when his sea anchor's halfway up.'

He turned to Asp.

'No pun intended, old girl,' he said, 'but in for a penny, in for a pound.'

*   *   *   *   *

15

To keep the rendezvous they'd improvised with Peter at such short notice now meant that they had to do the long drive north in one fell swoop. Paula did not feel happy driving on the right. When finally they fetched up at a pleasantly informal small hotel, some twenty kilometres south of Calais, John was bushed and dead to the world. The never-stopping whooshing onrush of the road seemed trapped inside his skull. The idiot bravado of the ceaseless procession of French death-wishers had transferred from his rear-view mirror to his retina: permanently, it seemed. He flopped out on the bed too tired to eat. Had he not been so tired he might have made more of a tiny incident that took place that night. Later, looking back, he was to curse that Paula's adamant refusal to co-drive had served to dull his wits.

It was Paula who told him what had happened. Saying that she must do something for the commonweal that day, however small, and that she would either call for help or lie back and enjoy the French variety of rape, she went out about nightfall to take Asp for her necessary walk. Too tired to sleep immediately, John was attempting to paperback the road out of his system when she returned shortly afterwards.

'All right?' he asked. He tossed the book aside.

'Fine,' she said. 'She is settled downstairs like a lamb.'

'Nice of them to be so nice.' He yawned enormously.

'Yes. You know, if we pull this off – as we will – I reckon we'll have got ourselves a damned good guard dog there.'

'Oh?'

'She's been as good as gold all day – wouldn't have known we had her with us. But just around the corner here she suddenly became transformed.'

John felt he'd fetched his next yawn up from deep within his scrotum.

'Won't be a sec, love,' Paula said. 'Anyway. There was this wooden fence and hedge and running up and down inside it obviously another dog. And, well, transformed is positively the only word. Hackles up, teeth bared, eyes white and rolling, legs locked – I tell you with looks like that if any burglar comes to call, Asp won't need to bark.'

'That's her,' John said. He yawned again. 'Her look's worse than her bite. Come on now. I'm putting out the light regardless. Tomorrow's going to last all day.'

CHAPTER TWO

Tomorrow had to start if not exactly bright, then early. There was one hell of a lot to get through by midday. By means of great cups of black, delicious, bitter breakfast coffee John was slowly able to get himself downstairs, into the car and, with their whole kit and canine caboodle, down the road to Calais. The grey and charmless town was quite indifferent to the seven millionth ferry-seeking tourist of the season.

First thing was their cover. John found a wine-shop not actively unprepossessing and, miraculously, a parking slot immediately outside. He settled for a case of Armagnac, his favourite evening tipple, a case of Beychevelle 70 and, from the same good year, another case of Pouilly Fumé. Part of his inner mind groaned in concert with his wallet, he dared not use a record-leaving credit card, but, he rationalised, looked on long-term it really was a saving.

It was, though, an indulgence that promoted an almost crucial hiccough to their tactics for the day. John was now dangerously low on ready cash. When in the drab lower town they found a boat yard where they could hire a sailing dinghy, he realised that he'd utterly forgotten a large deposit would be obligatory. The thin and sallow and, it seemed, indifferent proprietor stood aloof from all persuasion – the pointing out the BMW would stay behind as sure security and to the offer of John's Rolex as a guarantee of their good faith. In the event it was only after nearly an hour's perspiring in the dawdling lines of the main square bank to which they'd had to retrace their steps that John, via his Barclay card and umpteen phone calls, had access to the wherewithal to appease the laconic renter's sour reluctance. Now, at last, he cut them out an unlovely, but excellently nondescript, boat. As he did so, John let slip that although English, they lived in their cottage down in Brittany. The man just shrugged and for the first time thinly smiled. He had his money. What they did now with dogs or heavy cardboard boxes was meaningless to him. As they pushed off from the slimy quay Paula, who'd borne the interminable messing about with impressive self-control, suggested that the boatman had seen it all a thousand times before.

'But what a face to launch a thousand ships!' John said. Paula stuck out her tongue.

'Shut up and steer,' she said.

Asp seemed as much at home at sea as anywhere on land. Her tail wagged in the freshening breeze. The good luck she had brought was still blowing their way. The sun broke through the thin cloud cover and as the sea flashed joyfully with a ceaseless change of dancing glints, it suddenly was gloriously warm.

'You know, my love,' Paula remarked, 'I haven't once gone topless all this trip. I think I just might do that now.'

'Over my dead body,' John growled back. 'Peter's binoculars are ex-Navy. They've got a gadget built in that can pick out a left nipple at three thousand yards.'

He did not add that on the phone Peter had laughingly suggested that Paula's bra, run up the mast, would be the perfect homing device for their little marine caper. There were times when Peter pushed his luck. Especially of late he presumed a lot – even on a friendship that went back to a shared study at their public school and a record unbroken stand for the third wicket against Lancing. And yet . . . who else had stuck so faithfully over the long years since? Who else had given them such spontaneous fun and good companionship? People said more openly these days that Peter Halliwell should start to think of settling down. But, given his independent means, his Midas touch with property, it was hard to blame the man for refusing to constrict his buccaneering life-style with the ball and chain of marriage. Not with such a stunning parade of long-legged girl-friends lining up and lying down for him. If novelty was the spice of sex, well – John choked off his own envy.

It was absolutely typical of Peter to have sprung on them the small surprise of a 'bon voyage' cocktail party on the eve of their leaving for France. It was absolutely bang in character that in the course of it he'd proposed that they ought to do this sort of thing more often – in two weeks' time, say, and he knew an absolutely super little place just down the road about three sea miles off the coast of Normandy. And they could underwrite the thing by stocking up on personally imported duty free. . . . No, Peter had charm in spades and never more than when, with a wink, he let you know he'd just been sailing close to the wind.

John adjusted the dinghy's course a point or two and scanned the quicksilver sea. The lovely day had brought one massive disadvantage. As far as the eye could see, a host of other little boats bobbed up and down on every quarter. Peter would never pick them out.

'Love,' he said, 'got your bikini with you?'

'In the bag. I thought you said—'

'Peter'll never find us in this traffic jam. We need a signal. Watch yourself but see if you can tie the bra high on that shroud.'

'Like this?'

'Fine.'

'Surely it's much too small.'

'Remember his binoculars. A disembodied bra will bring him down on us like honey would a bee.'

It worked like a charm. Within ten minutes Peter's suddenly enormous Halycon Mark III was cutting through the water hard at them. For an instant John's heart was in his mouth. Peter had surely lost control of the one-man yacht. But no. At the last moment, with a smiling insolence, Peter had brought *The Teal* about.

'Haven't forgotten all I taught you then,' he yelled. 'I've been on the watch for life-jackets. Nearly missed you, actually. I've grown more used to Paula's knickers dangling in the breeze.'

John, making fast dinghy to yacht, was stumped for a

quick enough reply. As he looked up from the cleat he saw Peter already helping Paula up and over to *The Teal*.

'Best man's privilege,' Peter said.

His standing little joke. The brown helping hand was now round Paula's back. John found it hard to keep a friendly smile upon his face. That Peter had been a model wit of a best man a whole decade ago hardly still gave him carte blanche kissing rights to such an over-sociable extent.

'Hey, you two sex fiends,' he called out, 'knock it off at once or I'll set my dog on you.'

Peter and Paula broke apart.

'Knock it off,' Peter began, 'is just exactly – Good God Almighty! What the hell is that?'

Asp was scrambling after her new mistress.

'My sentiments entirely,' John said as he helped the dog aboard. 'In fact my very words as I recall.'

'Love me, love my dog,' Paula said lightly. 'Hey, the service – the *drinks* service – on this cross-channel packet's quite disgraceful. I've been aboard at least two minutes and there's no sign of a Bloody Mary.'

'Two Bloody Marys coming right up,' Peter said. 'Or should I make that three?'

'Asp's on the wagon,' Paula said.

'Look's like he's just been under it. . . . Short for aspidistra, I presume – another misshapen form of ornament found – '

'Asp is a she and very sensitive to ill-informed abuse,' said Paula. 'She's been known to tear the throat from those who take her name in vain.'

'Well pardon me, you lovely ladies both. Bloody Paula and, as I shall henceforth look on her, Bloody Mary. Two of the latter coming up.'

Peter disappeared below. Paula turned to John.

'Let me do the talking as and when,' she said.

'When did I ever not?' John shrugged.

Peter returned bearing three brimming glasses.

'The king sits in Dunfermline toune, drinking the blud-reid wine,' he said. 'Cheers! Have you by the way got some of the old contraband plonk aboard that sink of iniquity there, or was that just a gag to inveigle a free drink out of me?'

'Well we have, actually,' John said. 'If you don't mind the risk.'

Peter grinned.

'Risk? What risk?' But now for a moment his voice lost all its banter. 'Gosh,' he said, 'it's good to see you two. Missed you even these few days.'

'Well, come and have dinner next Saturday,' Paula said. 'Make up for lost time. Bring whoever it is these days.'

'Pam,' said Peter. 'And you're on. We'll come. Absolutely gorgeous she is. Slim and almost virginal. Like you, my love. You nearly got to see her here and now but she cried off on the phone last night. Said she's a rotten sailor and all that but the truth is, I fear me, she's only afraid to be at sea with me. Thinks I regard her only as a private poking post and that I might run out of petrol. Absolutely right, of course.'

John and Paula exchanged a look.

'What's for lunch?' John asked. 'I'm starving.'

The Dennings had brought pâté, Camembert, French bread. Peter had slices of roast beef, cold potatoes, salad and some blessed English beer. It was suddenly a perfect sunlit afternoon. Easy and civilised, it was one of those times that seemed to require the imminent outbreak of a war to set it off to full advantage. In the warm sun the men were just that little fraction drunk. Biding her time Paula leaned back and looked at them.

It was incredible, she thought, to what extent in their two cases you could judge quite safely by appearances. Peter, tall and almost thin, had a firm hardness the long length of his body. His tight jet-black curly hair, his sharply boned face had just the swaggering panache you'd give to a film highwayman more interested in ladies' hearts than purses. John, by contrast, would be everyone's idea of the good friend. Average in height, in build, his brown neatly parted hair was still in the same style he'd had when, thirty years before, his mother had motored with him down to his prep school. The faded little photograph now might have

22

been the image of John's son. If ever child was father to the schoolboy man. . . . Ah well, she'd made her bed and, all things considered, it was comfortable enough.

She stretched and threw a strip of beef-fat to Asp.

'It's all so blissful and idyllic here,' she yawned, 'I just hate to break things up. But if we're going to make tracks we really should . . . make tracks. Are we going to do this thing?'

Peter got slowly to his feet.

'Sure,' he said. 'Or how else do I get my cut? And having come this far you're not going to tip it all in the briny, are you? Three boxes is it then, me boyos. Hark 'ee, Jim lad, seeing's we've got this slave-driver here as skipper best you and me make up a chain gang 'fore we feel the whip across our backs. Lord, though, I'm sleepy.'

John was too. Yesterday's drive, the morning's hassle, the beer, were all causing him to function in slow-motion as he climbed down to the dinghy and handed the boxes across. It was as he slowly clambered back he heard his wife begin to get her matter of great moment off her mind.

'Oh, Peter,' she was saying, 'one other little favour I might ask.'

'Name it, my pet.'

'Well, to simplify our lives no end tomorrow, could we stick you with Asp until we get back?'

But Peter now was straightening up and looking at her with a rapidly sobering grin.

'Aha!' he said, 'aha! So that's it, is it, then? And all this time I thought you loved me for myself alone. It's not me, it's my boat.'

'Oh, Peter,' Paula pouted.

'Look, love,' Peter said, 'get caught with a few bottles and underneath all the official fuss no-one really gives a damn. Get caught with a dog, there's hell to pay. And I do mean pay. Bottles of booze don't get it in their French heads to bark just at the wrong moment. Come to that, bottles of booze don't suddenly decide to come on heat and bring down half the hounds in Hampshire yapping around your heels.'

'Oh, Peter darling,' Paula laughed, 'Asp isn't French. She's as English as you or I. Look, I'll tell you exactly what happened.'

Her face had gone abruptly to full seriousness.

'You know how George died on us a few weeks ago?' she said in almost matter-of-fact tones.

'Yes,' Peter said.

'Well, about a fortnight later, Asp turned up on our back doorstep, right out of the blue. She was at death's door too, starving. Didn't I go through this when we had drinks at your place just before we left?'

'No,' Peter said. 'You didn't.'

'Well, of course, I had to take her in. It was like a sign. But by that time we were committed to this jaunt and being my usual selfish self I swarmed all over John and said we had to take her with us. I was afraid, you see, if we shot off and left her she'd . . . well, six months doesn't sound much if you say it quickly but suddenly it's staring all of us straight in the face. I mean, as far as Asp's concerned it's like five years or more in jail. The quarantine, I mean. And I know it's my fault but I really don't see why she should be punished because John and I fancied a quick holiday abroad. . . . So, I mean, Peter, obviously I can't—'

'Paula, they throw the book at you.'

'Yes, of course. Forgive me, Peter, it was unfair of me to ask.'

John had sat silent, amazed at Paula's effortlessly fluent range of acting. Lying. He was beginning to consider their past life in terms of such a hitherto hidden talent when, stunning him a second time in moments, she brought him hard back to the present. Paula was playing her trump card.

'Peter,' she said, 'how would it be if John brought back the car alone tomorrow, and I came on with you right now?'

Afterwards John was to reflect this was the first time in his adult memory that he'd seen Peter visibly embarrassed. At the time, though, he was desperately trying to mask – no, to decide — his own emotions. The great thing seemed to stay straight-faced while he made up his mind.

'Oh, come on, Paula, that's not really on,' Peter was saying.

'Why not?'

'Well . . . you . . . John. I mean you are, one, my best friend's wife and, two, putting it crudely a more than winsome little piece. And, well, this craft is not exactly a complete stranger to scenes of unbridled lust and passion unsanctified by—'

'Oh Peter, don't be such an idiot! Thank you, I'm flattered but you know damn well my idea isn't to give you a quick jump and a whip it in and out and wipe it off. What I had in mind was to come back potentially to carry any can. In that sense, yes, I'll hold your hand. If some nasty little mean official meets us I'll swear blind upon a stack of bibles we were on our way to see Asp put directly under lock and key. If all goes really rotten and he won't begin to wear it – well, as I say, it's down to me. And me alone, I warned you: love me, love my dog.'

'Well. . . .' Peter looked at John.

For John the moment was a time of total illogicality. A small part of his brain quietly assured him and with complete certainty that in her machinations his wife was being utterly two-faced. The beat-up animal stretched out there in the shade was no more than a pretext. Her whole desire was to end up alone with Peter Halliwell and thus to start – no, by God! thus to continue! – in this sparkling mood of champagne holiday the obvious affair with his so-called best friend which her tongue was hanging out for. Obvious was not the word! Only it was *too* obvious. If she were going to do a thing like this to him she wouldn't do it in this way. And how, in any case, to now say 'No!' How to say that without implying the worst and insulting one and all. To do so would appear somehow soft and crassly unsophisticated. By acting like a figure in a farce, so totally uncoolly, he would make himself farcical. Not that he liked it. Not at all! Only . . . it came to him the most important thing was at all costs to preserve his savoir-faire.

'Peter, old lad,' he heard himself saying, 'I've entrusted you with my Purdeys before now and greater love than that no man can have. You think I'm going to jib at the prospect of placing my mere wife in your safe-keeping for a day or so? My dear chap, what's the odd wife between old friends?'

John was still waving to them across the rapidly widening stretch of water. Side by side, Peter and Paula waved back. The dinghy was gathering speed now as it found a serviceable tack. Peter still stared at it, at John, but from the corner of his smiling mouth he spoke to Paula.

'Looks nonchalant enough, I'll give him that, but I'll bet you he's really having kittens. You little Machiavellian marvel you – however did you get him to fall for it?'

'Oh John! He'll fall over backwards not to seem middle-class. Which, of course, is just exactly what he is. He wouldn't dare open his mouth for fear of seeming stuffy. Don't worry. I can handle him.'

Her fingers slid along the rail to Peter's arm.

'Careful. Keep waving. Don't do anything you really want to do until he's well and truly out of sight.'

'Like what?'

'Like falling right over backwards to please me.'

Paula laughed softly. Now Peter pulled her to him. And now at last, luxuriously, they kissed. She let his hands move over her at will.

'Peter, you pure swine. It's been so long,' she finally had opportunity to say.

'And just a moment longer. Let me set her on automatic.'

When Peter came back up it was just as he had hoped. Paula had removed her last and every stitch. She lay stretched out upon the narrow deck a knowing and a willing sacrifice. Peter caught his breath. The whiteness of her skin about her firm high breasts, between her waist and thighs was gorgeously provocative.

'You might have left me just a bit to do myself,' he complained in a tone of mock frustration.

'I have. There is. So don't just stand there, do it,' she replied.

He looked about him. A massive tanker lay far off on the

horizon and there were now no small craft bobbing about. Quickly he undressed. In every sense he stood above her.

'When you were on about that bloody pooch,' he said, 'I should have said you'll have to go on your knees to me. How about now?'

Paula grinned wickedly.

'One good turn,' she said. She clasped his legs and pulled herself half up.

'Like this?' she said.

'Yes,' Peter said. 'Oh, yes. Oh, yes . . .'

After a while he took her head between his hands.

'Let's go below,' he whispered thickly.

'No,' Paula answered. 'Take me out here. Now. Quickly! Hurt me if you like!'

So, fiercely and awkwardly, the spray stinging at their straining flesh, he had her on the deck. Paula's nails clawed at him for those furious shuddering seconds that she'd sought.

'Oh God!' she gasped, 'Oh God!'

Then they lay still.

'Tell me one thing,' he said after a while. 'That dog back there – disgustingly oblivious to our little ways – is he, is she here really for her own sweet sake? Or was she merely one more pawn in your incredible plan to get me all alone and wreak your wicked will on me?'

Paula reflected. When she spoke she had achieved a rare moment of virtual honesty.

'Oh, about half and half,' she said. 'I do like dogs, you know.'

She fondled Peter where he most wanted to be fondled.

'All shapes and sizes,' she went on.

'In a while,' Peter said. 'Hold me like this for a little longer.'

Revelling in the unaccustomed hardness of his body against hers, she did. A small tattoo of triumph beat along her veins. This was a hardness she had dominated. The pain and hardness of the deck against her back had been a token of her power to dominate.

'Peter,' she said.

'Hmmm . . .'

'I don't begrudge you all your other women. Not all of them. I like you for the sex. But this last year it's not been half enough. I like you in me and I want to see you more. You get my point?'

'It all comes down to opportunity. I can hardly—'

'Balls! John's away enough and you're at home. Now don't get angry. Simply take the hint.'

'O.K. Point taken. Will be acted on. You know it's suddenly got awfully California.'

'California?'

'Cold and damp. Come on below. This time we'll do it long and soft and slow.'

He held his hand out to her. This time she rose without demur and followed meekly as if butter wouldn't melt.

It was some time after ten when *The Teal* nosed her familiar way back up the Hamble and Peter made her secure.

'You know,' Paula said, 'your yacht's a bit like me.'

'Oh?'

'There are times when you can make both of us fast.'

Proud of his day's prowess, Peter grinned.

'I'll get the car,' he said. 'You wait here with it.'

They were quite safe. There had been no customs nonsense. A yacht had gone off pottering about the Channel, made no landfall and come pottering back. The question of a yellow duster had never been raised. The Scimitar now backing up to near the mooring would merely take the skipper and his crew back to their virtuous couch.

Tail swishing rhythmically, Asp followed Paula the few paces to the car. Obedient as a lamb she hopped in through the tailgate.

'Purpose-built for dog thieves,' Peter said softly. 'One down, three to go.'

Under a clutch of clobber he got the booze aboard. He turned the key in the ignition and the green dials and instruments leapt to life. The engine purred away.

'You did say,' Peter said, 'that John would be away until late tomorrow afternoon?'

Paula leaned her head across on to his shoulder. Her hand stroked up and down his thigh.

'Sealink can be so slow,' she said. 'You know – all the customs and formalities. Much better to go privately and miss the crowd. Much better to have your own most personal chauffeur.'

Peter bent round and kissed her.

'Funny,' he said, 'I'm not the least bit tired. Can I stay the night?'

'I would have killed you if you hadn't!'

Peter made as if to bite her. He set the car in motion. From behind them in the dark Asp let out a yawn, Peter gestured at her with a quick flick of his head. He chuckled.

'Home free,' he said. 'Abbotsfield next stop.'

'Yes,' Paula said, and knew a moment of achievement.

CHAPTER THREE

John arrived home the next afternoon as promised. He had
not enjoyed his trip. Apart from Paula he had fallen instant
prey to constant, nagging worry. Of course they wouldn't
get away with it! They were sheer utter fools to try! Paula
would be caught red-handed. As he had warned her
there'd be hell to pay. The law, the courts, the press. Even
TV. It could affect his job. Then there was the Peter aspect
of the venture. He drove the last miles home in a sort of
fatigued daze. But as he slipped out from behind the car's
wheel to open the iron gates to his drive, such was his
pleasure at being home that even this was forgotten in a
fresh moment of pride at his ownership.

John and Paula's house was Queen Anne. Not large, it
effortlessly conveyed that classic sense of solid graciousness,
of quiet symmetry which was the hallmark of that period.
Now, its red, matured bricks warmly mellow in the late
day's sun, it faced the world with a secure serenity as if
aware it showed to maximum advantage. Such assurance
came, perhaps, from its sustained acquaintance with its
owners. It had remained the Dennings' only home in the
ten years of their marriage – John had bought it during
their engagement. His great-aunt had expressed a keen
desire to sell it within the family in an attempt (quite
successful as it was subsequently managed) to minimise
death duties. She had lived just long enough to thwart the
clutching talons of the Chancellor and her satisfaction at
this victory was matched by John's at having come upon so
magnificent a bargain. Set in about five acres on the village
outskirts, Gunn House boasted a small paddock besides its
lawn, together with formal and vegetable gardens. Best of
all, its eastern boundary was defined by a typically narrow

Hampshire stream. Here in perfect peace John could keep in his hand at casting whenever the mood struck him. Only occasionally could he be persuaded to admit it, but in his heart he liked to think of himself as an outcast from the eighteenth century.

Gently, now, he crunched the car over the gravel to the free-standing double garage. (Paula had a Renault for her local running-around.) He hooted his habitual signal and Paula was smiling at the kitchen door to bid him welcome back. She kissed him warmly.

'All go well?' she asked.

He nodded. She smiled and stepped aside and he walked into his home from which, just two hours before, in bedroom and in bathroom Paula had carefully removed all evidence of Peter Halliwell's protracted and, at intervals, athletic bed and board. John set his over-nighter down upon the kitchen floor. In the corner, curled up asleep in what had been until recently George's basket was the cause of nearly all his recent worry. So far, so good. He took a breath. Having maintained his outward composure up to now, John was now free to ask the question gnawing at his mind.

'What about your end?' he asked meaningfully.

Paula smiled. She winked.

'Like a charm,' she said. 'Easy as pie. So easy I've hal. forgotten all about it. And Asp has settled in just as if she'd lived here all her life. Ah, look at her. She's so at home, she's not even bothered to wake up for you.'

'Peter see you all right?'

'He's such a darling!' Paula double-bluffed. 'You can understand why he's got all those girls of his standing in line. He dropped me off right on the doorstep.'

'What time was that?'

'About half-past eleven.'

'I was laid out like lino by that time. . . . Oh, I think I did a clever thing on the way back.'

'Oh?'

'I bought some extra bottles on the ferry. More than my allowance. Then I declared them and paid duty. Went down the red lane. I paid by cheque. That way, you see, just in case there's any feedback over Asp we've perfect proof – excuse the pun – we came through customs on the way back in.'

'You don't think they'll have noticed I wasn't there. If you see what I mean?'

'No,' John shook his head. 'Among that lot? Shouldn't think so for a minute.'

'Well, you have been clever, then. Have another kiss.'

'What about the booze?'

'Still in the hall where Peter left it.'

'You gave him some?'

'Yes. Three of each. Wouldn't take more. . . . Actually, the sun's well over the yard-arm. Do you fancy a quick snort to celebrate our feat?'

'It happens my feet are killing me. I'm still half dead. What I could really do with now is a nice strong cup of good old English tea.'

'And you shall have it, you poor dear.'

'God, it'll be nice to sleep in our own bed again.'

That night John was far too tired to feel he could do Paula justice making love. Paula seemed tired as well. Holidays are often followed by a sense of anti-climax.

Days passed. Not altogether happily. John felt on his return to work as if he'd walked into a meat-grinder. During his absence, figures had come in from Baltimore utterly contradicting their earlier projections for production output in his sector over the next three years. At such drastically lower estimates there was no way they could competitively launch the new brand in the UK in a viable down-market bracket. Unless . . . with Petersen more of a hindrance than a help he slaved away with a calculator against data constantly shifting and revised. He brought reams of work home. It sprawled across the darkened yew of the dining-table where he liked to work.

One night it suddenly all seemed too much.

'God!' he said, 'this bloody government! If only they'd stand honourably by Rhodesia and put an end to all this sanction codswallop. I mean look at us! Chasing tobacco in Jamaica, Korea now, for God's sake, all over the bloody shop. Still not finding enough. And there's stacks of it piling up and simply going to rot in Salisbury. Tons upon tons. I mean I wouldn't mind but the simple truth is until Rhodes got up there and brought in the white technology and know-how the whole bloody area was quite unpopulated. It was only after that the blacks—'

'How many more times!' Paula snapped. Her own exasperation helped her intervene.

'You know as well as I do,' she went on, 'that if you've said it once you've said it forty thousand times. Launching a new cigarette – spend what you like on market research and promoting a new image, all that crap – is absolutely hit and miss.'

'Well, thank you very much. My life and work. Hit and miss,' John said.

'I'm only saying what you've always said.' And with that she got up and left the room.

Possibly because they had been thrown back upon themselves, she'd seemed on edge of late. John's work had kept them in and the oasis of the 'Thank you' dinner they had planned for Peter proved only a mirage. He had called up and begged off. Obviously got something, someone rather, literally better to do, John had thought with a curious mixture of envy and relief. Paula, he had noted with relief, had not batted an eyelid at the news and they had postponed the evening by one week. But, generally, she was moody now and quick to fly off any handle. She spent long evenings working in the garden, cooked and, on the two occasions since their homecoming, made love perfunctorily. She seemed to prefer Asp's company to his own.

And Asp had seemed to catch the bug from her. She was growing more and more restless as the days went by. Forsaking what was now her basket, she sought out all manner of odd nooks and crannies in the house to lie in. But no sooner, it seemed, had she settled in one spot than she would get up again and wander off in search of corners new.

'I think I can see just why her former owners gave Wandering Nell there the old heave-ho,' John said one evening.

'You've had it in for her right from the word go! Ever since you first laid eyes on her!'

Not tempting fate, John had wisely held his fire that time. He'd gone back to his sums.

It was not without some gratification that the following Saturday he saw even Paula's partisan indulgence sorely tried.

'That so-called bloody friend of yours has really got a nerve,' she'd said. 'At the eleventh hour this time! Two weeks in a bloody row that makes it that he's phoned up casual as anything and announced he's cancelling us. Time you saw less of him.'

'But we are.'

'You know what I mean!'

Not untypically, the Dennings faced the prospect of two consecutive Saturday nights without social diversion. Their mutual company and television's lenten weekend fare, yawned heavily before them. Stretched out upon their chesterfield John had already succumbed to the electronic aquarium's light relief – well, he argued, Southampton's key result will be through soon – when Asp came padding in, pushing her black luck to its limits. Paula yelled with rage and jolted her painstaking flower arrangement utterly awry. Dangling from Asp's muzzle were the remnants of her prized suede handbag. Even such parts still visible were chewed to glory and beyond. John moved at once. He seized Asp by the haunches and forced her to sit down. He crisply rapped out one of the two commands, they'd found she'd answer to.

'*Couche-toi!*'

Paula, meanwhile, had torn the tattered strips of leather from the wetly gripping jaws.

'Ruined!' she hissed. 'You bitch!'

Several times she lashed her pet about the head and muzzled with the leather. Asp turned her head and cowered but beyond choking harshly in her throat took her punishment in meek silence as a penitent.

'What the hell's the matter with her lately?' Paula said. She pushed the animal away.

'She's your dog.'

'Oh! Suddenly she's mine! I expect she's bored out of her bloody skull. I mean, you never take her for a walk, do you!'

'Do you?'

'When did you last—'

'Oh, come on! That's not it and you know it. If a dog gets bored it goes off down the road looking for any trouble it can find. This is something else.'

'Is she coming on heat, then?'

'No.'

'Well what the bloody hell is it?'

'I don't know. It's all this restlessness.'

' "I don't know!" The great country-lover! You expect me to take her to a vet!'

Husband and wife looked at each other. They left unspoken the main issue.

'She's even worse than you for being restless,' John could not resist. 'Look, there she goes. Off again—'

'I'll ignore that, John,' Paula said acidly. 'Now—'

'Ah, you *do* admit you've been restless.'

'Go and take her for a walk this minute and don't start thinking you can start on me!'

'I'm not starting on you. I'm worried about Asp. I'm also, as it happens, worried about you. You've not exactly—'

'Your trouble, John – you worry too much. Now piss off and leave me alone!'

John drew a breath. He moved to the French windows. Distantly he heard Southampton had lost 2–1. Christ, he thought, this isn't right. This is too cheap. He turned to make another and more reasoned effort.

'Look,' he said, 'I shouldn't have said that. I'm sorry.'

'Oh for fuck's sake stop saying "sorry" every other word! You'd be apologising for your own existence if I didn't stop you.'

Out of nowhere Peter's name was somehow on his lips. With a conscious effort he managed to bite it back in time. He turned towards the windows once again.

'You seem to think I should, in any case,' he found he had to say. He looked at Asp.

'Come on, then, girl,' he said. '*Viens, viens.*'

After some hesitation Asp got up and followed him.

It was a perfect evening of late summer. Golden light flooded the world with friendly warmth. As, born of habit, his steps instinctively led Asp toward the Dog and Fox and the village green, John felt the past tensions already softened by the air's peaceful dying fall. The heavily thatched Hampshire cottages, half-concealed by climbing tangles of rose-vines, honeysuckle, had the look of magic yesteryear. Their heavy eaves were ancient eyelids full of dreamy memories. There were hollyhocks, marigolds, forget-me-nots, in garden after garden. Miss Maitland's ginger tom, stretched at full length in a green window-box, slept blissfully, his furry belly to the low rays of the sun, his paw curled over his nose. He seemed to be awaiting the little girl in a Victorian smock and straw beribboned hat to lift the front door latch and, hoop in hand, tickle him awake. The village street was an old photograph and like all old photos touched with a still and pleasing sadness. John's anger as he approached the village green had faded to a wistful melancholy. When in the distance he caught a glimpsed flicker of white figures and it belatedly came to him there was cricket on, he so far forgot his self-pity as to believe once more God was an Englishman.

Circled by elms and leafy beeches just about to turn, the handful of low cottages staring upon a game they had watched going on for some two hundred years, the green looked quite outrageously the stuff of travel posters. The players, gently strolling through the old and loved familiar motions seemed to have more to do with history than the present. John felt a sudden, different pang. It was so . . . right. Some years ago he'd turned out for the local team quite frequently. He'd got among the runs with flair and style more times than not. But Paula – ah, well, probably she had a point . . . He whistled Asp, drinking from the old horse trough, toward the Dog and Fox bathed on the south side of the green by the sun. A drink was just what he could do with, too.

A scattering of spectators sat at the wooden benches fronting the pub half-watching the game, half-nattering between contented pulls upon their leisurely pints. John knew them all and smiled to right and left as he came near.

'Still got that Black Beauty of your'n, then, Mr Denning,' Bill Gadney called out. 'Ain't run off back where she come from.'

'Black Ugly's what you mean,' Ted Rimmer's always surprisingly smooth voice slid in. As if to emphasise his point, he bent and stroked both of his two inseparable terrier companions, Chop and Chip, who were crouched at his feet. John grinned and let the wisecrack go.

'Oh, she's here to stay now, don't you worry,' he called back. 'Two square meals a day. She knows when she's well off.'

'Still on the thin side, though,' Bill said.

That was true. Despite her prodigious appetite Asp still displayed a lean and hungry look.

'Just give me time and a second mortgage and I'll soon have the flesh back on her,' John replied. He went into the pub.

Its cool dimness was the perfect complement to the outside warmth. Its horse brass decorated beams, its huge brick, inglenook fireplace the perfect adjunct to the echoing green outside. Lord of his own free house Wilf Hopper with impeccably old-fashioned natural taste had adamantly refused all truck with vinyl, plastic, plaster and keg beer. Behind the bar, he greeted John.

'Evening, Mr Denning. Pint of best bitter?'

'Pint of best.'

He pulled the pint.

'Still got her then,' he said.

'Oh, yes. Permanent fixture.'

Florrie Beeston, Wilf's cheerfully fat barmaid, was almost as much a permanent fixture as the faded hunting prints above the cracked oak mantelpiece. She came in from the pub's rear bearing a heaped tray of sandwiches for the cricketers.

'Evening, Mr Denning,' she called out. 'Still got her then, I see.'

John and Wilf laughed.

'Here to stay,' John said. 'Think I'll just watch the last few overs.'

He wandered back outside into the sun, and gawkily Asp followed. John had, did she but know, a small problem in village diplomacy. As he resolved it in his mind he temporised by drinking deeply from his cellar-cooled pint. Normally he would have crossed to Bill and Ted and joined them like a shot. But they had gained a third while he had bought his beer. Maggie Peacock. That made John pause. Maggie and he, well, put it this way, they weren't each other's cup of tea. In any case there wasn't a spare seat around their table. He sat down on a bench against the white-washed wall.

They were an odd trio, actually, although often to be seen together. Bill Gadney was the simple one to comprehend. Almost literally so. He was the proverbial gentle giant. A farm labourer, his well-over-six-foot frame seemed in its strength to make nonsense of half the complicated labour-saving hardware forever seizing up on the surrounding farms. His work rate was prodigious. But just as legendary was his patient tenderness in putting an orphaned lamb to a new foster ewe or seeing a straining mare through a long complicated birth. He had a face like a potato and, in truth, a brain to match, but his simple faith – on Sundays his base approximation to a hymn would boom right through the Norman thickness of the tiny church – and innate goodness enabled him to talk to duke or tramp with complete unselfconsciousness.

Ted Rimmer very nearly was that tramp. Old beyond anybody's guess his background was equally uncertain. His habitual garb was tattered and torn pickings that would have shamed a self-respecting scarecrow. He always wore, come rain or shine, a stained and greasy moleskin waistcoat. And always a three-day growth of beard. John used to wonder with amused amazement how old Ted could always keep it exactly at that length. There were as many theories in the village about him as villagers. On the run from Broadmoor was one lurid version. Others maintained that stuffed inside the mattress in the corner of Mullen's barn which, between his disappearances from the locality for days and weeks on end, made up the nearest thing old Ted had to a fixed abode, were untold thousands in crisp fivers, in gold sovereigns, in – well your guess is as good as mine. More certainly, Ted cashed his pension at the village Post Office, dabbled in the odd barrow-load of scrap-iron and, when the mood took him, picked up beer money as pot-boy at this very pub. In that capacity, in tones more redolent of Winchester than Mummerset he could charm Guinness from a stray American tourist as easily as Moses drawing water from the rock. And, certainly, considerable culture, not to say gentility, lay in his background. Amid the clutter of ragged and tin-kettled junk he woke to every morning, his row of books were always as dust free as thumbed. Drunk, he would quote Shakespeare like a Lord. And once, out of the blue, he had casually remarked that any fool with half an eye could see that Epictetus was ten times the weight of Marcus bloody Aurelius. Quite at sea, John had stood him another round on the sheer strength of his own ignorance. Old Ted in quite the best of senses, was what you had to call a character.

But Maggie Peacock now, she was something else. She was the village school teacher and a socialist. There were two teachers. She and Mary Burns. They were both young, both thin and both had come hard on each other's heels from London when old Miss Ryan had retired. Mary was tall and gangling – 'She goes up for the corners' Wilf had once said to John – but Maggie was almost tiny. She invariably wore heavy amber-framed and thick-lensed spectacles that with her sharp features gave her the general look of a fierce-willed owl. The two girls lived together in Medlar Cottage and the most obvious inference had long since been drawn by all the village gossips. The story went that young Mike Lawrence (trying his off-spin from the far end now and coming in for quite a bit of stick) had been so green as to make a semi-serious pass at Maggie one fine night. He'd soon backed off, so it was said, his tail down between his legs. In giving him a piece of her sharp mind, she'd chewed him up and spat him out a dozen different ways. John had been on the receiving end of that quick tongue himself. At several council meetings open to the public they had clashed over the new housing estate on the village's north boundary. To John it promised nothing but a badly planned, jerry-built desecration of a classic tract of countryside. To Maggie, naturally, it was a totally accept-able egalitarian extension of the rights of normal people into the undeserved preserves of a mere privileged few. Who cared if a few coverts were bulldozed flat to make way for some decent and long overdue housing. Or, John answered, for indecent eyesores. But Maggie was a hard one to keep quiet. Against his general stand or principle she'd quote the chapter and the verse of umpteen statistics – unemploy-ment, cost of living, percentage of people owning property. They had at first agreed to disagree. A year ago he would have probably been standing her the pint of bitter she was nursing now. But at one meeting her increasingly personal attacks had gone over the top: something about 'a disregard of those not born with silver spoons complacent to the point of Fascism'. John had held his peace, but from then on they had tacitly agreed to maintain a distinct distance. Hence John's quiet refusal now to turn the somewhat off-beat trinity into a¹ foursome with his presence. He drank more beer. A pity, he reflected, Maggie Peacock didn't stick more firmly to her last. By all accounts the kids down at the village school adored her and were improving in their work in leaps and bounds.

For a while in a pleasantly disinterested and vague way he watched the cricket. The exact state of play meant less to him than its soothing overall effect, the odd specific detail of good play. Then, perhaps because his thoughts had run on school, he found them moving on to Paula, to their childless marriage. Well, it was not her fault that they had no little boy or girl to send along to school each morning. Perhaps the time had come to go much deeper into the whole question of adoption that they'd rather casually discussed a couple of short times and shelved. Paula's reliance on the substitute of dogs had arguably toppled over into the grotesque this time. And while when Asp had walked into their lives all had seemed momentarily right, since their return the new *ménage a trois* had speedily degenerated into a sour, back-biting mood of grating irritation. The pressure he was under at the office didn't help but, putting that to one side, his marriage had known far happier days. The grey and worrying facts of domestic life had all but recaptured his thoughts when an untoward outbreak of farce brought him sharply to the present.

A useful-looking visiting batsman had swept a badly flighted ball from off his pads straight towards the pub. He had not timed it altogether right and a fielder coming fast around the boundary looked to have it well cut off. But Asp had meanwhile shot out from by John's bench like a black arrow. The black arrow had the ball before the white cricketer and with this latest piece of leather wedged between tight jaws, Asp was off and running. Immediately it became the great dog-on-the-pitch joke. Asp bobbed and ducked and weaved past the fielder in a Mad Hatter's version of sheep herding. A dozen or so sheepish creatures all in white were trying to round up one ludicrous lassie of a dog. To no avail. Growling throatily with tones much less than playful, Asp halted, sidestepped or accelerated, untouched by human hand.

John had been on his feet and calling her at once. The countryman in him was mortified by this lapse from grace of his own animal but, embarrassed as he was, he still had the presence of mind not to resort to French. Then he was on the pitch chasing with all the rest. And equally in vain. Breathless he paused. The faces of the players told him that good humour had soon turned to a more ugly mood. He heard resentful mutters about leashes, running wild, having more sense. He was on the point of thinking he might risk French after all – who here would know? – when somebody was at his side. To his further chagrin he saw that it was Maggie Peacock. In her hands she held two soda siphons. She gave him one of them.

'Old Ted says let her get close then try giving her a dose with these,' she said.

John looked back at the pub. Old Ted, his own two dogs annoyingly as well behaved as statues at his feet, waved encouragement. John shrugged.

'What have you got to lose?' said Maggie and he knew, once and for all, he'd never really liked her from the first.

Asp had meanwhile halted. Her tail swished ominously. She suddenly seemed grotesquely like a miniature black fighting bull grown wise to all the tricks. A player charged her from behind. This time as she came bounding past, John squirted her full bore. It was a bull's eye; he caught her square amidships while Maggie's aim went home even more effectively because more intimately. Asp yelped, skedaddled sideways and there was the ball, wet and sticky on the grass. Mike Lawrence dubiously picked it up.

'Blimey!' he said. 'Look here!'

They gathered round. A half dozen dents, two long deep grooves were gouged into the ball's tough leather surface. Mike whistled. He handed the ball over to Joe Dunlop, Abbotsfield's venerable archbishop of an umpire mentioned, it had been alleged, in the Domesday Book.

'Crikey!' Joe said. 'Whatever you got for yourself there, Mr Denning, I wouldn't advise you try it at retrieving. Leastwise, not less you're after rhino. But what about this ball, then, lads? Anyone got another? Can't use this'n now.'

An outraged cry was all his answer. Their heads all turned as one. Close to one set of stumps Asp was about her rather liquid business. The incensed batsman's hurling of his bat abbreviated this watering of the wicket slightly, but a glistening puddle gave promise that quite soon the pitch would take considerable if somewhat odoriferous spin. Now, encompassed in guilt, Asp sought out John less like a black villainess than a lamb lost but newly found. Maggie Peacock laughed aloud but the other visiting batsman was definitely not amused.

'You may laugh, young lady,' he icily observed, 'but I

prefer to see this episode as a most unfortunate slur upon an old and noble game.'

Maggie just laughed the louder.

'A cur, you mean,' she said.

She was still snorting as, the players making tentative motions of resuming, she, John and Asp walked back together toward the Dog and Fox.

'Just what the hell is quite so funny!' John rapped out. Then abruptly he was laughing too.

'His face,' he said, 'his po-faced face! Look, thanks for your help. What'll you have to drink?'

'Thanks,' Maggie said, 'I'll have a half of bitter.'

'Ted? A Guinness?'

'Wouldn't say no.'

His face like crumpled wrapping paper old Ted was grinning from ear to ear. Bill Gadney's huge moon face was crimson and tear-stained from his great bursts of laughter.

'A pint,' he grinned in answer to John's look. 'And mind you pays for all the soda you used up!'

Which set him off again.

They sat and drank a pleasant further while. The cricket finished with an easy win for the disgruntled visitors but John was much more pleased to think he'd made things up with Maggie. Avoiding politics, they talked without a sense of strain and he decided that, in certain ways, she was quite nice. She'd be quite pretty really if only she would throw away those bins . . . now she was rising to her feet.

'Must be off,' she said. 'Mary's expecting me.'

Ah yes. There was always that as well.

'Me, too,' John said. 'Or Paula will be filing for divorce.' Now why had he said that?

'I'll walk back with you,' old Ted said. 'Come on Chip, come on Chop.' The two Jack Russells scrambled to their feet.

'You're not helping out here?' John said.

'Come back later when the rush is on. That's if I feel like it,' Ted replied. 'Must stay a free agent, me old lad. 'Bye Bill. You be good now.'

' 'Bye.'

Mullen's barn stood in the field next to the Dennings' paddock. When old Ted was in residence beneath that leaky roof he was the Dennings' nearest neighbour. They strolled that way talking of country things. Ted was a store of knowledge. John questioned him about the prospects for the shooting season, just how long the chickens could be expected to continue in full lay. . . .

Their dogs, after the obligatory opening exchange of sniffs, trotted haphazardly behind, in front, about them.

They were actually in front when, without more warning than a sudden snarling growl and a strange bark, Asp viciously launched herself at the two smaller dogs. Their normal nimbleness was no answer to the fury of this un-provoked attack. With her first bound Asp had slashed a gash deep in the neck of Chop, the older of the pair. Eyes ablaze she turned at once on Chip. Slightly forewarned the youngster got off lightly with only a small bite on the hind-quarters. Game, he started to go on the offensive but by that time both startled owners were hard upon the scene.

John grabbed Asp firmly by the tail.

'Sit! Sit, I say! What the hell's got into you? *Couche-toi!*'

With his other hand John had Asp by the scruff of the neck. Slowly he forced her hindquarters down into a sitting position. She resisted stiffly then visibly relaxed. As quickly as it had begun, it was all over. The two terriers, though keeping their distance, also calmed down as Ted ordered them to sit. John shook his head. He could see Ted was looking at him strangely.

'What can I say?' he said.

'Oh, don't try. Can't be helped. Just one of those things. Certainly no fault of yours,' Ted diplomatically said. 'All the same, it might pay you to keep that 'un of yours on a mite tighter rein.'

'I don't understand it. That comic opera with the cricket ball. Now this. She's never acted up like this before.'

'Well, you don't exactly know where she's come from.'

'Er, no. She might be coming into season, I suppose.'

'Never. She ain't ripe for lining yet. You ask me, she may be sickening.'

'You think so?'

Ted shrugged.

'Funny look about her eyes just then,' he said. 'Often a sure sign of something wrong. You could do worse than have a vet run the rule over her.'

'Yes, maybe I'll do that. Gosh, forgive me – how's Chop? Or is it Chip?'

'Chop. You can always tell the difference by the brown saddle on his back,' said Ted.

He was examining the gash on the dog's neck. It was quite deep but not bleeding to any great extent.

'He's all right. Had many a worse'n off a rat.'

'You're not just saying that?'

'God bless you no! How long have you known me? I'll call a spade a spade as soon as I've got cause.'

John smiled apologetically.

'Tell you what,' Ted said. 'You take that thing of yours on home and I'll wait here a moment or two longer. Just in case. Oh, and I'll bring your eggs round first chance I get.'

Relieved at Ted's lack of indignation John took him up on his suggestion. As he and Asp walked off Ted called out after them.

'Love to the missus! *A bientôt!*'

And John had half-checked his step before turning to wave back.

On his return home, he did not, in fact, pass on Ted's message. Paula was stuck fast before the box with what seemed to be a triple gin and tonic in her hand.

'I knew you wouldn't bring me anything back so I got started on my own,' she said.

She was watching ballroom dancing.

'Exciting, isn't it,' she said.

He didn't raise the matter of Asp's attack on Chop either. Paula had come close to calling him an old woman once that day and he wasn't spoiling for a replay of that fight.

'Anything to eat?' he asked.

'There's some salad stuff and cold meat in the fridge.'

He went into the kitchen and found Asp hiding under the table.

CHAPTER FOUR

John and Paula passed the following week in a state of cold
war, being self-consciously polite. Their gin and tonics
tended to grow larger, their adherence to the television the
more unblinking. Paula issued invitations to dinner, drinks –
less from affection for old friends than need for diversion.
On the Tuesday evening John was tempted to take down
his very passable collection of British Commonwealth
stamps but, when it came to it he lacked the heart. It
seemed pointless to be fiddling with a hobby while thoroughly important issues were unresolved. Work was hanging
fire in a nerve-wracking way. Now that he'd thrown his
detailed counter-proposals back to Baltimore's court, there
was little he could do but wait upon their verdict. Time
dragged and he tried to make it pass with several long liquid
lunches. Increased heaviness was the thick-headed upshot.
And worry. He was worried about Paula and their marriage
naturally, even though, no doubt, they were just going
through a passing phase. He was worried, also, about Asp.

Asp's condition had quite visibly deteriorated. She seemed
now perpetually ravenous, her appetite virtually insatiable.
No sooner had she bolted down her regular meals than she
would go off in search of something else. Anything remotely
chewable. They had to keep her from the living room; make
sure that shoes and sealing wax were kept well out of her
reach. Often scolded, the poor animal constantly slunk off
to mope in thick shrubbery but there could be no hiding
the fact that she was now in a state of very considerable
distress.

Paula was distressed as well. She could not bear the
thought or sight of pain. Since childhood it had always
driven her close to panic, making a whirling chaos of her

usually clear-cut mind. Now, far more than John, she had illness, pain's cousin, thrust upon her constantly. At home all day, she had Asp's dark shadow perpetually underneath her feet, scratching to be let out. It worried her half sick. Had the bitch been, well, conventionally acquired, she would have taken her to be examined by a vet a week ago. But, as John wryly pointed out, Mr Townsend was a stickler for going by the book: if he found out that something alien was afoot . . . God! she could kill him sometimes when he used that phrase! And Peter, damn his eyes, refused to call. There were times when as she went about her housework her belly would contract from raw desire for him. She would run her own hands over it and try to think . . . but still the phone stayed mute and she'd be damned first before telephoning him! When she did an automatic answering machine informed her she should leave a message and, as she cradled the receiver, Asp was looking up at her with eyes yellow and somehow sideways. She did her sort of best. She found a musty packet of 'Conditioning Powders' (Put Pep into Pet) and mixed a couple of sachets in with some of Asp's meat.

But now for better or for worse – for better probably after all that indiscriminate devouring – Asp went totally off her food. Meat, biscuits – she ignored them utterly. And water. Perhaps that was more serious. She would approach her bowl time after time, but, after guttural choking spasms that made Paula feel quite literally sick to hear, shy away again leaving the water level undisturbed. Paula found it best to leave the bowl outside, but as she did so she was thinking if this state of affairs continued over the weekend they'd simply have to take their chances with a vet. Then the phone rang. She rushed to it. It was Frank Drysdale saying that they'd love to drop in for a pre-lunch drink tomorrow. That was the Friday.

Saturdays at the Dennings saw a different start to the morning than to the mundane working week. John and Paula would enjoy the luxury of a longish lie-in. Then, instead of the cornflakes and perfunctory toast that marked Monday to Friday, John would come down and, as a sort

47

of gesture to gracious living, prepare a full-blown egg and bacon and all the trimmings breakfast. Then, off trays, they would eat it in bed. Sometimes, afterwards, they would make love but right now, he thought, descending the stairs, chance would be a fine thing. He paused to peer out of the landing window. The balance of the year had tilted in the week gone by. There was still sun but there had been a touch of early autumn frost on the lawn and garden. Gosh! he loved the autumn, the cycle of the seasons. ... He pushed open the kitchen door and was stopped dead in his tracks. He was rooted to the spot with shock.

The cheerful, utterly normal kitchen was a sickening disaster area and for a moment he had the insane thought that the garbage waste-disposal unit had gone somehow into reverse. Spewed morsels of chewed-over wood, plastic matting, lacerated wickerwork, pot-holders, flex and items pulped into a gooiness beyond all instant recognition lay piecemeal across the entire floor like so much vomit. Overturned chairs, splintered, gouged, were strewn at random on their backs, their sides, as if after a brawl in some unspeakably squalid bar. But no human agency, no mechanical device had perpetrated this revolting mess. Crouched in a corner, oblivious to John, was Asp. Her coat, matted in filth, stood starkly up about her like so many spikes. Her eyes stared straight into madness with a blazing malignancy. With first this paw, then that, she tried incessantly to wipe away the loathsome glutinous discharge dribbling from her mouth. In vain. It clung about her muzzle with an obscene stickiness beyond all normal slaver. Not from fright alone but on account of something far more perversely subtle, John shuddered. Obscene seemed just the word. That so everyday and ordinary a room as this should have had its orderly brightness befouled and poisoned by such a vile unwholesomeness made his own skin feel dirty. He let the door swing to again. And, in the few instants that its solid four-squareness, travelling back across his vision effaced the nauseating scene beyond, he knew with utter clarity what he must do at once.

He found he was extraordinarily calm. Still in his slippers

and dressing-gown, he walked into the study. He stood before the glass-fronted cabinet and, dismissing his obscure reflection, opened it. He took down his gun. He took two cartridges out from the drawer. He loaded the gun. He did all this mechanically. All the time in a most curiously detached way his thoughts ran upon Paula. The situation was quite simple. It was all her fault. But he was the one to blame. He should have stood up firmly to her and not been so spineless. As simple as that. But now Asp would die and God knew what other. . . . He closed the gun thoughtfully, and walked back to the kitchen.

Outside the door he paused. He could hear a dragging noise of movement inside. Commonsense became the better part of foolhardiness. He turned, making for the French windows.

'John,' Paula shouted from upstairs, 'breakfast be long?'

He ignored that. He walked steadily around the outside of the house and peered in through the kitchen window. Asp had knocked over one of the bar stools and was gnawing madly at the metal legs. For a moment she looked up and John flinched with fresh horror. Her eyes still blazed as if focused on far distant suns and through the gluey, viscid whiteness all about the mouth, John could see the gums were red with running blood and he heard her odd moaning bark.

In recoiling, he had scrunched the gravel underfoot. That, perhaps, was why Asp had raised her head. Perhaps she saw in some dim recess of her consciousness a moving shape between her and the light, a thing, perhaps, responsible for all the torment of her feverish, wracked body. She rose and freezing in a stark and rigid pose of mindless hate bared at John the ground down stumps that had been fangs. John stared into a mouth from Hell. He did not dare try opening the window. Taking as steady aim as his unusually shaky arms and legs would let him, he fired. An ounce and a quarter of heavy lead shot blasted its way through skin and bone and into brain. A single shot sufficed. Without twitching Asp was quite dead. She lay the diseased centrepiece to all the shambles of the room.

John had scarcely heard the sound of the explosion at his

ear. Now a door slamming distantly upstairs jerked him back from the fixed, fascinated contemplation of the gruesome still-life he had just composed into the present. His flapping slippers trying to delay him, he rushed back into the house. He was just in time to bar Paula's entering the kitchen. Their eyes locked and he knew that she had already half-guessed what he had done.

'What the hell was that shot?' she said.

'Me,' he said.

'Christ!'

'I've just killed Asp,' he said.

'What!'

'I've just killed Asp.'

Without warning she struck him with full force about the face. He staggered back a good half pace and found he lacked all idea of how he wanted to react. Small mechanics came to his assistance. He remembered to unload the second cartridge. He put it in the pocket of his dressing gown. Paula was staring at him with distended eyes. Her breath was hissing sharply through her open mouth.

'I did it for your sake,' he said at last. 'And hers. Asp had rabies.'

It seemed impossible that Paula's eyes could open wider and yet they did. Then she began to weep uncontrollably. John moved toward her but she backed away.

'You murdering fucking bastard!' she panted out. 'You could have called a vet!'

'No I couldn't and you know it. I had to—'

But she had launched herself on him again kicking and pounding with a weeping fury. He tried to catch her wrists but she had the strength of the possessed. Pushing her off he lashed her once across the cheek. It was a milestone. He had never raised his hand to her before. Perhaps it was the shock of unexpectedness rather than sheer force that made the blow effective. Paula's hysterics stopped at once. She froze, then drooped. The fight went out of her. Then her head came up. Her resolution had returned. She made another move towards the door into the kitchen. John went to check her once again – and then held off.

'Perhaps you ought to know,' he said. And stood aside.

Paula opened the door. She stood upon its threshold. She said no words but a low, groaning, guttural moan came from deep within her. She closed the door, brushed back past John.

'It is incurable,' he said.

He heard her going upstairs and then the locking of the bathroom door.

He went back to the study and replaced his gun. He went upstairs himself. As he passed the bathroom he heard Paula being sick. He almost called out to her but if she'd locked the door . . . he went into his little dressing room and searched out his oldest gardening clothes. He had a full morning on his hands.

He went first to the garage. He had two sacks there that he used when working underneath the cars. He folded them and returned to the kitchen. Trying for as long as possible not to look at Asp's body, he went to the sink and put on the rubber gloves that Paula used for washing up. Now there was nothing for it. He turned and faced the corpse. It would be too big to fit into a sack. He spread one out flat alongside it. He stooped, gritted his teeth. Even through the rubber it felt shudderingly like handling a victim of bubonic plague but, grunting, he had heaved the body squarely across on the sack. He shrouded it with the second. Then, dragging the unholy sandwich after him he backed towards the door. A streak of greying slime trailed behind him.

He paused, straightened, looked outside. The postman would have been. The milkman didn't arrive until mid-morning. It should be all right. In any case, he hardly had a choice. The body bounced down the back step with a sudden and malevolent vitality. The top sack became all askew. At that moment a cock pheasant's hard crow screeched derisively from somewhere and, his heart pounding, he started up looking to right and left convinced that he was being watched. No-one was in sight. He bent to cover up the exposed corpse and as he did so heard the clink of milk bottles. His blood ran cold. Another, louder clink confirmed the worst.

Christ! Saturday! Reg Bates began his milk round early because it was the day he took the money. He always came to the back door. John pulled feverishly at the rubber gloves. Christ! They would not come off. He was all fingers and thumbs. At last! Stuffing the gloves in his hip pocket – oh Christ, his money was all upstairs in his other trousers! – he moved toward the corner of the house just as, bottles in hand, Reg Bates came around it.

'Good Lord!' he said with a naturalness that later as much disgusted as it now amazed him, 'you made me jump.'

'Morning, Mr Denning,' Reg replied. 'Sorry about that. Whistle I will next time. The gold tops, then?'

With false casualness John stretched out his hands. He was trying to stand square on to block Reg's view through to the kitchen steps. It suddenly came clear into his mind that when he'd covered Asp's gaunt body for the second time, the ragged tail had been left limply sticking out. He went to turn his head, then realised that at all costs he mustn't. Despite the morning's chill, he felt the sweat begin to break out down his ribs. And, in the same instant, he saw the broken kitchen window was no more than a foot from Reg's left ear. Inside was all the mess.

'Setting us a bad example,' Reg was saying.

'Sorry Reg. Not quite with you.'

'Out gardening so early.'

'Oh! Yes! Well, I've let things go a bit.' Theatrically he slapped his pockets. 'Er, be all right if we settle up next week? I think Paula's in the bath and I don't really want to traipse upstairs.'

God! The man must notice! The tail was a dead give-away.

'. . . no problem at all,' Reg was saying. Looking at his beaming, be-spectacled fat face, John realised for the first time how absolutely ugly Reg really was. He realised too that he must hold the piggy eyes fixed on his own.

'You're not so slow at getting started in the morning yourself,' he heard himself remarking.

'Good Lord, I'm more'n half done the time I get to you,' Reg said. 'Delivering's the easy part. It's loading up at crack of dawn, that's the real bugger. Specially in winter. And checking all me lists.'

'Oh, know what I wanted to ask you,' John said. 'Excuse me interrupting but I've got this kind of red spore on a bit of my wisteria. I was wondering if you'd know what to make of it. Blowed if I can.'

A look of expertise crossed the milkman's face. Gardening was his consuming passion. John, having steered the conversation back to it, took a short step to try to steer those beady eyes round in an arc that would not take in the window and what lay beyond. He was successful. Reg turned and in five paces they had turned the corner.

When John returned five minutes later – the spore had most mysteriously vanished, could have been dust from them old bricks, Reg said – he saw at the first glance his fearful memory had deceived him. No tail protruded into view from underneath the sacks. To a quick glance they could well have been laid just where they were, to stop mud being tracked in. He drew a deep breath. His legs seemed to be twitching of their own volition and the sweat was pouring out of him with relief, but he dared not take more time to let his pulse return to normal. He opened one door to the garage. Grabbing the sacks he dragged them inside without further incident or interruption. It had been so long since he had made use of it he had to think where he had left the padlock but, finally, he had the body under lock and key. He was, of course, behaving like a criminal but . . . well, whatever he decided, the kitchen had to be cleared up.

This time he took a large black dustbin liner. Using an untold number of paper towels, a dustpan as a scraper, his own gloved fingers, he managed to remove the solid and the semi-solid debris that was both the product and the evidence of Asp's last manic agony. He tidied up the glass. A sudden storm of rain raged at him angrily as he carried the half-full bag the long length of his garden. Ignoring it, he stopped *en route* at the garden shed, to collect an axe and a can of paraffin. As suddenly as it had started the shower had stopped when, three trips later, he deposited the last of the kitchen furniture alongside the rusty, perforated water tank that served as his incinerator. Finding release for much of the sick tension pent up in him, he smashed into the furniture. The axe reduced it to fragments and in minutes he was dousing them and the plastic bag with the can's contents. He dropped a lighted match and with a rebuking roar the paraffin flared up.

Its ferocity took him by surprise. He had rather over-compensated for the rain. Flames crackled and grey smoke ascended upward at a considerable pace. Well, it would be over the sooner. There was no danger from sparks. He went back to the house.

He was on his hands and knees washing and wiping down the kitchen with a strong solution of disinfectant when the door opened sharply behind him and Paula came in.

'John,' she said with biting alarm, 'you're not being such a fool as to try and burn . . . it, are you?'

'In the garage,' he said tersely. She had dressed. He felt a hard bolus of positive hatred for her forming. You might say she was back to her old self. He went on wiping steadily. They'd had rows before. Things would be better in the long run if he could keep his composure now.

'Well if you'd just deign to look out of the window – or what's left of it – you'd see you're letting half the county know that something is up. It's Saturday morning for Christ's sake. You know what they've said about garden bonfires.'

Standing, he looked out. She had a point. A column of black, oily smoke rose up in an uncannily tell-tale column. If you were superstitious you might have said it was a sign. It was probably that bloody bag.

'I'll see if I can do something,' he said.

'Do,' said Paula. Yes, she had recovered.

He was halfway down the garden path again when a familiar voice arrested him.

'Polluting the neighbourhood and environs thereto pertaining?' it said.

He turned. Grinning at him over the rough hedge that

separated the garden from the bridle path to Mullen's field was Ted Rimmer.

'Not sure what that is,' John said. 'Think an old car mat may have got in by mistake.'

'Like the old one about the Indians having a row with smoke signals: wish I'd said that.'

John's answering laugh was far too hearty. He could hear Chop and Chip scampering about the far side of the hedge as if the scurrying autumn leaves had already fallen to tease them.

'Heel, sir, heel!' Ted snapped at one of them. 'Behave yourself. That's better.'

He turned again to John, nodded at the smoke.

'Want a hand?' he asked.

'No,' John said as casually as he could manage. 'Be over soon.'

Ted shrugged. 'I was just bringing you the eggs,' he said.

'Oh, thanks.'

John took the container that held six of Ted's free-range eggs from the old man's mittened, bandaged hand.

'I don't have any change on me,' he said. 'Can I—'

'Oh that's all right. You'll be along to the pub before the day's out I shouldn't wonder.'

'Er, yes. I expect so.'

'Just come from hospital then?'

'Sorry?'

'By the pong on you.'

'Oh. Doing the loo.'

'Well, that's one less problem you've got now.'

Ted was gesturing in the direction of the incinerator. As if with malice aforethought, attention having been drawn to it, the smoke had almost stopped.

'Vanished into thin air, you might say,' John tried.

'You might,' old Ted said testily. Then he winked his face into its thousand criss-cross wrinkles. 'Then again you might not. *Auf wiedersehen*. Here Chop, here Chip – now, you stop that, boy!'

And he was gone at last. John walked back into the house. How many times was that this morning? Paula had not completed cleaning the kitchen for him in his absence so he finished what little needed to be done. He went upstairs and, after a very hot and thorough shower, he changed. All the while he was trying to direct his facing, whirling thoughts back on the straight line that led towards the inevitable Either–Or decision. Yes, all morning he'd been acting like a criminal. The criminal he technically – no, actually, damn it, was. When he came downstairs again he was none the wiser. In any case he had to talk to Paula.

He found her in the drawing-room. Although it was only just turned eleven she already had a king-size gin and tonic on the occasional table to her right hand. Yes, if not relaxed, she seemed to be her reasonably composed self again. And, he suddenly realised all anew, utterly lovely. The edge of tension in her had brought out the thoroughbred. He tried entering on a light note.

'No breakfast?' he said.

She shrugged. Everyone was doing that this morning.

'Bit late in the day now,' she said. She took a stiff pull on her drink. 'Well,' she went on, 'having seen the desert you've made of our kitchen I might say you've rather overdone the melodrama, but I'm glad to see you're acting in the only sensible way.'

'What melodrama? What sensible way?'

'Destroying the evidence.'

'I haven't destroyed Asp yet. Not in that sense. I'm thinking about that.'

Her head came round. Her eyes were steadier than his hands had been when levelling his gun at Asp.

'Meaning just what exactly?' she asked.

'I put Asp in the garage for one or two reasons,' he said. 'Possibly as a preliminary to telephoning the authorities to come and collect him. Possibly because it's much too difficult a job to risk burying her by daylight when anyone might wander by.'

'Two solutions,' Paula said, 'which may be regarded as final.' Her eyes had not deviated a millimetre from his. 'For her – obviously. But just as certainly if you call in some busybody in a white coat the end for us. I mean, if you do

56

that, it is goodbye to all this.' She gestured comprehensively with her glass. 'Goodbye to the house, the cars, the booze. Goodbye to fishing for sea trout. Good—'

'Oh, for Christ's sake!'

'And hello prison. Oh, and goodbye position as rising marketing manager and super-star executive. Or hadn't you thought of that, my pet?'

'Of course I have! God knows how many times and God knows from how many angles I've been thinking just those very thoughts all morning.'

He forced himself to lower his voice, to speak more slowly.

'And I enjoy these things,' he said. 'I'm not a saint hell-bent on martyrdom. I – well, let's not rush our fences. Let's start at square one.'

He moved towards the set of *Britannica* Rupert, his father-in-law, had passed on to them with some flimsy excuse to cover his generosity.

'I've already looked,' his wife said. 'All warm-blooded animals are susceptible.'

'Then you admit it!' he cried out. 'Asp had rabies. Then we don't have any choice.'

'I admit no such thing! There could be a dozen other explanations why she . . . she died.'

'Name two.'

'Epilepsy. Swallowing some pesticide. She was gobbling absolutely—'

'Like George? Lightning doesn't—'

'That's not fair!'

'Paula! You saw what it was like in there! I saw her while she was still alive. If you care to call it that. I had to kill her! Yes? She—'

'Perhaps your propensity for shooting things made you quicker on the trigger than you need have been. Perhaps if you'd waited, she would have recovered.'

'Paula! You saw her. You were throwing up. She looked like something out of hell. That wasn't Asp. That was a demented animal. If you seriously doubt me, go out now into the garage and take a hard look at her.'

'I don't concede that she had rabies.'

'Paula!'

'And since we don't know that she did have it – and since there's no way we can find out for sure, safely that is – I'm certainly not going to see us sacrifice our life-style, everything we've worked for these past years, just because you've a perpetual tendency for looking on the dark side and always fearing the worst.'

John looked at his wife. He weighed his words, delivered them in a scrupulously neutral tone.

'There's something you don't know,' he said. 'Last week Asp got in a fight with Chop and Chip. Ted Rimmer's dogs. She got her teeth in both of them. Drew blood. If she had rabies—'

'I keep on telling you! I don't admit that she had rabies! Everyone knows what terriers are like. I bet they went for her.'

He realised her face was set against all further offering of fact or persuasion. Yet he was honour-bound to try.

'Look,' he said. 'Frankly, I'm terrified – yes, terrified – of what could happen to us now. You ask me have I thought about it. I think I should be asking you. I honestly don't think you've begun to imagine the implications of what you've done.'

'Imagination has got absolutely nothing—'

'*Realise* what you've done then!'

'And now it's what *I've* done is it?'

'Yes. Yes it is. It was your idea to smuggle Asp to England. I tried my level best to talk you out of it and so, to give him his due, did Peter.'

'Best! Some best! We're all in this together and the sooner you get that into your holier-than-thou milk-and-water head the sooner you'll see reason!'

For a brief moment John thought that he might go for her with his hands a second time that morning. He made himself walk around the room. Inconsequentially he saw that she had put the volume of the *Britannica* she had consulted back in the wrong place. That was most unlike her. . . . It came to him that perhaps it was total panic that

drove her to this hateful, unyielding, hard-as-nails per-
formance.

'Yes,' he said at last, 'of course. Of course I'm just as
guilty as you. Perhaps more so. I meekly went along with
you on it – in my milk-and-water way – even when I could
see much more clearly that what we were doing was
thoughtless and illegal. And that's really my crime, isn't it?
As so often, I was guilty of being weak and not standing up
to you. For just one reason. Because, as you so diabolically
know, I love you.'

And now to his amazement Paula was laughing. She was
laughing loud and raucously.

'Love? Love? Don't make me laugh, John! You don't
know the meaning of the word! Face it! You're so inadequate I can't even screw a kid out of you.'

'God! What a bitch you are! What the hell has that
got—'

He made a final effort and bit his last words back. She
was not herself. However crucifyingly hurtful that had been,
hysteria was rising in her once again. He had heard it
crackling on the edge of speech, behind her strident
laughter. And yet – in anger people spoke the truth. An
enormous fatigue washed through him. He had been
stretched to utter limits all morning, it seemed, and now he
felt devoid of anything but tiredness. He turned away and
moved to stare out of the window but, before he did so,
Paula had seen the colour drain from his face to leave it
greyer than she could have believed possible. He was
standing without any movement. His mind obviously a
million miles away from the familiar view, absently twisting
the heavy signet 'wedding' ring she had given him on their
first anniversary. Or were his thoughts so absent? She had
enough *Reader's Digest* psychology to feel a stab of real
alarm.

'I've gone too far!' she thought. The destroying whip of
her hysteria flicked at her mind to urge her on to a full
confession that would burn all her boats. Peter would have
her. Peter would take her. The judge would never sentence
a mere woman . . . but would he? And would Peter really?

She could not face up to the truth and an age-old cunning told her she should hold in cold-blooded reserve the ultimate disclosure. She carefully controlled her voice.

'Do you love me?' she asked quietly.

John turned from the window. He was not unaware of some degree of artifice.

'Yes, God help me,' he said with complete accuracy.

Paula was at a loss for words.

But then the door-bell rang. John gave her a look somewhere between straight enquiry and last-straw desperation.

'Christ! The Drysdales,' Paula said. 'Drinks.'

John winced. He shut his eyes. It was a long time before he opened them and, when he did it seemed a great effort. The bell rang a second time.

'I could tell them that you're sick or something.'

'No, no,' John said. 'Too late for that. Come one, come all. Come hell or high water. Come the Drysdales.'

'But John ... what are you going to do? ... About the other. ...?'

'How do I know until I've done it?' John said. His voice was infinitely weary.

As Abbotsfield weekenders the Drysdales came at best in the acquaintance bracket and owed their presence at Gunn House almost entirely to Paula's tactics for diversion via a host of invitations. They had a sumptuously appointed cottage at the far end of the village which stood deserted during the weekdays they spent in Blackheath, an area that had formed the nucleus of Frank Drysdale's large fortune from the lush fields of property investment. They were older than the Dennings. He used a sort of barking bluffness to mask shrewdness; she, more obviously *parvenu* and less reconciled to the idea that money could buy respect, took refuge in a rather overdone genteelness.

They were not really John's cup of tea and in present circumstances almost the last people he could wish to be stuck with. But there they were and here whisky and sherry and conversation flowed. They talked about the usual things. Inflation (especially in terms of cars and houses); television (there had been a predictably risqué play on television which Paula had found unpleasant); the folly of the district council in sanctioning the Roseberry housing estate. From a far place somewhere at the back of his mind John watched and listened to his and Paula's every word and gesture. Again he was amazed, and frightened by the charming ease with which, so much else to worry them, they both were able to roll out their meaningless contributions to the small talk. If they could be so practised at such short notice who in the world was there to really trust when anyone could smile and smile and be a villain?

'More ice,' he was saying. 'I'll be right back.'

He rose and went into the kitchen. As he reached for the freezer section of the fridge he realised Frank Drysdale was hard on his heels.

'Sorry,' he was saying, 'but could I muck you about and alter that to something long if— Good Lord, you had the bailiffs in?'

'Er, no, not exactly,' John improvised. 'We've had a bit of a cock-up in the delivery of some new kitchen stuff. Let's see, will lager do?'

'Just the job, thanks. So you were more or less caught between stools, eh?'

'Between about half a dozen, actually. We let the other stuff go – there's a charity down in Southampton Paula has a bit to do with. So now for a few days we're pigging it in the dining-room.'

He was pouring the beer. He noticed how steady his hand was. Drysdale was pacing around the all-at-once much too large room.

'Do you always have it smelling like a hospital?' he asked brusquely. 'Or is it me?'

'Oh,' John said, 'just trying to make a virtue of necessity. While it's empty and we're not using it much, I thought I'd give it a quick wash down with disinfectant.'

He made a move towards rejoining the ladies but at that moment Drysdale's ox-blood brogue crunched on a shard of glass and he was looking at the broken window. John cursed as Drysdale chortled loudly.

'Been taking pot shots at that lovely wife of yours?' he

said. 'I'll take her off your hands if she's too much for you –
save an awful lot of mess.'

He's pushy and nasty with it, John decided. I don't like
him. I really don't. He smiled as he handed the beer to his
new enemy.

'Cheers.'

'Cheers. Was a gun, actually.' The best lie was the one
nearest the truth. 'A bit embarrassing, twenty years I've
been handling the things and never an accident before.
Just shows you. Paula gave me a right royal bollocking –
and quite right too.'

'What – were you cleaning it?'

'Yes.'

'Outside?'

'No. In here.'

'Then how come the glass is in here?'

John felt it was the time to kick against the prick a little.

'Well,' he said, 'if you insist on playing detective I can
see I'd better come clean. We've had a lot of trouble from a
fox up this end of the village. Got in amongst a neighbour's
hens some time ago, made one hell of a mess. Anyway.
First thing this morning I saw the bugger in the garden,
bold as brass. I rushed for the gun, loaded it, sneaked out
the front door and round. But he was gone. I did a sort of
token dawn patrol around the garden but no sign and in the
middle it came pissing down. I dashed back in. Didn't
unload. I went to the loo. When I came back and began
wiping the gun down one barrel went and bloody well
unloaded itself for me. I'd completely forgotten. You know
foxes in this day and age are virtually urban creatures.
Suburban anyway.'

'Good lord, yes. We've got tribes of them in Blackheath.
Packs. See them trotting down the streets. Here, I say,
talking of hens, shouldn't we go back in?'

They did and John was off the hook. A further twenty
minutes of inconsequential talk prevented any further
cross-examination. Even so they nearly failed, all four of
them, to rise to the last few moments. The thought of lunch
was hovering about. Yet neither pair were so insincere as

actually to suggest they corporately do something about it. It had been nice, yes, but you wouldn't want to see too much of them. . . .

'So nice, dear,' Mrs Drysdale said, smiling, to Paula as John gave her assistance with her coat. 'You must come over soon and see our little country *pied-à-terre*.'

'And have the other half, old man,' Drysdale was pumping John's arm now.

'That would be nice,' John said.

They waved goodbye. They closed the door. Paula leaned back against it and, eyes closed, let out a long sigh of relief.

'Funny,' she said at last, 'they didn't once ask after Asp.'

'Well they wouldn't, would they? They're only around at weekends. They don't know us that well and they don't think in terms of animals.'

He looked at her.

'You know,' he said slowly, 'I think it might be an idea to drop in on Jock Reid and put Asp's disappearance down on record. Officially. I'll say she seemed a bit off-colour. Who knows, maybe those swines who pick up dogs to sell for vivisection got their hooks on her.'

This time Paula's sigh was short.

'Oh, thank God,' she said. She came to John and held him. She was shaking now. 'I've been so petrified, just rigid, thinking you'd do something noble and land us absolutely in it.'

She had a knack at times of telling more truth than she knew. And now she had made John the one excuse he was prepared for and prepared to understand. All the same, he did not yield utterly.

'Better be careful about putting the idea back in my head,' he said.

He did not eat lunch either. Worn thin he lay down for a while. No sleep came or ever seemed like coming. After a while he got up and, changing again, forked over his main rose bed. That way there would be no village comment on its having been disturbed.

That night working alone he dug a hole in that same spot. A grave. It took forever and the night was alive with noises and, surely, with eyes. But no one interrupted him and at last he was spading soil back in upon the stiffened body he could not see. Only the differing sounds of earth on earth, earth on fur, and his own shoulders aching from the dragging confirmed that Asp was there. Her last, mortal remains. Poor Asp. Well, out of sight and out of mind. She would not rise from under that lot. He would sleep well tonight.

He did not.

CHAPTER FIVE

At the far end of the line the phone rang. Some kind of static crackled up and down.

'He may well not be there,' Paula said. 'It is Sunday. He's probably away sailing.'

'Or in some other bed.'

'More than likely.' Paula thought she controlled herself quite well.

The phone twelve miles away was answered.

'Peter Halliwell.'

'Peter,' John said, 'John. John Denning.'

'The John Denning who should bloody well know better than to call me out of bed at this hour of the morning?'

'Well that's a risk that for one reason or another I have to take at any hour.'

'*Touché* as we say in the New Forest.'

'Actually, it is something rather important. I'm not too keen about telling you over the phone.'

'Oh? All sounds very dire and dramatic. Something, er, personal, would you say?'

'Er. Yes and no. Not really. Reason I rang early, actually, was partly to catch you in case you were going out early or had plans and—'

'Well, as—'

'—and partly to see if there was any chance I could pop over this morning and have a chat with you on it over a pint, say.'

'Yes, well, as a matter of fact, I do rather have my hands full at the moment, if you see what I mean.'

'Well, it is rather urgent. Would there be any chance that the pair of you might be over this way in the course of the day?'

'Sorry, John. No chance. Not today.'

'Peter, it just could be I might be in some quite serious trouble. And, by extension, so could you.'

'Trouble? Oh, would all this have something to do with that aspidistra I ran over to you from my Aunt Frances the other week?'

'Yes. Yes it would.'

'Got the mange, has it?'

'Pretty much, yes. It died on us, in fact.'

'Oh dear, Auntie will be sorry. She wanted it to go to a good home so much.'

'Peter – it's not exactly a matter for joking. The good home could be in Winchester prison.'

'But I don't know anything about it, do I, old son?'

'Well . . .'

'And what's dead is presumably buried.'

'Yes.'

'Well, there you are, then. Keep your trap shut and Bob's your uncle.'

'Peter, are you sure I couldn't come across and see you sometime?'

'I do think you're going a bit overboard on the cloak and dagger stakes, old chap. Lie low, keep mum – who's to know?'

'That's what I can't be absolutely certain of. Nobody – I think.'

'Well, there you are. Look, John, I've really got to hop around the cage a bit this morning, as it happens. Going sailing. Annual fire drill, don't you know.'

'God damn it, Peter, this could be serious! We could all be well and truly in the shit over this one!'

'You could, old lad. I thought I'd made that clear. . . . But I'm sure you won't. Now just relax and I'll call you in a few days when things are a bit less hectic at my end – ha, ha.'

'Peter—'

'Love to Paula. *Ciao*.'

And he had hung up.

For a half second John refused to believe it. Then in a

rage he slammed the receiver down. He slewed round angrily on to the pillow and the breakfast tray tilted perilously. Coffee spilt and became an instant stain upon the duvet.

'Sod it!' John exploded. 'Now look!'

Too late he dabbed wildly at the vanished liquid with the corner of his pyjama sleeve.

'If that's how you treat it, I shan't trouble to bring you breakfast in bed in future,' Paula said.

'Yes, well, I can get by all right without a blue moon in my life once a year!'

There was a pause. When Paula next spoke there was measurably more sweetness in her tone.

'Sorry, my love. It was, actually, believe it or not, intended as light relief. I did rather get the message Peter-wise.'

'God how I hate people who say "*ciao*". My best friend! My schoolboy chum! I've heard him say – you're my witness – "if the going gets rough, try calling me first." Well, I just did. Look where it got me.'

'What did he say?'

'If anyone asks he wasn't involved. Shut up and it'll all go away. Prick!'

'Well, he's right in the second particular.'

'And I am in the third.'

'What was that about "the pair of you"?'

Paula had managed to keep her voice rock steady.

'Oh, the obvious. In every sense. He's got some bird with him.'

'Well we hardly want some total bloody stranger coming over to sit on a post-mortem and alibi session. The fewer who know the better.'

'It was his tone of voice. His whole manner.'

'You did call him rather early.'

'It wasn't that. I'm worried, Paula. He'd shop the both of us to save his neck. Oh, he sends his love, would you believe.'

'How nice of him.'

Paula bit hard upon a crust of toast. Propped up on

pillows, man and wife lay side by side. Neither was quite aware of the rare unanimity of thought that, even if for different reasons, they temporarily shared. Both were thinking Peter Halliwell a Grade A shit.

John had had another reason for telephoning his friend so early on a Sunday morning. He had woken up early. He had woken up early because he had had a nightmare.

It had seemed to him that he was on a seashore. He had a sense that he was on an island. A Caribbean island or one in the South Seas. Turquoise seas ran in to break under blue skies on a beach that stretched its old gold sand away in a vast curve to the world's rim. White foam frothed where the breakers finally died like everchanging lace, fluid, hypnotic, never the same. Only – the tide was running out. It dragged and sucked the sand out with it. With each fresh wave it brought some back upon the beach but always it took out more than it returned. And somewhere on the water's edge was something buried. Something vague but black and terrible. Something he had put there. It had all but broken through the shifting surface of the sand. Black and terrible and he had put it there. To hide his guilt. He was guilty. He had done something terrible. To the black thing. At any moment now it would roll forth. A black arm would rise. All would know what he had done. The blue skies would turn black and a head, a head without a face, or with a face he could not quite see but black and terrible and laced in a now hideous foam. Clawing at his throat, he had reared up in bed panting and drenched in sweat. Now, remembering, he still shuddered. He poured coffee from his slopped saucer back into the cup. It was stone-cold. As cold as he now felt.

'Well,' he muttered, 'this won't do. I've got to see about that window.'

Two hours later he was hot and sticky. Replacing windows was not his thing. His long acquaintance with country matters had given John a high level do-it-yourself skill but this self-reliance came close to shattering after he had broken his second pane of glass. The trouble was the silly little wheeled thing you were supposed to use. He had several sheets of glass left over from the installation of the greenhouse and even though they were of an inferior quality and slightly thicker it was obviously much better in the circumstances to do the job himself rather than call in an expert from outside. A badly bleeding finger and two false starts later he was almost thinking otherwise. But third time lucky. He carried the hard-fought-for pane and the putty over to the window. He knocked out the remaining glass, gouged the old putty away. Holding his breath he put the new pane in place. Yes, a fair enough fit. Now just the putty. Without the proper tools he found it sticking, crumbling, most difficult to smooth. Blood was mixed in with it from his finger wound. The sun was on his back. He should have taken off his pullover but somehow, though he was sweltering now, it seemed the few seconds it would take would be a terrible waste of time. A chunk of old putty, flying out from his chisel, had stuck in his hair. Becoming fully aware of it at last he took a step back to brush it away and felt his heart miss a beat. Staring at him from the glass was the thoughtful reflection of P.C. Reid.

It seemed most monstrously unfair they should have found out right away.

'Hello, Jock,' he said. 'Long arm come for me at last?'

Unfair. He nearly had gone along and made a full confession. Honestly.

'Couldn't stand the strain, Mr Denning,' Reid said. 'All that paperwork. We have a technical expression in the force you know, for what you're doing there.'

'What's that?'

'We call it a right balls-up.'

'Well . . . I haven't got the right tools.'

'A bad workman. Here. Let me remove the evidence.'

Reid stepped forward and took the trowel from John's hand.

'Better wash that before you get dirt in it,' he said. 'Now.'

He made some passes at the putty. Small for a policeman, he was the son of a Lanarkshire Scot who had moved south in the Depression. He was as Hampshire as the Test.

'What did they do?' he said suddenly. 'Effect entry by

breaking a window and then make off with your kitchen furniture?'

'That's what I'm telling the insurance company,' John said. 'No. Getting some new stuff. Rake handle went through the window.'

'Oh, ay,' Reid said. He spat into his hand. 'Reason I called is I'm on my way in and your firearms certificate's due for renewal. Can I take my yearly butcher's?'

John's relief welled up in such a flood he felt light-headed.

'Of course,' he managed to say. 'I've half been expecting you. Come in when you've finished doing my work for me.'

'Well, that's about it. Not perfect but improved.'

'Much better. I'm really—'

'Let her dry and then a lick of paint.'

They went into the study. Paula was there.

'Hullo, Jock,' she said smiling at once.

'Jock's here to check the guns,' John said, perhaps a shade too quickly. 'He's also done the window for me as windows should be done.'

'How nice. Well, the labourer is worthy of his hire. What'll it be, Jock?'

Reid grinned.

'I shouldn't really,' he said, 'but we all bend the law, don't we? Scotch, please.'

John got the guns while Paula poured. The .22 rifle and .22 revolver were restricted for use on authorised ranges and, for the purpose of killing vermin in three named locations. Glass in hand, Reid glanced cursorily at them checking their numbers against his record.

'Fine,' he said. 'If you'll just sign the application and let me have the fee, I'll be on my way. You'll have the permit back with the Chief Constable's compliments – for what they're worth – in a week or so.'

John reached for the cheque book on the desk.

'We can kill a third bird,' he said. 'Window. Guns. And, you may have heard, we've been putting up a stray dog, bitch actually, the past few weeks.'

'I did hear, yes, sir. Never saw her to my knowledge.'

'Big black mongrel. Anyway, she's run off. I've been

meaning to drop in and see about a licence – we'd just
decided she was here to stay – but now I suppose I should
report her missing.'

'Answer to any name?'

'Not really. We called her Asp. She's got poor George's
choke-collar on.'

He described her. The collar was three feet under too.

'Well,' Reid said, 'I'll circulate this. Keep my ears open.
If she turns up you can come in and reclaim her and get a
licence. Bit funny a bitch running off. Not like a dog
feeling it's time to go off getting his end away – saving your
presence, Mrs Denning.'

'Some ugly customers about when it comes to animals,'
Paula said. 'They could've got her.'

'True,' Reid said. 'Possible. Thanks. Here's your receipt.'

'Thanks.'

Reid nodded. 'Paper work,' he said. 'Nothing but.'

He took his leave. As had become their habit, Paula and
John looked at each other like conspirators.

Their lunch was a light ham salad. Their conversation
was lighter still. Paula dropped the only memorable remark.

'Well,' she said, 'now we'll just have to wait a while and see.'

Neither of them actually went on to say what they were
waiting for.

In fact, because they were so busy, Paula very much
enjoyed the next few days. Her schedule was so suddenly
crowded it was a real blessing she had her Mrs Hicks coming
in three days a week to do for her. From one of Southampton's better shops she bought a really very nice kitchen table
and the matching chairs. They were Italian and really
rather expensive but the flair of perspex and chrome was a
big improvement on the old stuff. Thanks to her best line
in shy smiles she managed to get delivery from stock within
two days. Meanwhile from their favourite nurseryman just
outside Stockbridge she bought some summer blooming
roses as a cover for the newly dug flower bed. Next year the
dark dusky red would make a brave show there.

At work, though, time for John reverted to a crawl.

There was still no feed-back from Baltimore and it took an increasingly major exertion to maintain the low-profile nonchalance made obligatory by the company life-style. He spent much of his desk time, his commuting hour each day behind the wheel, trying hard not to think of Asp. He had had no further nightmares. But how do you not think of something that constantly returns unbidden to your mind? It had taken all his willpower to go out and plant the new rose bushes. He tried to pull himself through the long week with the thought that come Saturday he would be going shooting. Normally that would have given him a different impatience altogether, lively, active, not wanting to sit still. But everything was now a dull kind of strain. All he wanted to do was to sit around. But Paula, obviously trying to be as nice as possible, deserved some kind of matching playing up from him. They went out to eat Chinese in Andover. They went to see a film. Three nights consecutively, most comprehensively, Paula and he made love. And yet . . . Thursday evening he went out for a walk.

Though he had a simple reason to, he owed him for some eggs, he didn't go to see old Ted. That was, well, like meeting trouble half-way. He set out in the opposite direction. There was no breath of wind. The air was warm and sleepy, hung with the evening scents of flowers, the notes, liquid and thick, of evening birds. From one of the clutch of cottages down Parson's Lane there came the sound of 'Jesu Joy of Man's Desiring' played with a charming childish hesitation that was exactly suited to his mood. Ah yes. The Mallet's. That would be young Johnnie, his namesake. For a little while he managed, free of thought, to lose himself. Then just as, circling back, he came upon the village green, he was aware increasingly he felt some sense of loss. Had he been carrying a stick, some kind of parcel? Ah! His peace of mind was gone again. The strangeness was the lack of need to turn occasionally and call on an eager, scampering, insatiably curious companion of a dog. Once again he had nothing better to kill time with than thinking everything over as if he could in some way discover a happy ending to all his worry.

He sat down on a bench. If he just put his mind to it something remembered would convince him all was well. It seemed hard to believe the worst could ever happen with such a scene as this before your eyes. Autumn browns and reds were beginning to creep into the still full-leafed trees. Where at the far end the golden light of the late sun still flooded one last corner of green, flame was to be seen on a lone beech. That and the cries of a few distant children scampering about in a last game provided just the edge of contrast to bring home to him all the serene, unruffled timelessness of what he saw. This was a safe place. In a few days he could be sitting here a weight removed from his mind forever and a gentle unforced happiness gladdening his heart. It would be like. . . .

John had a little secret. Three years before on an extended business visit to South Africa he had spent some nights with a tall secretary from their Cape Town office. It had been as much an affair of alcohol and physical relief as anything. Almost a means of getting a good night's sleep. That she was blonde and curvy as well as a receptionist had seemed to throw a sanctioning cloak of cliché over this pleasant little interlude. He had known, of course, that it was safe enough. They had kissed goodbye. . . . Then, trapped in the return plane's sickening air-conditioning, he had come out in a muck sweat. What if she talked and it got back? What if she were serious and wrote, came over, even? She could trace him easily enough. Of course, she wouldn't, it was just – God! what if she'd given him a dose? That was much more likely. That brought in Paula. Of course, he had behaved badly. He would tell Paula everything now, naturally. She would understand. A good marriage should have no secrets. He had landed at Heathrow consumed with guilt. Paula had been there to meet him and he had not told her. Unable to face the indignity of going for a check on his most immediate fear, he had sweated out a few weeks, imagining symptoms, fearful of what both past and post might bring. Nothing had happened. It had all gone away. When months later the girl's name had cropped up at Southampton in a routine telex he had had to think a moment to remember who it was. . . . So, surely, it would be with Asp.

Cheerful, friendly, the lights of the Dog and Fox clicked on to his left. He was tempted for a moment for a change of faces and a bit of company. But no, he might see old Ted. And he felt pleasantly tired now with the acid bite of his anxiety all gone. He'd been washed through, somehow, into a calm as peaceful as this setting. He would go home.

He stood up, began to look about him and then checked himself. Just habit. Things were so often best when left alone. He was convinced. All would be all right.

CHAPTER SIX

Saturday dawned clear and bright, promising one of those crisp days when the sun climbs high enough to clear away the whiteness of the overnight ground frost. They would use the Renault. John loaded the back with the cases, his gun, the cartridges, boots and, you never know, their waterproofs. There was one sourness. He had neglected to remove the dog guard. It caught his eye and for a moment George's bright cream shadow ran across his mind. Then Asp's. The black one lingered obstinately and he felt the ice beginning to form deep in his stomach. No: he wasn't going to spend this day under a black cloud. This day of all days. This autumn sharpness had always been his keen delight. The school team clattering in studs from the pavilion, the sportsman making for his covert. Nothing would mar his aim today. He wouldn't let it. With a supreme effort he willed the black shadow to go away. He slammed fast the Renault's tailgate. In action was relief. He called out for Paula not to take so long.

Meticulously punctual, they drew up outside his in-laws' Tudor house. Crook-beamed, crook-roofed with dark, moss-covered tiles, it was the stuff retirement dreams are made of. But dreaming hadn't made it come about. In the army, later with the farm, Rupert had worked damned hard for this. And had to still. Conventional retirement for him would spell ruin. On his father-in-law's behalf John fiercely resented both those who hinted it was owed all to a silver spoon and, again, those unacceptably faceless Governments eroding someone else's success to shore up their continuing failure. If it should ever be that England had no place for Hilary and Rupert Marsh, then, for John, the time had come to be done with the whole damned shooting match. They were in his eyes what it was all about. It was, for example, typical of their selfless consideration, that hearing the car, they should be halfway down the path to greet their daughter and her husband.

'Darlings!'

'John!'

'Hello, you two!'

Amid kisses and hugs everybody talked at once from sheer delight.

'Come on, my boy, we'd best get your things upstairs.'

Rupert had got a word in by John's ear.

'Something I'd like your considered opinion on,' he added.

He said no more. Stooping to avoid the low ceiling John followed him up the twisting oak stairs to the guest room in no way the wiser. He put down Paula's case.

'Well?' he said.

'Well what?'

'You wanted my advice.'

'Ah, that! Ah yes. Well it's nothing of great import. Still – look, be a good chap and follow me.'

He led the way downstairs and then out to the kennels at the back. John had, he found, to check his pace. Rupert was walking noticeably more slowly than he could remember. The silver hair was just as spruce but the bantam figure had lost much of its jauntiness. The sports jacket was stretched a little tighter at the waist and there were the loose folds of age about the neck. On the watch for such signs John felt a pang. He had first known Rupert in the formal role of suitor to his daughter. But within minutes of their meeting the older man's quiet-mannered genuineness had made them friends for life. Rupert was, in two words and in one, a gentleman. The retired officer was now the perfect type of English squire. If squires had hearts with pronounced murmurs. A few months earlier he had taken John aside and let him know.

'Just between ourselves,' was how he'd put it. 'In case anything should happen suddenly. Seems there might be a limit on just how many shoots I may have left me.'

John had been sick in his own heart to think he must lose

this loved friend and now, crossing the kennel yard, he was sufficiently upset by the new evidence that death would separate them sooner, probably, than later, to be slow in noticing that Rupert had doubled up his dogs.

In here were the familiar liver-coloured labradors, old and tried and true but, in the next kennel, heads as eagerly high, tails banging away in just as rapid fire against the wooden walls were two cream youngsters.

'Funny the way they always know when we're off shooting,' Rupert said.

'I've always guessed they smell the powder and the gun oil in our clothes,' John said.

'Could be. Could very well. Now, er, my boy . . . that is to say. . . .'

Rupert with all his ease was so very seldom embarrassed or at a loss for words, John felt a quick jab of alarm. It proved quite false. Rupert was instantly back into his stride.

'The thought struck me,' he said, 'even before that ghastly business with poor George that, like ourselves, like me at any rate, none of our dogs were getting any younger. So I went out and ordered a pup for both of us. And here—'

'Really, Rupert, I couldn't possibly—'

'Now hold your peace and hear me out. Of course you can. I was, I tell you, planning to give you and Paula the surprise and pleasure of a young dog. That would be my pleasure too, you see – I'm being selfish. After what happened to George, I'd hazard a large wager that a newcomer's more than ever necessary. There they are. They're both fully trained to the gun. I've had Jason, on the left there, for a couple of months. Yours arrived this morning. The trainer brought him across and he'll work him for you today.'

Now it was John who was lost for words. In equal measure he was overwhelmed by gratitude and sadness. The new dog was so like his old beloved George. He felt a need to fight back tears. To give himself something to do he opened the kennel door. The two dogs bounded out.

'Sit,' said Rupert quietly. Both animals fell back on to

their hindquarters. Their tails swept the ground in unison as they took turns at yawning with anticipation.

'He's so like George,' John managed finally.

'Yes. That's really the nicest thing about it. I didn't tell you but when you kennelled George with us the time you went to Ireland, I borrowed his services. I asked for the pick of two dogs from the litter by way of a stud fee. The owner agreed like a shot so you can tell what she thought of George. So, you see, they didn't cost a thing.'

'Come off it, Rupert, you don't keep and train a dog for nothing. It must have cost you a fortune.'

'That, as I said, is my pleasure. I've been out with Jason a few times after duck and he's shaping up well. Ackroyd the trainer, tells me yours is the better of the two – provided you don't let Paula ruin him.'

'Well, I'll do my best!'

'I took the necessary liberty of naming him. His mother was a prize-winning bitch and called Helen – Helen of Hillsthorpe. So we christened him Troy. I reckon my fellow will see me out, so I named him after my very first spaniel. . . . Anyway, I hope you will like each other.'

On instinct John reached out and gripped Rupert's forearm.

'Father-in-law,' he said, 'I simply – truly – don't know what to say.' Curiously, he always used this most formal form of address when feeling closest to his friend.

'Then let's take it as read. Come on – we'd better get back to the front and meet the others.'

Accompanied by all four dogs they made their way toward the front of the house. Any last doubts John might have had concerning Asp were washed away. He had a renewal of complete faith that all was well with the world. Paula's tough commonsense was right. He knew, he positively knew, that, starting with himself, everything was fine.

On the front lawn a gathered sea of mainly familiar faces – other guests, beaters, keepers – smiled at their approach. There was a flurry of handshakes and slapped backs. As might be expected, Troy had trotted straight off to his trainer, Ackroyd, and in quick succession John was introduced to both this quietly spoken small dark man and to Colonel Poskett, an old Army friend of Rupert's former days who had recently retired and come to live nearby. There was just time for him to dart into the house and bring out Paula. Told about Troy, meeting him, she was reduced to hugging, tearful raptures. John got a quick, anxious look from Ackroyd straight between the eyes but he could see in Paula the same total dropping away of doubt and fear he had experienced a few short minutes earlier, and he was happy she should let her tensions melt away in this spontaneous outpouring of emotion. He watched her kiss her father on the cheek and then softened, her best old self, she was kissing him.

'Have a good day,' she said.

Then it was time to move off and he was strapping on his cartridge belt and assembling his gun.

Except in the most shaded spots, the night frost had vanished. It was going to be a fine warm day with just a suspicion of breeze. Avoiding the one tree in the long hedgerow so as to give himself a maximum field of fire John took up his assigned position. He was on the far wing and the south side of a broad uprising field of barley stubble. Ackroyd stood with him and, in undertones, they chatted. Colonel Poskett, to the right, was their immediate neighbour. Somewhere in the distance a whistle blew. Almost simultaneously a fusillade of shots crashed out as a twelve-strong covey of partridges, correctly guessing the safest line of retreat lost only one of their number in flying over the party's older members. Now another covey was flashing between John and the Colonel. John fired both barrels and missed twice but his neighbour dropped two in the front and, reloading a single cartridge, killed a straggler behind.

'Some shooting,' John whispered to Ackroyd. He felt a fool at having fluffed a straightforward chance in front of him. The Colonel, obviously, was mustard. But he had scarcely time to dwell on that. A single cock pheasant, must be an old bird, was coming straight at him, high and handsome. Not his favourite. He never fancied his chances at really high pheasants. Could be another miss. No – a hit! In classic style the bird crashed stone-dead on to the stubble twenty yards in front of where he stood.

'Good shot,' Ackroyd said and John could sense his admiration.

The drive completed, John didn't get another chance. Troy picked up the dead cock and brought it straight back to the trainer. The Colonel's three partridges apart, the rest of the line had mustered only five pheasants to pick between them.

It was a pattern that continued. Through successive drives, John shot well and consistently, but he looked mediocre compared to the Colonel's brilliance. Yet John was free from envy. The acrid tang of powder on the breeze, the waiting, the sudden beating need for instant action and decision combined to send champagne bubbling through his veins. When Troy distinguished himself with a spectacular retrieval of a hen pheasant that had struggled whirlingly on for some three hundred yards before collapsing in thick cover, his day was made.

Like all openers it had not been a particularly noteworthy day and at its end they had run up a mixed bag of just seventy-nine head. The Colonel had contributed a redoubtable thirty-one; John at nineteen had offered up the second highest tally. But it was not the numbers. It was the unalloyed joy he felt that was important. As back on the long-shadowed lawn before the Tudor house the company exchanged goodbyes with handshakes and broad grins, even the old Naval man whose one and only bird had given Troy the chance to show his mettle was beaming. Paula had slipped out the moment John returned.

'How was Troy?' she asked.

'Magnificent,' he said, 'an absolute delight.'

They went to thank the keeper.

'He'll come even more into his own when the leaves go and you can do the big woods,' Ackroyd said. 'It'll be good pickings in there this year, too.'

'That's something like,' John said. 'That's what year-to-year I'm really looking forward to.'

He looked quickly around. Rupert was busy bidding farewell to some of the other guns. Now was his chance.

'You must have some idea,' he said, 'how indebted my wife and I are to you for the way you've brought Troy along. You will allow me—'

But with a deft and curiously final motion of his hand, Ackroyd was making it quite clear he would have none of it.

'Thank you, there's no need,' he said. 'Mr Marsh has seen me all right. Thank you just the same.'

He held out his hand and John shook it. Ackroyd seemed to hesitate. He seemed to want to say something. Now he shook hands with Paula.

'Mr Marsh is a good man,' Ackroyd said. The statement was more subtle than its face-value simplicity.

'Yes. He is,' John said. 'A gentleman.'

Ackroyd nodded just once, smiled and moved away. Troy made to follow but Paula gently restrained him.

CHAPTER SEVEN

The remainder of the weekend passed by all too quickly amid good food and drink and the easy friendly talk of a happy family. Wishing to settle Troy in to his new and permanent home well before nightfall, John and Paula made their fond farewells immediately after Sunday lunch. Troy sprang into the Renault on the nod and the thought came home to John that the dog-guard he had neglected to remove had been, all along, a good omen kept intact by his subconscious.

There were waves and laughter and a little sadness and then they were cruising down the road. For a while they drove in silence. Then to his mild surprise Paula was snuggling across and up to John.

'You're happy now, aren't you?' she said.

'Yes,' he said simply.

'You have to make allowances for me. I know you do. I know you know it but being worried brings out all the bitch in me. I get tough and edgy because I pretend to myself that will make me look efficient and frighten trouble away. But really, of course, I'm just a spoilt and frightened little girl still.'

John kissed her forehead briefly and Paula thought of Peter in the Scimitar. She was not sure how much of what she was saying she believed.

'I was awake last night,' she said. 'I was thinking about what that man said yesterday. The trainer, Ackroyd. About Daddy being good. He is, of course. And you're good too. That's why you both get on so well together.'

'Oh, I'd say that I was pretty ordinary – deadly dull.'

'You're not! You're nice, kind and considerate.'

'There you are – dullsville. I don't go swinging around the Channel in a yacht the size of a Cunarder.'

'Oh John! Let's leave that – that vulgar man right out of this. No! Let's not! He exactly makes my point. You're everything he's not. He's flashy. Unreliable. You'd never walk out on a friend. On him. He's what he is and, admit it now, you're good. I'm the one who's not, if truth be told.'

The conversation's shape seducing her, for a dangerous, delicious moment, Paula again stood above the attractive precipice of giving John a full and frank confession. Her affair with Peter – if something so intermittent could be raised to that dubious dignity – obviously no longer existed. In confessing she could, she was quite sure, make John forgive her. Perhaps, her offence revealed, their marriage would be stronger, freed from an underlying strain of poison. But he would be so hurt. And it would be so awkward.

His 'Oh? How's that?' had hung for seconds in the air. She must take it up.

'Daddy does have one fault,' she said. 'He'd have been very good with boys but blessed – or cursed – with two daughters, he spoiled us rotten. That's what I am – spoilt.'

John grinned.

'Maybe,' he sang. 'But he spoiled you just for me.'

Troy took to Gunn House like a well-disciplined duck to water. After a house-warming drink from a temporary bowl he set about establishing the extent and lay-out of his new territory with commendable method. John led him up and down the garden path while Paula picked some velvety red roses.

'Ouch! I've pricked myself,' she said.

'Now you'll sleep a hundred years.'

'I've told you once today. I've got my personalised Prince Charming built in.'

'I think I'll just stroll round and see old Ted. I've owed him for those eggs for days.'

It was silly that he hadn't gone before. There was no reason not to.

'You mean you're simply dying to show off Troy to him. Honestly, John, you're positively transparent. Be off, then! Quickly! Both of you!'

With mock severity they were dismissed from the royal presence.

John whistled Troy along. O.K., he was transparent, but old Ted had always had a soft spot for George and it would gladden him to see his son. He took the bridle path to Mullen's Field. Troy sauntered along happily. With so many new bushes and trees and unfamiliar smells to be investigated, progress was leisurely. But there was no need in the world for haste. People so often forgot that. . . . Troy was indicating the greatest interest in a patch of dying briars.

'Seek on then,' John said.

With a bound the dog flushed out a rabbit. It tore off down the hedgerow in frenzied search for the haven of its burrow.

'Ware rabbit!' John shouted. 'Leave it, Troy!'

To his surprised delight the dog made no effort to pursue. John realised he'd really got a topper here. How typical of Rupert to reserve only the second best for his own use. He gave Troy a good patting and showed his pleasure at such disciplined obedience.

Perhaps he was premature. About twenty-five yards from the barn Troy capriciously stopped dead. He sniffed once or twice at the air. He sat down on his haunches. He began to whine.

'Come on, Troy, come on – what's the matter with you.'

Troy would have none of it. The more John commanded him forward the more steadfast he remained. Each time John tried to coax him on his tail would wag a fitful moment and then stop. His whole appearance gave off the smell of fear. John was considerably mortified. Curtly turning he began to walk alone toward the barn. With every step he took Troy's whining became louder and the more insistent. Curiosity now mingled with John's chagrin. Was all this fuss just on account of Ted's two terriers? Hardly.

'Quiet, Troy! What *is* the matter with you! Ted? Ted? It's John, Ted.'

There was no answer. He slowly pushed the door open. Troy grew absolutely frantic. John hissed his annoyance. This was no prize exhibit to show off! He peered inside. A parallelogram of dusty sunlight lay aslant the mud floor. Nothing. A rat squeaked and scuttled from the shadow through the light and back into gloom again. Somewhere outside, chickens cackled on the edge of sound. John took a step across the threshold. He waited as his eyes became accustomed to the further darkness. Then he made out Ted. He was lying, his back towards the door on a mattress laid upon the floor. A moth-eaten sleeping bag and several sacks served to cover him.

In that instant, terror like unholy lightning etched certain knowledge acidly upon John's brain. He had the total recall of a sudden snapshot. When old Ted's mittened hand had profferred him the eggs it had been bandaged too. How could he have been blind to that until now. John hesitated, driven into shock, vaguely aware somewhere he owed an apology to Troy. Then, sleepily, Ted stirred himself. Relief shot through John. He could move forward. How many times in the past week had he been on this switch-back?

'Ted,' he said, 'Did I wake you up?'

Ted moved but did not speak. He might be sick. John went down on one knee and pulled away a sack. And knew full horror. He screamed in disbelieving, all believing, shock beyond all shock. Rats had leapt from underneath the covers, from on top of the unrecognisable. The corpse was eaten half-away. What had been eyes were accusing blood-dried sockets. The lips were chewed away. The nose. The throat had been laid bare down to the windpipe. And the stench! The overpowering stench! Ted who had lived in tattered dignity had died robbed of that one quality he prized. John wanted to be sick. But, powerless, he was held. A howling, high-pitched siren flared in his skull transfiguring him. The sightless eyes burned into his, a ghastly mesmeric spell binding him to the spot. The sockets forecast, the black gummed teeth smiled, assurance of revenge. He knew this face reduced to obscene carrion was promising to poison his every night, his days, until the end of time.

And he, in turn, confronting it, guilty, must feast his eyes unstintingly on flesh gone to corruption. This was the ultimate – but no! His heart stopped utterly. The grinning corpse was twisting round the better to confront him . From deep within the deliquescent bowels a last and blood-bespattered rat was squirming – John shrieked. An animal too in his reactions now, he dropped the sack he'd clutched throughout. He staggered, fell, clawed to his feet and to the door. He retched but once and, as the smell of flesh long putrified, gathered raw in his throat, he vomited back his very bowels.

He ran down a long tunnel that led to the world's end. The earth reeled under him tilting him down to the horizon. The sky crashed down upon him, receded to the far side of infinity. Before him the vision of what had once been a living face fixed him with a look of implacable and merciless revenge. The ground rose up and smashed into his face. For timeless moments all was dark. Then John Denning heard a whining sound and found himself lying full-length among the first leaves of the autumn in a country lane. Panting he rose to his knees. A dog, his dog, unsure about this game was looking at him with his head enquiringly cocked to one side. John stood. The world swam, blurred, then held still. He was bathed in fiery sweating ice, he'd never felt such cold. He lurched towards a gate and began to take great gulps of air.

Twelve minutes later he walked back into his house. Paula was in the drawing-room smoking a cigarette as she read a paper. She glanced at him then looked at him.

'My God!' she said, 'whatever's happened?'

He brushed straight by her and went to the corner cupboard. Glass rattling against glass he poured himself a near half tumbler of Armagnac. He gulped at it. Again. The spirit scorched his throat and with harsh paroxysms he was coughing till it hurt. He saw that Paula was upon her feet.

'Whatever is it?' he heard her say. 'For God's sake tell me! Let me know!'

He saw that Troy was in the room. He couldn't bear him to overhear.

'Please take the dog out to the kitchen,' he heard his own voice say.

Paula looked at him with widening eyes. Then, abruptly, without more ado, she did as he had asked. When she came back to the room he was able to sip from the glass without an immediate desire to gag. Nor did his wife, standing and looking at him, still seem to be at the wrong end of a telescope.

'Ted Rimmer's dead,' he said.

Paula's head came up a fraction.

'When?' she said. 'Who told you?'

'No-one. I found him dead myself. Just now. In the barn. He's been there . . . days. Paula . . . he's been eaten half away by rats.'

Paula blinked just once.

'Where are his dogs?' she said.

'I don't know. Not there. I didn't see them.'

'Then Ted can't have died of rabies.'

'Paula, that doesn't follow for one second. If you'd seen what I've seen.'

'Exactly. Listen, my love, listen I implore you. You've obviously just been through the most horrendous, vile experience. When you came in you looked as if – John, I beg you, in your present state, I beg you – not to over-react. . . . Old Ted was just that. Old. From the creases on his face he could – John! Are you all right?'

'Of course not, for God's sake!'

But Paula would not leave it.

'He could have been past eighty. The logical thing to presuppose is that he just pegged out. Heart failure.'

'Paula, the fact the dogs aren't there doesn't mean a thing! He could've realised and put them down. Buried them.'

'In which case we have nothing to worry about.'

'In which case we would have killed him! We don't know what – who – else they might have bitten. They may still be alive and wandering at large. We have to assume they are. God damn it, be honest for one second! We both know! – we brought a rabid animal into the country and it's started off a chain whose end—'

'I've said before I don't admit that.'

'Well I do! I know reporting this to the authorities means a plain and utter ruin but for other people—'

'It would finish Daddy. His heart would never stand it.'

John looked at her. His horror knew a new dimension.

'You, me in prison,' Paula was saying. 'Especially you. Let's face it.'

John held himself to the one course that still contained some honour.

'Paula. People will die.'

'Let them!'

'Paula!'

'People! Them! The masses! They're not us! What have they ever done but try and ruin us? Unions striking to way past the point of suicide. Governments taxing us into the grave. Beyond. You know damned well they stole your parents' capital and hounded them abroad. They've nearly driven Daddy to his grave with worry. To keep the estate going, his employees' jobs secure, is just one treadmill for him. That's who I care about. Us and those few close to us. And if you really want to know I don't give a single solitary fuck what happens to anybody else at all!'

Her voice had risen to a strident vehemence. He stared at her caught somewhere between disgust and astonished fascination. He had never seen her selfishness so naked and so shameless.

'That's just about the nastiest little speech I've ever heard in my life. From anyone.'

She ignored him.

'Asp is buried. There's not a shred of evidence against us.'

'She can be dug up.'

'We don't know that she died of rabies! We don't know that Ted did either!'

'I do!'

'John, for Christ's sake! Those bloody cancer tubes you peddle have brought about more hideous deaths than all the bloody rabies the world has ever known!'

She'd gone too far with her wild rhetoric. The shift to an

old argument brought home to him the crooked depths his wife had sunk to in her self-centred defence of their small world. Now he had arrived at his decision he was calm. He walked towards the telephone and lifted the receiver.

'All right,' Paula said. 'You had to know sometime. If you call the police now, allowing for the speed at which the full and awesome majesty of the so-called law is nowadays made to move in bloody England – allowing for that, then my baby should just about be born in the hospital wing of Winchester prison. Or in a cell. I don't suppose there's all that actual difference.'

For a long, long time husband and wife looked at each other. John put down the receiver.

'You're lying,' he said.

'Am I?' She looked at him. Marble could have seemed softer.

'You're lying in a last ditch effort to prevent me calling.'

'So call. I've gone past caring now. It is true, though.'

John walked to the French windows. It had grown dark outside. His own reflection stared back gauntly at him. For a reeling moment Ted's death-mask superimposed itself on his own features. He blinked and thus effaced it. He had that power now. A crushing weariness made that nightmare now seem very far away. For many years Paula and he had been aware the reason they were childless was that he was sterile.

He turned back to the room and faced her.

'Peter?' he said. He had always known, of course. Now that he knew. It had just seemed easier not to.

'Yes,' she said.

'When?' he asked. It seemed important.

She shrugged.

'On his boat – just as you feared. That's the one that counts. But times before. On and off. Three years ago the first. When you were in South Africa.'

He shut his eyes.

'You may as well know this as well. There never was a phone call on the day George died. The reason that his

89

bowl was dry was because I was stretched out on my back upstairs with Peter jumping up and down on top.'

He crossed the room and struck her several times about the face. He could not tell if it was from his outrage at the unforgivably pointless way that George had died or in an effort to remove the picture of four sprawling legs that her words conjured up. Paula resolved his difficulty. She had not attempted to defend herself and beyond hissing had not cried out. Now, cheeks livid from his blows, tears of sheer pain flowing copiously, she spoke.

'For George's sake I grant that I deserve all that. And no doubt much, much more.'

There was a thin trickle of blood on her cheek. He must have caught her with his signet ring. No doubt the gentleman in him would later be conscience-stricken over such heavy handedness. For the moment his prime feeling was a gleeful satisfaction.

'Regarding Peter, I reserve defence,' she said.

'Peter's a shit.'

'Peter is a shit. No doubt, again, it was like calling to like. The first time, you know, it was as much out of curiosity as for any other reason. I wanted to find out again what it was like with someone else.'

'You were searching for a yardstick.'

She returned his sneer.

'Perhaps I felt stuck in a rut,' she said.

'And he was better!'

'No. Different. I won't lie and say I didn't enjoy it. He was fierce, aggressive where you—'

'You can spare me the blow by blow comparison.'

'He's given up on me,' she said. 'That's why he's been avoiding us.'

'Until the next time.'

'Perhaps . . . he's his own worst enemy, of course.'

'Not while I'm alive.'

'He's dreadfully insecure. Has to go endlessly round re-proving himself. Hence the ageing playboy act.'

'Will there be a next time?'

'That depends.'

'Depends!'

But she was circling away from the implication.

'Funny,' she said. 'Ironic. He drops me when . . . that time on the boat – it was like flipping a coin. I never use anything, of course, with you and being on holiday, living out of cases, well I could hardly tote my little extra-marital bag of tricks around with us in my purse. So when I let him have me there, I was sort of gambling with the future. Or rather letting Fate decide if we were going off down a new path. If I got pregnant it would be our child, yours and mine, and he would never know. You have to give me that.'

'You expect me to believe that?'

'You don't have to. You don't have to believe this either. Probably you won't. Coming back in the car this afternoon I almost told you all this anyway.'

'I still think you're lying. Bluffing. Because of this . . . this other.'

'Ring up Doctor Moar.'

'You didn't mention it to your parents this weekend!'

'Of course not. I hadn't told you. I wasn't about to go through this in front of them. Besides I've been weighing all the possibilities that go along with a woman's right to change her mind.'

'What's that supposed to mean?'

'Everything from kidding you it was our child to your routine abortion. And everything between.'

'You were going to leave me?'

'No. I wasn't planning to. As I said in the car I like you. And I like the things we have. Sorry – but that's part of it. But as I also said – just now – now it all depends.'

'On what?'

'If you persist in picking up the phone and insisting we're responsible for old Ted's death, I promise you I'll walk straight out on you.'

'To him?'

'If he'll have me. I think I can make him. Yes. But if not, I'll publicly proclaim that he's the father and you're not and fend for myself somehow. I won't go home to Daddy and Mummy.'

'How do you know I'm not planning to throw you out this minute?'

'I don't.'

'If you did all that, you'd be left worse off than anything the authorities might do to us.'

'Perhaps. Probably. What I'm offering you, no, both of us, is an all or nothing. . . .'

'Deal.'

'Deal. If you want your whole life laid in ruins. If you want total exposure, to be plastered across the headlines twice over – Rabies Killer, Husband Who Didn't Know – then go ahead. Pick up the phone. It's a simple choice. Things as they are or lose the lot. Me. The house. Your job. Our child. It will be our child. I promise that as well.'

'We know what your promises are worth. Your deep concern for others.'

'Rules about sex and rules about the law are not the same for people like us. I've been faithful to you in my fashion.'

'Ha!'

'I've run the risk of sacrificing everything just to protect you from yourself. You might consider that. . . . It all comes back to one clear fact. At this actual moment there's no real proof and certainly less evidence that Asp had rabies. Still . . . do as you must. I've said my bit.'

Her voice tailed lamely away. Her hand gestured feebly. Blood still trickled from her cheek. Her face was a mess. But he saw it from beneath so great a weight of weariness there was no importance in the fact. He saw she had a kind of calm and that she did not know what he would choose to do. They were still standing. The room had been exhausted of all air. Breathless, unbreathing, they faced each other in a vacuum of time as if embalmed. The accumulated details of ten years' life together crowded upon John's mind. It came into his mind from nowhere that the name of the blonde secretary in Cape Town was Anne.

He moved towards the telephone.

'We'll call your bluff,' he said.

CHAPTER EIGHT

'I still can't bring myself to believe it's true,' Rupert Marsh said flatly. 'I just can't take it in. You two!'

'I certainly thought your phone call was the routine got-home-safely one,' his wife took up. Grey-haired, trim and petite, she seemed the less unruffled.

'After letting it go for so long!' Rupert said. 'Here, perhaps another go at the old champers will drive it into my thick skull.'

'Coming up in the next bucket! Good job it's champagne. I'll have to forswear mother's ruin!' Paula was instantly on her feet and pouring freely from her parent's magnum of Veuve Cliquot Ponsardin.

'Now, now, my girl,' Rupert joked inevitably, 'you should be resting – lying back with your feet up.'

'How do you think it happened?' Hilary Marsh said in a sly aside.

'Mummy! We've been through all those jokes already.'

Considering it was her mother she addressed, there was an unusually sharp ring to Paula's tone. That was perhaps understandable. It was the following evening. She and John had been unable to prevent her parents driving over to celebrate the joyful news that she was pregnant.

'We'll prematurely wet the baby's head,' Rupert had chortled down the line to John.

'John's the one it really seems to have knocked for a loop,' said Hilary. 'Hardly a word all evening. White as a sheet. Shadows like nobody's business round his eyes. You'd think he was the one expecting. And any moment now.'

'It has been quite a shock,' Paula said quickly. 'After so long. And the poor dear's been positively savaged by all those brutes he works with at the office.'

She could have bitten off her tongue. Why had she put it like that? Because, of course, it was the one thing pounding through her brain. Ceaselessly. She must watch herself; use more control. She could see that it had cut into John's conscience like a knife, see the effort it had cost him not to wince.

John smiled at Hilary in a vague way. What Paula had maintained, might or might not be true. He had no idea. His office day had passed a nightmare montage of strange shapes and distant sounds. All meaningless. All that concerned him was if a phone should ring with the news that a body had been found in Mullen's Barn. It hadn't. He had floated in a limbo of suspense and by mid-afternoon, unable to bear it any longer had announced that he was sick and leaving for the day. No-one had objected or seemed at all surprised. No news, he had discovered getting home, was still bad news.

'If I hadn't been so flabbergasted,' somebody was saying, 'I wouldn't have tried to put an end to all of it by slamming the door in Paula's face.'

'Mother and child in one fell swoop,' Hilary said. 'I think there's probably a teeny-weeny law against a thing like that.'

Suddenly they could all hear the approaching crescendo of a clanging bell.

'And here come the police to nab you now,' Rupert was saying jovially.

'Good Lord the ambulance is early. There's the best part of eight months to go.'

Paula had spoken instantly but had not forestalled the ashen look that swept across John's face. Through the half-opened panels to the dining-room they caught a stabbing flare of headlights slewing in a rake across the house. There was a throb of engines idling.

'Probably that water main again,' Paula said. 'They never get it right.'

Rupert had got up.

'You know,' he said, 'I'm an old codger and a bit slow on the uptake but I think at last the message has got through.

94

Matter of fact, I'm sure it has. Thing is, at last, long after I had given up all hope, I'm going to be a grandfather. Well, excuse the descent into speechifying — but, dash it, let one just put on formal record that nothing in this life could have so gladdened my old age as knowing now one day you two will be enjoying the same role that at this time is such a privilege and a pleasure for Hilary and me.'

A corner of John's mind was able to acknowledge the perfect niceness of the old boy's gesture, but as he raised an answering glass to his own lips, he was straining every nerve to avoid an appearance of shock when the doorbell rang. But no ring came. Instead, he had a sense of lights, of distant footfalls hurrying down the path to Mullen's Field.

'A very pretty speech, my dear,' Hilary was saying. 'Sentiments I thoroughly concur with. And evidence, I think, beyond all question that I shall do the driving on the journey home.'

'If a man can't get a little squiffy on hearing—'

'Talking of which,' Hilary went on, 'I think perhaps we'd best be making a move.'

'Oh, you will have coffee,' Paula said brightly.

'Well, thank you—'

'Won't take a minute. And I've got some absolutely scrumptious *petits fours*.'

Inwardly John groaned. How much longer was the knowledge of that thing inside the barn to hold him in this vice? All his life? Forever? All was quiet again outside. . . . There was this other thing in Paula's body. . . .

'I'll just grind up some coffee-beans,' Paula said. 'I shan't be a moment.' She left the room. John tried to think of something sane to say.

They were midway through their second cup of coffee when, without warning, the doorbell rang. Eyes turned to John. It would seem unnatural for anyone else to go to the door at this late hour. He set his cup aside and went to the front door. He opened it to P.C. Reid. His face in the porch light was white and drawn.

'Sorry to be disturbing you so late,' he said.

'Oh, that's all right.'

'It's bad news, I'm afraid, that brings me. Old Ted Rimmer's been found dead.'

'No!' Tension made John's shocked surprise seem genuine.

'It's true, only too true. Maggie Peacock went to see him earlier this evening. She'd missed him for about a week and started to get worried.'

Behind him John heard the phone begin to ring. He heard Paula answer it.

'She had good reason,' Reid was saying. 'He'd been dead several days. Not a pretty sight.'

'But . . . this is terrible . . . awful . . . How? I mean – do you suspect foul play?'

Reid's face contorted to a grimace.

'There'll have to be an autopsy,' he said. 'Not a pretty sight is not the half of it. Well, I'll spare you the details but I doubt if I'll forget them in a hurry. I shouldn't think so. Foul play, that is. Everyone liked old Ted. Who'd have it in for him? Where would be the profit? Still, on those lines, I thought I'd just come and ask if you'd heard anything. Shouts? Strange noises? Seen anything at all that you'd consider untoward?'

'No. Not a thing. I saw Ted the weekend before this one just gone.'

'Where was that?'

'In the path just down the side here. He brought us round some eggs.'

'Seem all right then?'

'Well, yes. Just his normal self. I don't know if Mrs Denning saw anything. Look, excuse me, Jock, I should have asked you in.'

'No. That's all right, thanks, Mr Denning. I'm not much in the mood for company right now, to tell you the honest truth. I can see from the car outside you've got people in. But if you wouldn't mind asking Mrs Denning the same questions when you have a moment, I'd be much obliged. If by any chance she does think she might have seen something, perhaps she'd be kind enough to get in touch.'

'Yes. All right, Jock. I'll ask her; tell her what you said.'
Reid made to move, paused and looked at John.

'I know you and old Ted were . . . well,' he said, 'I'm sorry to have been the bearer of bad news.'

John tried to offer back a similar sign of fellow feeling. He found his smile stuck in his throat.

'Everybody liked him,' he mindlessly repeated.

'Yes.'

'. . . what about a funeral?'

Reid grimaced again.

'God knows,' he said. 'But the quicker the better and let it be cremation.'

He nodded. John nodded back and closed the door. For a few seconds he did not move. He stared at an arrangement of oak panels that meant less to him than the craters of the moon. He turned and faced the hall. The blue and white umbrella stand. The sporting prints. They were two weeks ago, a thousand lives away. He saw again those eyes that could not see and yet saw right through him. They scorched a new word on his brain: autopsy. He realised he was back in the drawing-room with everybody looking at him.

'Don't keep us in suspense. What was all that about?' Paula said.

'Oh. Nothing. Jock Reid. Er, wanted to check something about my gun permit.'

'At this hour?'

'He saw the lights.'

'The phone rang while you were at the door.'

'Yes?'

'It was Petersen. There's a bit of a flap on, it seems. The great white chief in Baltimore.'

'Mike Kaminsky?'

'Yes. Him. He's decreed there should be a gathering of the clans. You're to—'

'What! Go over there!'

'Yes.'

'I can't do that on top of all this mess! I can't!'

Paula's face froze, he had nearly given the whole game away.

'Mess? What mess?' asked Hilary sharply.

John caught his breath.

'That wasn't quite the truth just then,' he said. 'It was Jock Reid, yes. But he had some rather upsetting news, though, I'm afraid – Ted Rimmer's been found dead.'

'Oh no,' said Paula. 'Not old Ted!' She did it very well.

'I'm afraid so. I didn't want to spoil our celebration.'

'Appreciated,' Rupert said. 'I thought you looked a bit subdued when you came back.'

'More like a man who'd just seen his own ghost,' said Hilary.

'Well it was a bit of a shock. I was quite fond of Ted.'

'The famous educated-tramp chap?' Rupert said.

'Yes.'

'Well, he was quite old.'

'Yes. . . . What was all this nonsense about Baltimore?'

'Not nonsense,' Paula said. 'You're expected there on Wednesday. You're to fly to Dublin late tomorrow morning and meet up with that Caroll fellow. Then you go straight to Shannon and on to Washington D.C.'

John shook his head. It was impossible.

'Now come on,' Paula said. 'A change is as good as a rest. Your Dublin flight leaves Heathrow at eleven thirty-five, so I can drive you up. Then you can sit back and relax. You know these jaunts are all perk and no work.'

She stared at him.

'There's always the telephone if you miss me,' she said, with even emphasis. 'It's only like Newcastle.'

'But better,' Rupert said. 'Gosh, jet-setting young executive. All right for some. Now you make sure you bring me back some of those MacGregor hunting shirts.'

John didn't hear him. He was looking straight at Paula screaming at her with his eyes he couldn't go on, he was down and out and longing to fall into a soft, soft sleep where all of this would be a distant dream.

'Why didn't you call me?' he said. 'I could have talked to him myself.'

'I didn't see the need. You were tied up at the door. It

was only taking down the details of the trip. I've got them here. You can always call him back.'

He felt so tired. There were so many variables. So many questions. . . . But part of his mind, the part that all along had watched him from afar now whispered to him like a dark bad angel. Go on, it seemed to say, you'll be well out of this. When you come back you'll feel much better. You won't feel tired, and everything that's nasty will have blown right over.

Hilary, Rupert and Paula were all looking at him once again.

'No,' he said, 'I won't do that. I suppose there's no real need.'

CHAPTER NINE

To the considerable surprise of the hard-core businessmen who were the majority of its passengers, John's flight to Dublin took off exactly on time. His insides washed dry with fatigue after a sleepless night, John stared straight into the featureless plastic back of the headrest before him. He closed his eyes and after a short while he slept.

He had, in a sense, chosen an apt moment to leave his native land.

It was no great surprise to Florrie, the barmaid at the Dog and Fox that when she turned up for work that morning one of poor Ted Rimmer's terriers was nosing among the dustbins. She did not know that just about this moment John's plane was taking off, but she did know the sad, bedraggled little mite was now without an owner. In a village, gossip travels fast and bad news travels faster. Several days, they said: the poor thing must be starving: come here from force of habit. Chop it was. As she had done so many times before, she bent to pet it. Chop drew his lip back in the briefest snarl and the next thing Florrie knew she had received a sharp and smarting bite.

'You little devil! What you do that for then?' she said.

Admonished, the terrier seemed to grow aware of what he'd done. He slunk away. Sucking blood from the pierced skin on two fingers, Florrie watched for a few seconds till he had disappeared into some bushes, then turned and walked into the pub. She could tell at once from the noise, that Wilf was shifting barrels in the cellar and she called out to him. In a few moments he came up the steps. His broad round face was without a smile and he made no attempt to greet her.

'Bad day for all today,' he said directly.

'And no mistake,' Florrie said. 'Poor Ted. Poor old boy.'

'You hear what they're saying. Maggie was hysterical.' Florrie shuddered.

'I don't want to know about that side,' she said.

'Here – what you done to your fingers?'

'I just got bit. And it was by one of old Ted's dogs. I just seen him round by our dustbins.'

'Hungry he'll be.'

'I expect how he's upset at losing his master, poor little bleeder. Never saw the other'n.'

'You want to watch that, Florrie. Dog bites can be bad.'

'No, t'isn't nothing. I'll just hold it under the tap. Won't even need a plaster.'

As John Denning's flight levelled out at fifteen thousand feet and the Captain woke him with his crackling efforts at P.R., Miss Weldon was on her regular Tuesday morning expedition to the corner shop. Her matching corgies padded squatly at her side. A middle-aged spinster in her prime, somewhat corgi-like in appearance, Miss Weldon did good works. She might well have been a figure of some fun. But few in the village mocked her. They saw the work she did as Chairwoman of the Women's Institute and as a Parish Councillor and she was much respected. Now, however, without warning, there came a rude and sudden interruption to the even tenor of her ways. As she passed close to the Dog and Fox a small dog hurtled forth from a clump of bushes and viciously launched itself upon the two unprepared and unsuspecting corgis. The instant result was a snapping, barking, snarling mêlée. To an onlooker it might have had something of a Keystone comedy about it but mild Miss Weldon was appalled.

'Get away you nasty little brute!' she shrieked.

To no effect. The small dog, a terrier, was twisting, turning, biting like a thing possessed. The game and plucky corgis were trying to give as good as they had got. Long submerged protective instincts overcame Miss Weldon's fear. Taking her life into both her hands, her shopping bag in one, she aimed a swinging roundhouse blow at the whirling little dervish of a dog. It leapt aside and she had clumped one of her darlings about the ribs. Almost over-balancing, she dropped the bag and half on the ground committed herself to a policy of no-holds-barred counter-attack. She grabbed at the dog which in its teeth-bared fury looked like a scalded cat and it bit her for her pains. She cried out and lashed out with a stoutly brogued foot. This time her aim was true. Caught in the throat the terrier ran choking back to cover.

Miss Weldon fought to regain control of her own breath and of her bristling corgis now worked up to a ferocious indignation in their own right. However, when Miss Weldon entered the village shop a few minutes later, the corgis were at peace again and Miss Weldon was sucking the blood from the bite on the side of her left hand. She bought some sticking plaster there and then.

'Twenty-three years I've lived here,' she righteously proclaimed, 'and I've never been subjected to such un-warranted unpleasantness before.'

She stuck a plaster home. The rest of the shop's congre-gation of morning gossipers exchanged sly looks. It was a rare sight to catch Miss Weldon with her feathers ruffled. It was hard to know quite where to hide your smile.

'What dog was it?' Tom Durrant thought to ask.

'You know, it all happened so quickly I'm really not at all sure I know,' Miss Weldon said. 'A small one. Yes. I'm sure of that and from the council estate I've little doubt.'

There were more grins. Tom, a pensioner, felt it might be kind to pour some oil on Miss Weldon's troubled waters.

'Well,' he said, 'if you've lived in these parts twenty-three years and never had a nip from a dog afore now, then you've been right lucky, Miss. Why, I've been bitten more times than I've had hot dinners and it ain't never done me no harm.'

'It's not myself I'm worried about,' Miss Weldon said in mother-hen solicitude. 'Look what the savage brute has done to Jane and Emma.'

* * * * *

A half-hour later John Denning's plane was cruising high above the Irish Sea. He had relapsed into a fitful, twitching compromise between consciousness and sleep. At Abbots-field Primary School the fun of the lunchtime break was in full swing. In a kaleidoscope of whirling noise and move-ment the six, seven and eight-year-olds were acting out, on their own compressed scale, all of the tragedy and comedy that some would experience again as adults. Some.

For Marion Gadney and Tricia Mallet it was a time of bitter recrimination. During sums that morning Charlie Swinton had whispered he was fed up with Marion always trying to copy him. From now on Tricia was going to be his proper girlfriend. Marion had retaliated by saying that was just because her mum was the headmistress and was now shrilly accusing the pig-tailed other woman of aliena-tion of affection. Meanwhile, true to his first true-love, tennis-ball football, Charlie was oblivious to this affair of the heart. He, and his side of Johnny Mallet, Robert Park and Bryan Moore were busy emulating their television heroes in reacting to a goal that Bryan had just snapped up. Amid so much fervent drama nobody noticed the small dog, its coat stark, its eyes staring, that had slipped in under the gate. Then Charlie noticed it.

'Look,' he called out, 'there's Chip, old Ted the tramp's dog.'

'Old Ted's dead,' said Robert.

'I know!' said Charlie. 'He was in the barn. Miss Peacock found him. That's why she's away.'

'That's not Chip, that's Chop,' said Johnnie. 'He's the old one. And Chip ain't got a brown back neither. Here boy, come on, then.'

The footballers, their game forgotten, advanced towards the dog. Chop did not move.

'Here, boy,' Robert said as he knelt down.

Chop nervously approached the outstretched hand and in doing so was transformed. A spasm juddered through his body. His lip was curled, his teeth bared. A queer bark came from his throat. The boys looked at this sudden nightmare monster and then at one another. Nobody quite wanted to let on how scared he felt. Four very ordinary small boys, they hesitated doubtfully. And were too late. With all the speed of a good ratter, Chop had pounced. In split seconds two bitten hands, an ankle and, in Charlie's case a copiously bleeding ear marked his demented progress. The boys shrieked and yelled out. Then with that utter bravery that only children are compelled to show, each held back the tears that, alone with his mother, he would have let flow unchecked. So it was the screams of the two girls that now brought thin Mary Burns at long-legged speed out from the tiny staff room.

She saw a group of fearful boys and girls huddling toward the further playground wall. A growling dog was crouched down on the asphalt fixing them with yellowed, glaring eyes. The children! With no thought for herself she moved to put herself between the dog and them.

'Mary! Stay there! Don't move!' Saving her life, a sharp voice stopped her in her tracks. She whipped her head around. Coming into the school yard was the burly shouldered figure of Mike Mallet.

'All right,' he said. 'You just stay there.'

Mary sighed with unreserved relief. Nobody better could have turned up. The headmistress's husband, Mike was the keeper for the local syndicate. He was slipping his gun from off his shoulder now and whistling once, made the panting terrier shift its glassy stare in his direction. But, surely, in front of the children, he wasn't going to . . . no . . . his gun laid down Mike was gently removing his jacket as all the time he sneaked nearer to the dog. The jacket in both hands, he had drawn close. With no warning he had thrown the coat. His aim was true but the dog quicker. Alarmed it bolted for the gate and, as it had entered, squeezed itself under and away. As if exhausted, it settled down in the grubby, unused field right opposite the school.

'I'll fetch Celia,' Mike called out. He picked up his gun and jacket and disappeared into the tiny school and Mary smiling reassuringly, began to quieten the scared and chattering children. Perhaps a little uncertainly, they were starting to smile back at Miss Burns when their head-mistress and her husband came out from the school.

'Wasn't Mr Mallet brave, children?' Mary asked in her best classroom voice.

'Yes, miss,' came the chorus.

'Hands up those who actually got bitten,' Mrs Mallett said. 'Those the bad doggy bit. Charley, I can see you were.'

Six hands went up.

'Hmm. Our two,' said Mrs Mallet in an aside to husband and colleague. 'Bit of luck there. I'll only have four incensed parents to deal with tomorrow.'

'If Maggie had been in, we would have had someone on playground duty,' Mary said.

'Yes. Well. Never mind. Goodness knows she's got good reason to be off.'

'That's one of old Ted's dogs,' Mike said. 'He may have had reason to be upset and all, but six kids bitten's too much for a dog without a home.'

He glanced eloquently at his gun.

'Couldn't in all conscience recommend him anywhere else now,' he said. 'You get the kids inside. Then ring the bell right good and loud.'

With brisk cheerfulness the two teachers began to march the children in. Loading his gun Mike crossed the road. Chop was still lying in the same position where he'd come to rest. His eyes were dulled now almost as if with absent-mindedness. Mike closed the gun and the terrier turned as the school bell began to ring. Mike aimed and fired. One barrel at that range was adequate. The second was a gesture towards mercy. Chop kicked two or three times and was still. The school bell ceased to ring. Mike tucked the gun under his right arm and, stooping, picked the body up by its hind legs. He made towards the woods. Shortly, using the spade he kept in the old charcoal burner's hut, he was starting on a grave. By about the time that he was finished, his wife had just completed washing the bites of her 'poor wounded soldiers'. To err on the side of safety she had used rather more antiseptic in the solution than she would have for a playground graze. Her soothing words had had effect. Even Charlie with a bitten ear was back to normal, boasting a little as the bites became a source of classroom pride, that his head bled the most. Only as she packed away the first-aid kit did it enter Mrs Mallett's head to wonder why her husband had been looking in on her.

All Irish eyes a-smiling and a broth of a boy to boot, Sean Carroll was waiting to meet John at Dublin airport. The blarney came out nineteen to the dozen. John parried with some token nods and smiles. It was a pity, he reflected, that on this trip they were teamed to trouble-shoot together against Baltimore. Carroll was a man who knew the price of everything and the value of always being charming, and personally John didn't like him one least little bit. He wouldn't trust him further than he could throw Trinity College. As the taxi crossed O'Connell Bridge, he continued going through the motions of rapt attention but Carroll's talk of European non-viability for the bracket given an unchanged U.S. tar-rating had him all but screaming. His heart sank. The whole trip would be no more than extended going through of just such motions. How did you shoot trouble when you no longer gave a damn?

At about the time that John was forming these conclusions in the back seat of a Dublin taxi, a second car, a Triumph station wagon was drawing to a halt outside a pleasant modern house in Midhurst, Sussex. George Wrinch was returning from picking up his two teenage sons from a long weekend spent with their mother at her home in Abbotsfield. George was in peevish mood. He was not yet reconciled to his former wife's new-married bliss. Additionally, she had worked a cheap trick on him. The two boys had been walking in the woods when a small terrier had playfully made friends with them. It had stuck to them refusing to go off. It had followed them back to that bitch's place and, thanks to her encouragement, been fed and consequently was still there in the morning. When he'd turned up the boys had asked to keep him. He'd naturally said not: the dog must have an owner, you couldn't just waltz off with it. But like a Cheshire cat his former wife, whose name just now escaped him, had gleefully announced she recognised the dog and knew for an actual fact the owner had pegged out a couple of days before. He was an old recluse who lived alone.

'So you see the dog is just like you are, George,' she'd said, still grinning from ear to ear. 'Completely up for grabs.'

The German bitch had known the boys would take against him if he kept on refusing so, now, here they were back home and here was he saddled with this canine liability while that bloody kraut of an ex-wife died laughing. Would that she would!

'O.K.' he said. 'Out you all get. And, remember, I'll say it one more time – that pooch gets fed from your own pocket money.'

'Dad, we've already promised twice,' Terry Wrinch answered back.

His brother Dominic was opening up the tailgate.

'Here Chip. Nice dog,' he said.

Towards six o'clock that evening both John and Paula Denning were sitting in the lap of well-upholstered chairs. Some little distance parted them. John was twenty-six thousand feet above the Atlantic in a droning west-bound Boeing. To ward off further punishment from his mono-loguing colleague he was busy feigning sleep. Paula was in Abbotsfield. Curled on the chesterfield, Troy sprawled before her, she was watching Southern TV's early evening news. It too was something of a bore. The pound had fallen once again to set an all-time low against the dollar. The trade deficit for the last quarter was the second worst on record. The National Union of Students were talking of a wholesale boycott of all institutions unless their claims for 'no-string' increases in grants were met. Not really tasting it, Paula munched on a chocolate mint. Then, suddenly, alarming Troy who started up, ears pricked, she was reaching forward to turn up the sound. Assuming his best human-interest face, the newscaster had mentioned Abbotsfield where, the previous night, the body of a man had been discovered in a disused barn. Despite certain macabre circumstances identification had been possible. The deceased was known in the neighbourhood for sleeping rough. An autopsy had revealed that death was due to natural causes. Thieves in Southampton had made off—

Paula switched off the set. She smiled at Troy and winked. 'I told you so,' she said.

Troy wagged his tail in happy ignorance.

Paula picked up the phone. She dialled the village police force.

'Jock,' she said, 'it's Paula Denning.'

'Ah, good evening, Mrs Denning.'

'Jock, I've just heard on the news about old Ted and it reminded me that I was supposed to call you.'

'Well, only if you had some information.'

'Well, no, I don't. Just making it official, as it were.'

'Right, well, thank you—'

'They said it was from natural causes, anyway.'

'Yes.'

'Can you, er . . . what . . .'

'Heart failure. Cardiac arrest associated with pneumonia.'

'Oh dear. If only— We're so close.'

'Yes. If only. Still, it's happened now. Anyway, thank you for phoning, Mrs Denning.'

'No. Not at all. . . . Sorry I forgot.'

'Not to worry. Goodbye.'

'Goodbye.'

Grinning again, Paula replaced the receiver. She settled back. She began to work out when she might expect John's call. She patted the sofa loudly with her hand and Troy jumped up beside her. Soon she was letting him help her finish off the mints.

CHAPTER TEN

'Hold the line a moment, please,' the English operator said.

There was a sound of electronic gremlins skittering back and forth the three-thousand-mile length of the line. There was a sharp, dry click.

'Hello, Paula?'

He sounded louder and clearer than if she were calling him at his Southampton office.

'Hello, my love. How are you?'

'Fine, fine. A bit tired. It's very hot here. Sticky.'

'What time is it?'

'About two in the afternoon. I'm calling from the hotel. We had a meeting scheduled for this morning but I knocked them for a loop by standing up and saying I was exhausted, suffering from jet lag and in no shape to do any kind of business. You should have seen Sean Carroll's face!'

'John – was that wise?'

'It was necessary. I was dizzy with fatigue. In the long run I think it may serve me in good stead. Paula . . . I've been half sick to death with worry. I can't sleep or—'

'Well you don't have to anymore. Worry. Darling, there's wonderful news. About old Ted. Wonderful for us, I mean. There was a what do you call it a—'

'Post mortem. Autopsy.'

'Yes. And it was natural causes.'

'Paula! You're sure of that?'

'Yes! Positive! Heart failure with complications from pneumonia.'

'Paula, you wouldn't—'

'Darling, I'll send you the page from the local rag as soon as it comes out. It was on TV as well and I spoke to Jock Reid just to make sure they weren't doing a cover up.'

'Oh, Paula, you can't know how relieved it makes me feel to hear that. It's like a ton of lead's been lifted from my mind. Gosh – I'll be able to think about other things now. The job, for instance. You've no idea, it was like being hypnotised, unable to—'

'You might credit me with some fellow feeling, darling.'

'I know. I'm sorry. It's been a strain for both of us. What about Chop and Chip? Have they been found?'

'Oh, Mike Mallett's taken care of them,' Paula said.

She hadn't planned the lie. She had opened her mouth and it had come out. There was a grain of truth in it.

'That's just like Mike,' John was saying. 'But they'll be good ratters for him. Listen, it looks as if I'll be here several days. You'd better take down the hotel address and number.'

She did so. It was the company's money so they talked on for a good five minutes. By that time they were exchanging remarks that at home, side by side on the chesterfield they would not have wasted breath on. But it was a good sign, Paula thought. She'd get him back to normal.

'Goodbye then, my love. I'm missing you already,' John called out.

'Goodbye, darling. You go to sleep now and sleep well.'

Paula put down the phone and scratched absently at the back of her right hand.

In the scrupulously sanitised and vinyled hotel room, John was suddenly wishing they were still talking. Belatedly, even as he was replacing his own receiver, it had come to him that according to the encyclopaedia, rabies was a virus and as such the bugs would probably be so small that unless you had a special microscope or were actually on the lookout for them. . . . Oh, sod it! he told himself, knock it off. Paula was right. He did go out of his way to make himself a nervous wreck. It was good news, full stop. Or period as they said over here. Now, sleep, beautiful sleep. If he could just get this air-conditioning monster to shut up. He was just dozing off when the smiling image of Peter Halliwell came to disturb his rest.

Although she had spoken of even more trivial things,

Paula had neglected to tell John of a small function she had attended earlier that day. There was no obvious reason for this: their chat had simply not gone off on that particular tangent.

That lunchtime, from duty as much as pleasure, Paula had gone to a sherry party. Miss Weldon had been her hostess. Wearing the hat of Secretary to the Village Preservation Society, Miss Weldon had taken this daring and dashing step as a first manœuvre towards diverting the proposed route for a motorway link that now threatened to come within two miles of Abbotsfield. Paula had been sort of irritably amused. Miss Weldon's indignation was overly protective: resistance on the scale that they could offer to the juggernaut of Government bureaucracy would be pointless. And those two damned corgis wouldn't settle down. They were roaming about listlessly and getting under everybody's feet.

Paula tended to parade her affection for animals and she had an opportunity to do so now. She knelt to one of the small dogs and, hand extended, started to make soothing noises. The corgi waddled forward, licked her hand in tentative fashion once or twice. Standing on its hind legs, it transferred the show of its affections, kissing her with rough-tongued messiness about the face. Paula laughed, twisted her head this way and that to escape the hot and heavy licking. The dog dropped back onto all-fours. It sniffed her hand again. Abruptly, its eyes blazed and its sharp, pointed muzzle was snarling at her with bared teeth.

Perhaps because she didn't quite believe her own denials about Asp, Paula's reaction had been very fast. As the dog snarled she'd drawn her hand away. The corgi's lunging bite closed only upon empty air. It moved to try again, but with a sharp, instinctive kick, Paula, in straightening, sent it yelping back. She was immediately non-plussed at having been seen publicly as less than dog's best friend but Miss Weldon was an instant flood of mortified apology.

'There's been no living with them lately,' she gushed on. 'I don't at all know what's come over them. You're quite sure Emma didn't get you?'

'Quite sure,' Paula smiled. 'Please don't worry, really.'

'Well let me get you just another drop of sherry. Was it the cream or medium . . .?'

Miss Weldon banished her two pets from the room. The slightly amused gathering were able to resume the motions of a motorway resistance cell.

It was a hot cloudy day without rain and it felt as if thunder was in the close air. Yet as she walked the short distance back home Paula felt a chill. Twice, involuntarily, she shivered. It was nonsense, of course. There was nothing in it. But she wondered what course she would have taken had she been actually bitten. No doubt she would have thought of something. It might have been awkward, though. Good Lord, what was that? Ugh! At the road's edge she saw the contorted body of a rat. Its legs were rigid and about its jaws blood and mucus had drawn several late flies. Yet again she shuddered. It reminded her of Asp.

Three days later, as she had promised, she forwarded John an account cut from the local newspaper of old Ted's death. There, she thought, he's got it in black and white. There was some chance her letter and he might cross but, although the house seemed far too large and lonely, she rather hoped that John's return would not be quite that soon. Her scissors had been necessary. On the same page, next to that very account, had been a report of how Ted Rimmer's dog had run amok in the school playground. That was a bridge she was proposing to cross as late as possible. If John were to come home soon and see that page with his own eyes – well, wait and see.

And yet she missed him more than she had ever done before. After the long luxurious lie-in on his first morning away, she found bed, in every sense, a bore. Time hung heavily on her hands. This was his third, no, fourth trip to the States. You'd have thought by now they might have stretched a point and let her tag along. These trips could not be as grim as men liked to make out. She tried to work off her impatience on long hours in the garden. Remembering to wear her gloves more often now than not – she had picked up a nasty scratch on the back of her right hand – she hoed and tidied it to new immaculacy. The latest additions, the rose bushes, were promising great things and what lay beneath their roots was, as far as she was concerned, quite out of sight. Then she received a US air letter. She tore it open eagerly. Before she was halfway through its quite short contents, her legs were weak and trembling. It was one of those letters that in putting down on paper ideas or thoughts usually left unsaid, floods the recipient with embarrassment. And yet the contents were most tender. The letter was from John and ran as follows.

Dear Paula,

It may well be that I am speaking to you – even seeing you – about the time that you get this. But this is something special between us and I want to mark that fact by putting it on paper. Putting it on record, if you like.

You well know (and for what very good reasons) I've been a worried man these past few weeks. That, thank God, is now all in the past. It leaves me free to think of something else: what you have told me about you and Peter.

In a way the other business insulated me from the shock of what you told me. It is clear grounds for divorce, of course, but somehow, at the time, I didn't completely take it in. Perhaps there is a Providence that shapes our ends because had I not been so preoccupied I might have blown my top and done something I bitterly regretted afterwards. You see, darling, writing in this antiseptic shoe-box of a hotel room so far away from you, I know now more than ever that I love you. Divorce is the last thing I want.

Just as, in a way, I respect your honesty in telling me about you and Peter, so I accept your word that all is now over between the two of you. Which leaves us with the child. Our child – as you also say. The full implications of our finally becoming parents are only now beginning to dawn upon me. Let me just say that the same joy is beginning now to blossom in me as we could see in Rupert and in Hilary the other (terrible) night.

I am going downstairs, shortly, for the inevitable choice of Roquefort, Thousand Islands or Blue Cheese upon my salad, but I wanted to first write you this in case, left to yourself, you might be wondering if I were going to come the deeply wronged and outraged husband. Judge for yourself, my darling.

All my love, John

Tearfully, Paula read the letter a second time. She then flew to the phone. She had the receiver in her hand before she remembered that in Baltimore it would still be the small hours of the night. By the time she did get through, the other part of her had had enough time to reflect that at such a distance, John had small choice but to believe that she and Peter were all through. She did not like herself for thinking that and now she was at pains to say how much he meant to her, how much in the one way that truly mattered she had always loved him.

'I wish you were here so I could tell you properly,' she said.

There was a little pause.

'I've got bad news on that, my love,' John said. 'I won't be coming back quite so soon.'

'Oh, no!'

'I've got to go down to Arkansas for a week to look at plant and discuss changes. My hard-line policy seems to have put the fear of God into the lot of them.'

'But John—'

'Tell you what. Why not start getting used to putting your feet up and go and spend a few days with your parents. Can't be bad, now, can it, and they'd love to have you.'

She did and, John was right, they were. But inexplicably however much Troy might enjoy Rupert's attention, Paula found the change not a welcome diversion but a yawning, dragging bore. Usually she was nothing loath to have the whole world fetch and carry for her, to be waited upon hand and foot. Especially at her parents! But pregnancy had made her fidgetty. She could settle, she found, to nothing. A book, television, a simple conversation with her mother – it made no difference. Her attention span was down to minutes if not seconds. She was beginning to swell up. If her parent's bathroom scales were to be believed (and her own tightening skirts confirmed they were) she had put on some five or six pounds. The hot and puffy cut on her face obstinately refused to vanish, and she felt generally ill; either complaining of a headache, a sore throat or aching limbs – all the symptoms of 'flu which never materialised. Roaming from room to room, from chair to chair, in a house grown strangely pokey, she found what she positively wanted was to be left alone.

'Good lord, girl,' Rupert had joked, 'anyone would think you had ants in your pants!'

'For heaven's sake, Daddy,' Paula had snapped, 'if you can't say something witty or original, why not say nothing at all!'

Rupert had blinked. He was not used to having his own daughter bite his head off. But he had followed her advice. You had to make allowances. Funny things women. In Hilary's case it had been mustard pickle.

Then the phone had gone. It had been Petersen from John's Southampton office.

'Sorry to disturb you, Paula,' he familiarly said. 'I got this number from the woman who does for you.'

Paula had kept her voice at a good arm's length.

'That's all right,' she said. 'What is it?'

'Got a bit of news for you.'

'Good, I trust.'

Petersen unctuously laughed.

'That depends,' he said. 'Depends on you. No, the thing is, it has been decided that your better half should do a bit more travelling for us before he heads for home.'

'Travelling? Where to now?'

'He's the best part of the way there now, it could be said, so we're sending him on to Aussie-land as soon as he's through in the Deep South.'

'Australia! How long for?'

'Just a few days. It's his own fault really. He's driven those tough Yankie wheeler-dealers into the ground by the stumps of their own knees. Then on to Seoul.'

'Where?'

'Korea. Positively the last port of call. He'll be back home safe and sound in – oh – ten days at the outside.'

Petersen was having fun. He could not keep the chortle out of his voice.

'Well you don't have to be so bloody jubilant!' Paula shouted.

'What? Oh, well, sorry. But that's the old cigarette game for—'

But Paula had hung up.

Illogically, she had gone off back home that same day. She could tell that Hilary and Rupert were both mildly hurt but, what the hell, they'd had their emotional pound of flesh for the time being. At least back here you could walk around without them breathing down your neck. Christ, she thought, am I going to feel so awful for the next seven months?

Sleep was a problem too. Feverish, she'd twist and turn. In princess and the pea fashion she found the least ruck in the sheet a thorn to her hyper-sensitive flesh and even as she missed the comforting bulk and weight of another body in the bed, she'd find that her restless, twitching legs had left her sprawling more out of the bed than in. The bed, in fact, at one and the same time was too big and too small.

One morning she woke up wanting a man. She couldn't remember when she last had felt the urge so overwhelmingly. She spread her legs apart upon the bed and pressed into the mattress with her arms, the whole weight of her body. Her limbs seemed hollow and a soft warm liquid of desire running up through them to her belly. She thought of Peter Halliwell. To call him up, of course, was quite unthinkable. But she could think about him . . . she saw him standing above her, lean, grinning, erect. She saw the ridge of hard flat muscle across his stomach. She felt again the sinews of his shoulders and his back working beneath her touch. She shivered now with pure desire and in the shiver found the ghost of climax. Why shouldn't she call Peter? What could be the harm. Now of all times. The deed was done. What was it they said? You don't miss a slice off a cake already cut? No, it *was* unthinkable. Just on grounds of pride. She tried to think of other sexy men and realised, these days, she knew virtually none. He had been so tanned. So hard. She had a sudden fierce desire to strip off her pyjamas and still lie there. Knowing what must then inevitably ensue she forced herself up. She went into the bathroom for an aspirin for her nagging headache.

That day dragged on one long eternity. No-one came or called. She lacked the will to get out of the house. She nibbled through the day on little snacks – chocolate, a crab-paste sandwich, cheese. Recurrently, melting her from within, the raw desire came sweeping back upon her. Peter! She could feel how it had been to have him in her, those strong firm hands touching her, controlling her. . . . The memory was cruel. Not enough, it put fresh edge on appetite. A dozen times that afternoon she fought off the temptation to pick up the phone. Then suddenly she was inspired. She should have thought of it before! She'd been cooped up all day, she was famished and to cook was just a bore. O.K.! She would go out and eat!

She bathed luxuriously, a vision of handsome men floating upon her mind; she lingered at the soaping of her breasts, letting the nipples tauten as she tried to give a perfect face to one of them. Somehow she could not. Their faces stayed obscure and fluid, tantalisingly veiled. She powdered and perfumed with an elaboration she had not used in years and then, feeling a clear *frisson* as she did so, put on her merest see-through wisps of underwear. She chose the dress with care. Provocative, its extreme expensiveness was guarantee against it being obvious or common. With like concern she opted for the BMW.

She went out to the garage. The lure that sex compelled her toward, for all its vagueness, had almost total power. There was a body of a second rat stiff upon her driveway. She saw and was at pains to step around it. But she did not wince and was not disturbed. In backing out she squashed it spatteringly flat.

As do most women, Paula drove well. Tonight she pushed that talent to its limits. Tyres squealed in rising protest, the gears crunched and other cars running for cover hooted and flashed. Paula was oblivious, or, rather saw from afar with a wild, exultant disinterest. She had no plan. There was this restaurant by the road. It had a bar. Unescorted, hell, so what, she would have a drink. There would be a table and she'd eat. Somewhere there would be a man. Tall. Romantic. Courtly. Somehow in an aura of *Vent Vert* the two of them would come together. Her blood was pulsing to a rhythm. Her eyes were luminous, her cheeks hectic as she screeched the car into the parking lot and to a savage halt. The rhythm sharply ceased. The car that she had threatened with her final power-steered turn was one she recognised. The next slot housed a yellow Scimitar.

Her visions wavered, almost broke. Her chilled heart began to beat the signal for retreat. And then her mouth tightened, her chin came up. If it had to be, let it. She had done her part. She had refused to phone. If Fate had ordained that Peter was to be inside waiting for her, then it must be. Why else had she had this overwhelming impulse to come here like this tonight? She suddenly knew why all the men floating in her young girl's dreams had all refused to take on clear-cut faces. Her inner self would not allow it. It was dishonest to deny it. The man she'd wanted all day long was Peter Halliwell. She took a deep breath, steadied herself. Making a meal of it, she swept in through the doorway of the Golden Pheasant.

He was the first person she saw. The bar was fairly crowded but as she smiled and indicated to the girl that she would keep her coat, Peter was the first person she saw. And he saw her. A quick frown of recognition crossed his face; then he was smiling too. She crossed towards him. In good time he could more intimately take her coat. He rose from his bar stool.

'Paula! Sweet!' he said.

He bent and kissed her on the cheek. She'd had the

quick presence of mind to turn to him the other cheek, to proffer her best face – the side without the irritating little festering sore. As his face moved back from hers, she saw the girl that he was with and a mailed fist seemed to smash across her mouth.

'Veronica, meet a friend,' he was saying. 'Veronica, this is Paula Denning. I'm sure you've heard me talk of her and John, Paula, this is Veronica Hartley.'

There were how-do-you-do's.

'Would you believe we've just become engaged,' Peter said with an embarrassed mixture of the throw-away and formal. 'A Bloody Mary, is it, then, to help us celebrate?'

Paula believed she said 'Yes' and that she had smiled as she offered her congratulations. She would have preferred a pint of lager as she felt quite thirsty, but that wouldn't have seemed chic. She was saying something idiotic now about young Peter holding out on them and where on earth had the two of them met. Meantime she tried not to look at the girl.

The girl was quite exquisite. She was ash-blonde, small-boned, dressed in a soft silver two-piece. Her hair was sculpted to her head as if she wore a helmet. Her petiteness had the strength of self-possession. She made Paula feel obvious and coarse and cheap. The dress was no help after all. She made Paula feel large and bloated. The corner of her mouth felt like the eye-sore that she knew it was and she wished she had done a better job of covering it with make-up. She tried to hide it with the glass.

'Cheers. Congratulations once again.'

The vodka burnt, all but stuck in a throat she suddenly realised was sore. She wished she had not come.

'Does it always take John this long to park,' Peter was saying. 'Or does he have a deep-laid plan in leaving you a prey to passing wolves?'

After his first confusion he had become his usual brazen swine of a self. She babbled some rubbish: away in Australia but a company 'do' she'd just had to attend – a ghastly bore – dying for a decent drink – popped in solo on the way back home.

'I'll believe you, thousands wouldn't,' he had the gall to wink and say. The young bitch with him actually smiled.

'The two of you must come over as soon as John gets back,' Paula heard herself say a long giddy way away, 'and we can celebrate in style.'

She put down her drained glass.

'I've been on the point of calling you to let you know the good news,' said Peter.

'Yes,' said Paula, 'well, we're in the book. Goodbye Veronica – so nice to have met you.'

'Farewell, my pet,' said Peter. 'Oh, any repercussions on that import deal of yours?'

Shit, Paula thought. Coward.

'None, darling,' she said, 'none at all. Our new roses should look very nice next June.'

She stuck out a finger, the thumb raised above. 'Pow!' she said.

'Ah yes, the Asparagus Beauties always make for a brave show,' he said. '*Ciao, cara mia.*' And winked again.

As she drove home, Paula once more failed to see the road. This time because of her hot tears of rage and humiliation. She should never have gone! Acting like a girl! And now the tears were colder, filled with melancholy. She was no longer young, she was going to be a mother. Take away the comforts and what sort of life had she and John really achieved? They might just as well have never been born. What was there to look forward to? Where were they going? Christ!

Entering Abbotsfield too fast she almost collided with a speeding ambulance. She slowed to forty for the last three hundred yards.

Her throat was really sore. And she was feverish. She must be sickening for tonsilitis. In the bathroom she reached for two barbiturates to help her through the night. Swallowing them half killed her. Her throat kept locking. She seemed to have lost the knack. By the time she'd got them down she was literally gasping for breath.

She awoke next morning feeling worse. Much worse. Thirst as she had never known it plagued her. She went into the bathroom and picked up a beaker. She filled it from the tap. She raised it to her lips and was confronted by a reflected face of horror. She could not swallow. Just that. She physically could not swallow. Her normal efforts to drink, were triggering off an agonising spasm in her throat, her chest. Gasping great guttural heaves she fought for air. Now . . . if she didn't think about it. She tried again and all but passed out from the agony. Iron bands were upon her windpipe tightening and strangling her to death. She swayed, the beaker splashed away. Her lungs were bursting as if she were trapped under water and the bathroom reeled about her in a whirling submarine dance of death. Ah! . . . The spasm had passed. She shuddered again for breath. My God! This was beyond belief! To have no control over the simplest, most basic actions. Something as natural as breathing.

Head down she leant forward for support on the wash basin, gripping it with both hands. After some panting moments, she looked at herself in the mirror and her gaze fell upon the cut on her cheek, and as it did a dreadful trap was sprung within her mind. Through it leapt the figure of her death. She saw in a vast and lucid close-up the corgi licking her face where John had struck her. She saw the glazed look in its eyes as it had tried to bite her. In that fatal cut and in that look she knew her death-sentence was confirmed. She knew what she had always known. Asp had had rabies. Now she had it too.

She found she at last felt calm. There was no cure. The pain, the disgusting, obscene spectacle she would become were quite unthinkable. She must therefore kill herself. Rationally and fatalistically, that was what she had to do. Therefore she must get dressed. And there were letters she must write. First, she must wash.

She largely failed. The sight and sound of water splashing from a tap were of themselves enough now to induce another choking, locked-throat spasm. Unable to do either, she wanted simultaneously to swallow and throw up. It was as if a metal tube had been rammed down her throat into her lungs and then sealed off. In an agony of panic she beat her hands against the wall. Somewhere in her grasping mind she saw the slavered mouth of Asp. This time the fit had only just passed when she staggered to the bedroom. She controlled herself and slid open the door to her long wardrobe. Dozens of dresses, costumes, hung in waiting. Which to choose? Which to choose for dying? As if it mattered! As if it ever had! Her vanity was suddenly brought home to her. She went to laugh and in trying felt saliva in her mouth. She felt a seizure start its stranglehold and in new terror, terror of sheer pain, she spat. Shocked, she cleaned the carpet with a tissue and knowing herself now to be living on short rations of control over her body and mind, willed herself to put on jeans and a plain denim shirt.

She went downstairs. Troy swaggered happily to greet her but she pushed him from her. It was all will-power now. A few more minutes fighting the thick resistance at the bottom of this terrible pit and then she could have peace. That inner hardness so often party to Paula's worst instincts now became her best ally. She went into the study. She sat down at the desk and taking a pen and a sheet of their printed stationery started at once neatly and legibly to write.

To whom it may concern,
I, Paula Denning, wish to make known that I am the person responsible for my own death. I, and I alone, am guilty of illegally importing into the United Kingdom a diseased—

She had thrown the pen down. A maniacal fit of berserk excitement was upon her. She rose to her feet and the chair sprawled away. As Troy reared up from the floor in surprise she kicked him with wild viciousness. He yelped, skittered away. Even as his sad eyes looked reproachfully at her, she was seizing a glass ash-tray and hurling it with a possessed strength at her frenzied image in the facing mirror. In a raucous chatter of disintegrating glass the teeth-bared fury disappeared from sight. And Paula, left to her grinning self, was racked by another seizure. She writhed, clawed at her throat. She was drowning! Drowning in her own spit! Oh God! . . . Then somehow she had spat out a viscid lump of mucus onto the Khelim rug and had been released again from madness to disgust.

She knew now there was no time for niceties. She sat again and straightway tore into fine shreds what she had written. Lucid, she knew that confession was a prerogative of the dead that did not extend beyond the self. She had done far too much to John in her lifetime to crucify him in her death. She took a piece of fresh paper and began to write.

My dearest John,

The other day I had a letter from you of the greatest love and charity. Although, God knows, I was unworthy of it, to have received it from you was the dearest honour of my life. You see that I write 'was'. After such a letter from you there is a terrible, grim irony in the fact that you must soon read this from me. Darling, by the time you do, I shall be dead.

Words are, of course, inadequate. Like time. I don't know what to write. Unless it is everything, it seems it must be nothing. I've been so rotten. Such a bitch.

Perhaps you will understand if I beg you to try to remember only the good times. The salmon was one. The one I caught when you hadn't had a take all week and you were so proud of me. There were good times a lot of the time, weren't there?

I'm so sorry about the baby. You know it would have been ours and I know how much you wanted it. I feel like the lowest thief that ever walked the earth to rob you of it but you understand it is not what I am about to do but what already lies behind that has doomed the child I carry. Forgive me this above all else.

Please keep your friendship, your love, with Mummy and Daddy. They love you, I think you know, like their own son and they will have great need of you now.

I have much to be ashamed of and I feel that I am

being punished justly. I hope you will understand I cannot bear the thought of the awful suffering and final indignities. I wrote above of a 'grim irony'. The appropriateness of all that's happened lately is enough to make me think there is a God. Of some sort. Perhaps you can pray for me. I give you my last, and I swear my best word, that if such things are possible, I will love you always.

                                    Goodbye my darling.

She signed it. She took an envelope and wrote her husband's name. Her handwriting had been as clear as when she had begun. She placed the letter in the envelope, the envelope upon the desk.

As a considered return to her old style the third letter was much easier to write. The intense concentration she had willed out of herself had kept the spasms in abeyance. Now as she got to her feet she felt the onset of still more constrictions in her throat. Spitting as she stumbled to the kitchen she kept the horror of her own saliva in some sort of check. She let Troy out. He looked at her in sorrow as he had not been fed but that she could not face. And, oh, he looked so beautiful! So golden and good. She slammed the door and lurched back to the study.

She did not trust herself to manage with the key to the gun cabinet. Taking a brass paperweight she smashed the glass front in. Absurdly careful not to hurt herself on the sharp remaining fragments, she reached in and took out the little .22 revolver. She sat back at the desk. After a pause for a clear moment she loaded three of the six chambers. Her fingers were trembling by the last, and another terrible spasm came upon her. It was the worst she'd suffered. Aghast, revolted, she felt her jaws snap like an animal's beyond all her control. She prayed amid her agony that she might die and be spared her last intended act. Her mind slid from the pain into white darkness and for a moment she believed she had been heard. Then all had passed and she was conscious once again and knew that there would be no easy drawing of a veil, no last remission.

She braced herself, reached for the phone. She dialled. It was a woman at the other end.

'Mrs Reid,' Paula croaked, 'it's Mrs Denning. Will you please ask your husband to see me as soon as possible. It's urgent.'

'Hello? Mrs Denning? I could hardly hear you? Are you all right?'

But Paula had hung up and was spitting on the floor.

She rose at last and went to the French window. She opened it. She took a last look at the everyday. It was prosaic. The weather had stuck at dull and overcast. And windy. Fallen leaves danced a melancholy, aimless jig at the far end of the lawn. In the rose-bed a blackbird mercilessly wrestled with a worm. The rose-bed. Asp. Paula closed her eyes. From somewhere in the paddock a cock pheasant rasped out a crow to bring her to her purpose.

She understood. Returning to the desk, she took the pistol. She pulled the hammer back. She raised the muzzle to the side of her right temple.

'John,' she whispered.

She pulled the trigger. The gun had jumped a fraction but her grasp had remained firm. In a while the blood ceased to flow and began to congeal.

Part Two

CHAPTER ELEVEN

Ambulance driver Stanley Holland had truly earned his money the previous night in managing to steer clear of a hurtling BMW. He'd had his own foot down. He was trying to make Southampton General in an all-time best. He was pretty thick-skinned by now – you had to be in his line – but this job had him as upset as any he could remember in his five years on the blood wagons. In the back, before the wide-eyed stare of his shattered mother, a little boy was being bodily held down by Stanley's mate and by his weeping, praying father. It took the two of them to contain the animal ferocity with which the childish frame tried to cast out its choking agony.

Not so many days before, that same seven-year-old had been bravely trying not to cry after a nasty dog had bitten him on the ear. Charlie Swinton, in a sense, was victim to his uncomplaining courage. Proud of his visible badge of gallantry, he had made light of it at home. His father had been tired, his mother, busy cooking, was a bit slow, sometimes, to take things in. When in the middle of the following week he'd started saying that his throat was sore they'd both forgotten anything about a bite. They'd kept him home from school. For two days his mother had been run so ragged by his perpetual restlessness and bad-temper that, as much in self-defence as for other reasons, she called the doctor in. Dr Holmes had at once identified some childhood virus infection. He had prescribed antibiotics. Then the next evening the convulsions had begun. Called to the phone from his old-boy reunion, the doctor had organised the ambulance himself. He would be waiting for it at Southampton General.

School numbers at Abbotsfield Primary were down that

week. The headmistress's own children, John and Tricia, had both complained of throats and headaches in the course of the same morning. Mrs Mallett had tried to let them soldier on but when at lunch they had conspicuously left their food, she had thrown convenience to the wind and called her husband. He had stayed in and she had sent them home. They were, if anything, worse the following day.

Police Constable Reid returned to the police house just after six that evening. It was uncanny, he thought, the times he missed the early evening news. Ah well . . . He ran his eye down the short list of messages that, with routine procedure, his wife had given him as he came in.

'What's this Denning one, love?' he called to her. She was in the kitchen.

'Don't know exactly,' she called back. 'She didn't say. It was a very bad line. But she said it was important.'

He telephoned the Denning house at once. There was no reply.

'Probably gone out,' he said. 'Well, a real emergency, she'd have dialled 999. I'll go around a bit later.'

'You can eat this first,' his wife said coming in. 'You didn't get no lunch to speak of.'

He washed and settled down to his pork chop.

'You know,' he said, his mouth pleasantly full, 'I'd've been in earlier tonight by far, only I had to do something about these rats.'

'Rats?'

'Rats. Dead rats. There were about six of them in all. All scattered—'

The phone rang. He was so used to being interrupted he did no more than raise his eyes to heaven.

'Probably her again,' he said. He took a large bite from his chop to sustain him in his absence from the table.

'Abbotsfield Police,' he muttered. 'Reid.'

It was not Mrs Denning. It was the desk duty-sergeant from the Lyndhurst station.

'Listen, Jock,' he said, 'you sitting down?'

'Just tell me anyway,' Reid said.

'We've got the makings of the mother and father of all flaps on here. I've been briefed to get on to you right away. Looks like you're sitting in the middle of a class one panic.'

'Hey. Mike. Wait a minute! Just slow—'

'Sorry. It's all been going on here. Listen, there's a boy in your village name of Charlie Swinton, right?'

'Right.'

'They admitted him to Southampton General last night.'

'Yes. I know.'

'Seems the poor little bleeder's gone and kicked it.'

'Christ, no.'

' 'Fraid so. The thing is – they're almost certain he had rabies.'

'Oh my God. He was round here only— How?'

'This is it. He was bitten by a dog about ten days ago. His parents were with him at the hospital. They're still there actually under sedation.'

Reid drew in his breath.

'Yes. You can imagine. They say they're sure that several other kids were bitten too. . . . You got that?'

'I got it.'

'You got an idea just exactly what that means?'

'I have. Go on.'

'That's why it's panic stations. There's been calls to London and I don't know where else going out of here like it was war.'

'What am I supposed to do?'

'Stay right there. There's a mobile on its way to you right now. Be with you soon. And hang on to your hat. The Chief Constable is coming up to run it all in person. Lucky you. Just do what you're told and everything else will be down to him. That's probably him at the door now.'

'Yes,' Reid said, 'thanks.'

He hung up. His wife was looking at him.

'Finish your food before it's all cold,' she said. 'Do you want me to warm it up?'

'I'm not hungry,' Reid said. 'Charlie Swinton's dead.'

'The little boy with glasses? The one who was always shy?'

'Yes.'

His wife began to cry.

'Make us a cup of tea,' he said, 'I won't be going to bed tonight.'

He turned back to the phone. P.C. Reid was not ambitious. But, if Abbotsfield was all he asked, he still liked to keep abreast. There had been considerable talk of rabies in the past few months and he had a pretty clear idea of what must happen now. He started to put through a call to Mrs Mallett.

It was a quiet beginning to the evening in the Dog and Fox. The weather had turned cold and was keeping people in. Wilf Hopper strolled towards the bay window to see if the threatened rain was holding off. A few regulars would be looking in a little later but the busy summer days were gone. Well, in a way he wasn't sorry.

'Quiet we'll have it tonight,' he said.

He had just treated Florrie to a large brandy. She was a bit under the weather too. Something outside caught his eye.

'Good Lord!' he said. 'Look at this!'

Florrie rushed to join him. She was in time to see a Police Range Rover pull on to the green before the pub. Within seconds, three other squad cars had jolted to a halt. Policemen, uniformed for the most part, were jumping out of half a dozen doors. They were beginning to do something with jacks built into the large trailer when yet another vehicle, an ambulance drew up.

'Blimey,' Wilf said. 'It's either the Great Train Robbery or they've found out about us. Christ, look at them go!'

Grinding tread marks deep into the turf, one police car and the ambulance had shot away. In thirty seconds they were skidding to a halt outside the police house. A tall man got out of the first car, muttered a quick instruction and marched up towards an already opening door. The squeal of brakes had alerted P.C. Reid to Chief Constable Morant's arrival. He led him straight into his one-room office.

'You know just why I'm here, what this is all about?' Morant said in a low fast voice.

'Yes, sir.'

Morant was looking round the tiny room.

'There's no doubt now it's rabies that we're dealing with,' he said. 'We'll use the mobile as our base H.Q. and work from there. Easier all round.'

Reid nodded. This room was purely village-bobby size. Morant had seen that in one stride of coming in. He seemed severe and formal in his uniform but the heavyweight's tough face promised he had risen by ability as much as by freemasonry. He looked like a good man for fast decisions.

'We know other children were savaged,' he was now saying. 'The absolute first priority is to contact the school's head and find out just who.'

Reid reached for a list of names.

'I've already done that, sir,' he said. 'The headmistress is a Mrs Mallett. There were six children bitten in all.'

'Six!'

'Six counting poor little – counting the one who's dead. Mrs Mallett is quite sure of the number because she was the staff member who gave them first aid.'

Morant threw a quick look at the slight, dark constable and began to be impressed. His first break of the day. He'd got a man upon the spot able to use his head. He took the list and started to study it.

'There's one thing you ought to know,' Reid went on. 'Mrs Mallett has two of her own children at the school. They're both—'

'Both on the list. Poor woman. We'll make her our first stop. Now. What about the dog?'

'Dead, sir. Shot.'

'Shot? By who?'

'Mr Mallett, sir, the husband.'

'It was the Mallett's dog?'

'No, sir. It had belonged to an old boy who died round here the other week. Ted or Edward Rimmer.'

Reid winced as he remembered what he'd had to go through in that barn. Morant's head had turned to look at him.

'Rimmer? he said, 'an old tramp?

'Well, yes, sir.'

'There was an autopsy, yes?'

'Yes, sir. Heart failure.'

'I want a copy of that in my hands tomorrow. Burial or cremation?'

'Cremation, sir.'

'Damn. . . . Now, Mallett. If it wasn't his dog, how come he shot it?'

'Coincidence, really, sir. He came to the school and walked in on the tail-end of things.'

'You're not telling me he suspected rabies and kept quiet!'

'Obviously not, sir, with two of his own kids bitten.'

Reid darted a quick anxious glance at his superior. That had been a bit strong to a boss, he knew. He saw that it had registered and Morant was making a considered effort not to snap at him.

'Arguably, then,' Morant said, 'he was being a bit high-handed.'

'He's a gamekeeper, sir. He'd just seen it bite those kids. He knew it no longer had an owner. He'd've shot it in cold blood as all in the line of work.'

'I see. Well, he did the right thing and a lot of people a good turn when he did. You know all these households?'

'Yes, sir.'

'You come with me, then. We'll talk in the car.'

'Sir. There's something else you should know.'

'For Heaven's sake, man! Time is precious! Every—'

'Ted Rimmer had another dog.'

Chief Constable Morant turned slowly in the doorway. 'What?' he said at last.

It was not really a question and P.C. Reid made no reply.

'Sorry I yelled,' Morant said. 'You were quite right. No question but we must put this second dog down right away. Where is it?'

Reid shook his head.

'It's disappeared,' he said, 'not been seen for days.'

'Oh my God,' said the Chief Constable.

In their brief, terse meeting Morant had impressed Reid. He continued to do so in the next half-hour as they visited, in turn, each of the houses where the children at risk lived. Morant asked for a pen picture of each family and, using the familiar face of Reid to ease the way, was subtly different in his blend of firmness and concern according to the parent he was facing. The Malletts, knowing already of the death of Charlie Swinton, were white with anxiety but calm. Their children went from their beds to the ambulance on stretchers. It was a stroke that brought belated tears to the headmistress's eyes.

'I should have thought,' she said. 'I should have thought.'

'There was no way you could have known,' her husband said.

'I should have thought!'

'This is England. Not France or Germany.'

He made to follow her aboard the ambulance. Morant reached out to intercept him.

'Mr Mallett,' he said, 'I want to ask you an enormous favour. I know right now your only place is by your children's bedsides. I've got two of my own and, well, I've some idea of how you feel. Only it happens you're a gamekeeper. And it happens we have reason to believe a rabid dog is on the loose round here. Tomorrow we'll have all Whitehall and half the world down here but one hour from now, off my own bat, I plan to start setting up the biggest shoot this area has ever known. Domestic, wild, if it's an animal I'm going to see it shot. I need help for that. Local help. Local professional help. That's the favour that I ask.'

Mike Mallet looked down at the ground. He looked up at his wife paused in the doorway of the ambulance. She nodded.

'All right,' he said. Morant nodded.

'Thank you,' he said. 'We'll be back for you in half an hour.'

None of the other children needed stretchers. Marion Gadney was having her hair washed and climbed into the ambulance in her dressing-gown. Robert Park was watching television and it took Morant's forbidding uniform to snap him into an obedience less indignant and disgruntled. An only child of a widowed mother, he had grown used to ruling the roost. When his mother went to kiss him and

135

Morant said that it might not be wise there was suddenly a scene. Without further warning the thin and large-eyed Mrs Park was screaming piercingly.

'No! He's not going! I won't let him! You can't just come and take him away like this!'

Morant looked hard at Reid. Reid took the boy outside and down the path while the Chief Constable stood up to the hysterical mother's wildly beating fists. When five minutes later the two of them emerged Mrs Park no longer fluttered like a distraught bird but walked controlled and subdued. Morant himself helped her aboard the crowded ambulance and as he did, said something to its uniformed attendant. Reid was impressed. And as much so by a comment Morant made a short time later.

It came as they left the last ill-starred house, the Gadney's. Given the circumstances Bill Gadney's reaction had been as matter-of-fact as Mrs Park's had been extreme. Even more gigantic in the cramped dimensions of his labourer's cottage, he had listened without comment. His potato face, ruddy beneath the flat hay-coloured hair, had nodded almost amiably as Morant spelt out the situation. Alone of the parents, he and his wife had not pressed to accompany their child: she was a big girl able to take good care of herself, he had an early start tomorrow over at Johnson's Farm; they could go in and visit in the evening; she seemed all right in herself.

'He took that well,' Reid said as the ambulance flashed off into the night. Then had come the comment.

'He hasn't grasped it yet,' Morant had said. 'When it's sunk in I'd hate to be in front of him.'

And Morant was a big man. Reid took the point. As they turned back toward the green, the driver switched the wipers on. Driving rain had begun to fall.

Emergency. Repeat, this is an emergency. An animal or animals thought to be suffering from rabies is known to have been loose in this vicinity. Anybody who has been scratched or bitten by an animal during the past six months . . .

. . . this Jack Russell terrier, answering to the name of Chip. C-H-I-P. Chip must on no account be approached by members of the public. Anybody thinking they have seen him, or supposing they have information that could establish his whereabouts should report at once. Please keep all dogs indoors and under control. . . .

Few people in Abbotsfield passed the evening undisturbed. Two loudspeaker police cars crawled slowly through the rain over every inch of road and track within a six-mile radius of the Dog and Fox. Steadily they broadcast the grim news, whilst the villagers alerted one another through the always open phone circuits. Those who had called to warn friends stayed on to elaborate and speculate. No dogs were let loose that night.

Plainly, some houses were deserted at this particular time. The Dennings' was one such. He was in the States, she with her parents. The converted farmhouse where George Wrinch's German ex-wife now lived also stood empty. She had returned to her native Bavaria for the Munich *Oktober-fest*. Unusually, no false-alarm reports came in regarding Chip. No-one, it seemed, had seen him or could say where he had gone.

Varied only by odd gusts of wind, the rain beat savagely down upon the aluminium a foot above their heads. Steam rose in spiralling columns from the mugs of coffee Florrie had brought over with the sandwiches from the pub. It was cold outside as well as wet, but inside the overcrowded trailer sheer numbers kept the temperature well up. Cars had been drawing up at regular intervals. Two new ambulances were now standing by outside. A black Rover with official numberplates had brought down from Whitehall James Henthorne of the DHSS and Dr Valerie Colburn of the Ministry of Agriculture. They were present now as were two vets from Porton Down, who because of their animal research work were already inoculated against rabies, and therefore had volunteered to be on hand. The first of many, Reid was sure. He sipped his coffee. It was funny, he was

137

thinking, there'd been an odd pattern to the meeting. The experts were present but so far had only showed their professionalism through the sense with which they'd held their peace. It was those without letters following their names, himself and most especially Mike Mallett who had born the main thrust of Morant's quick questions. In asking Mike to stay and assist, Reid thought, Morant had already justified his own presence as a field commander. There couldn't be too much doubt either whose executive decision it had been to set up shop hard by the Dog and Fox. It was a racing certainty the law would turn a blind eye on any breaking of the licensing laws and pretty likely, too, there'd be some ad hoc kipping down in the lounge bar before the night was through. Wedged in the corner, he shifted his weight back on to his other foot.

Morant had just finished minutely cross-examining Mike about the fracas in the playground. Untiringly, his voice continued to drive through the rain.

'Which brings us to the other dog, Chip,' he said. He looked around. 'Within these walls I'll be quite frank. The thought of what he could have done and could be doing now, has me running scared. As far as we know he could be anywhere.'

He paused again. No-one was fool enough to look for a bright side.

'When I got wind of this, the first thing I did,' Morant continued, 'was to contact my opposite number on the Surrey force. He's an old friend. Also, he dealt with the last rabies scare in this country – the one in Camberley in 1969. I believe you were on that one Dr Colburn?'

She must have been very young, Reid thought, she's not at all bad now.

'Yes,' she was saying. 'The dog in question had in fact passed its six months in quarantine in perfectly legal fashion. Released to its owners it displayed rabid symptoms ten days later and ran off.'

Morant nodded.

'To anticipate your question,' he said, 'the next thing I did was check with Quarantine. No animal, they told me, has been released in the past few weeks to anybody living in this area. We're checking on the whereabouts of all those animals who've been let go this calendar year, but I don't think it's going to be that easy for us. Frankly, my guess is we're up against a criminal action here. A smuggled pet.'

'But who'd be so thick?' Mallett, the professional keeper was incredulous.

'It might interest you to know that prosecutions for attempted smuggling of pets into this country now run at over two hundred a year. That's the ones who get caught. How many get away with such madness – your guess is as good as mine.'

Mallet's indignation began to harden visibly to thoughts of personal revenge.

'Who would it be?' he said.

Morant shrugged.

'A tourist. A long-distance lorry driver. If it's one of those . . .'

Eloquently he let his voice tail off. Their imagination could do the rest.

'The Surrey police were very lucky,' Morant continued. 'The dog's owner had lived in India. She recognised the symptoms from her experience there. Very responsibly – very courageously – she went straight out after it and at the cost of getting bitten managed to trap it. Oh yes, it was just trying to board a taxi full of children. Think about that one. Her neighbour by the grace of God was an Army vet. Between them they had the situation back under control, almost before it had begun.'

He leaned forward across the table.

'I tell you all this to emphasise our problem. Our dog has got away. That must be our premise. It is rabid and it has got away. On those assumptions I'm instituting a massive shoot under the Rabies Control Order of 1974. What that means is the extermination of every living warm-blooded animal within a twelve-mile radius of where we sit.'

'Christ,' Mike Mallett simply said.

'To save human life, maybe across the country, I have no other option.'

'It's not just that,' Mallett said. 'It's the scale. Who's going to do it? A radius of twelve miles is – well, have you thought what that takes in?'

'I have. The long-term answer to your question is the Army. But I want short-term action too. Fast action. There's a good chance that the disease won't have travelled anything like that distance from here yet. What I'd like to see is a locally organised shoot at work here right after to-morrow's meeting. Local guns. As many as can be drummed up between now and then. I'll understand if, for your own reasons, you say "No". I can't insist, but I'd like to ask you to organise and manage that for us. . . .'

The rain swirled a new rhythm on the roof as everybody looked at Mallett. For a moment he deliberated and in that time he looked, Reid thought, enormously tired and grown old overnight. To his own shame, Reid realised he'd already half-forgotten Mike had two children whom right now he must be picturing lonely and lost in white hospital beds, whom, separated from their toys, the thousand little taken-for-granted things of home, he right now had every reason to suppose were beginning to die. It's one hell of a bloody choice, he thought. Mallett's shoulders straightened.

'O.K.,' he said, 'I'll try.'

'Thank you,' Morant said. His smile was quick and short. It had nothing of the official about it. 'What I had in mind is that you try for a chain-letter strategy. Get the grapevine working. Call friends. Get them to call friends. Sergeant Fielding there – there, yes, that's him – has got a list of all the holders of shot-gun permits and firearm certificates in Hampshire. Go on to those when you run out of mates. If you go up front you'll find two phones patched in. Be sure you call the hospital first.'

Mallett nodded. He looked suddenly at Reid.

'John Denning back from foreign parts?' he asked.

Reid shook his head. Hell, he thought, I had to call his wife.

'Why?' Morant was asking.

'Oh, nothing. A good gun that's all. Do better by us than most. Right let's – oh, there is one other little thing.'

'Yes?'

'You said last time something like this happened, the owner was "responsible" was that what you said?'

'Yes. She was.'

They all waited. All could see what would come next

'If I ever – if I find out who the bastard is responsible for this mess, I swear to God I'll use this gun on him.'

'I didn't hear that,' Morant said.

'It's not just my kids, it's—' Mallett's voice choked. 'We've had one,' he said, 'and one is too many.'

People looked at their feet, avoided eyes in the respectful silence. Only Morant looked at the father.

'Listen, Mike,' he said, almost in a whisper, 'it is possible there's a natural, an innocent explanation for all this. But if there's not – if it's down to somebody – when we get whoever it may be – and I promise you a second time we will – I won't throw the book at him. I'll throw the whole damn police station. My fist first. He, she or them – they'll wish they'd not been born.'

He paused. Mallett nodded slowly. Morant snapped the mood.

'O.K., Sergeant,' he said, 'perhaps you'll just show Mr Mallett where the two of you can get to work. I'll be with you shortly. First, though, Reid, I want to see we've got this meeting all tied up. Church, school or village hall?'

'Village hall's biggest, sir. There's a stage.'

'Right. We'll need to fence off part of the green as a make-shift helicopter pad.'

Reid blinked.

'Yes, sir,' he said.

Morant briefed him for some five intense and detailed minutes. Reid made full notes. He normally prided himself on being able to keep things in his head but his failure to bear Mrs Denning's call in mind had shaken him. At four o'clock the coming morning his worn-out brain would need all of the chapter and verse he now took down. He'd get around to Mrs D. some time tomorrow – maybe.

'What about those rats I mentioned, sir?' he said at last.

Morant looked at Dr Colburn. She grimaced anxiously.

'They scare the hell out of me, too,' he said. 'When will we know—'

Without warning the flimsy trailer door crashed open almost off its hinges. Florrie, drenched, her hair like a mop and her haggard face yellow with a total, distraught fear, staggered her fat weight among them. Morant frowned.

'If you need the empties—'

'No! Not them! Me! God! All this time and I've forgot! I got bit and I've not felt right for days!'

Reid just managed to catch her as she crashed out cold into a faint. Outside Wilf was already making signals to a reversing ambulance. As they dragged her back towards it, the phone began to ring.

For another resident in Abbotsfield realisation had been slowly dawning that she was entering upon a crisis that promised to have only one way out. For poor, gentle Miss Weldon it was a double grief – a crisis not only of the body but of conscience too. In her busy but placid life she had, with cause, never admitted to a day of illness. Her beliefs as a Christian Scientist had never had occasion to be tried.

Until the present. The disease which for days had been advancing on her had brought her now to great distress. In the moments of clear thinking still allowed to her, she was aware something malign and evil had been visited upon her. And upon her dogs. Her own pain, perhaps, she could have born with patience to magnify the Lord's Almighty Will. That they, dumb innocents, must suffer too was a cross too much to bear. . . . Yet, after the children of the village, nobody was more righteously innocent than Miss Weldon.

Lucid, for the moment, she had chosen to open the window to her cottage garden. The rain could not beat in under the over-hanging thatch and perhaps the coolness it had brought, the evening scents it raised from the plants would bring a healing sweetness. Instead she heard a police car's bleak loudspeaker warning. And she had known that others were involved. She had just had time to phone the strange, emergency number before another choking

142

fit delivered her a shuddering captive to the sickness's power.

The ambulance driver had to come in through the window. Miss Weldon was inside but giggling hysterically.

'You're not a lady doctor! If I must have a doctor, I must have a lady,' she hissed breathlessly. Spittle flecked her lips. 'Where's that man going? You leave my dogs alone!'

Out of her head, she had backed into a corner. Now, even as Dr Moar was nodding grimly at the driver and attendant, she flew at them. Possessed by the disease, she was possessed of the strength of devils. Grimly, panting hoarsely, the three men fought to contain her.

She had seen the government vet pass through into her kitchen. He was a married man with children. One glance at what he saw there, had him drop the hypodermic on the floor and reach hastily for his gun. Without moving further into the small room he aimed at the first dog. Miss Weldon heard both shots. For an instant as they registered on some still-reasoning corner of her mind, she went inert. Then, screaming she launched into a bucking, wrenching paroxysm that outdid all her previous fury. Then she was slumping forward in their arms like a rag-doll. Moar felt her pulse and took the chance to inject her with a sedative.

Another hour and he felt sick. Miss Weldon had died while on her way to hospital. Perhaps if he had not . . . Beside himself with self-reproach he stayed awake all through the night until the early morning autopsy. Only then could he feel relief.

Miss Weldon's lifetime of perpetual good health had caused a heavy run upon her credit with the law of averages. Unknown to anyone and most of all to herself, she had been developing an aneuristic condition in the brain over the past few years. The rabies virus, ascending her nervous system and reaching her brain had driven her to frenzy and caused the aneurism to burst. She had died, technically, of brain haemorrhage.

Over a post-mortem cigarette the consultant chose to be philosophical with Dr Moar.

'Things sometimes go the kindest way,' he said. 'It was

only a matter of time for her and, in the event, she was spared a great deal of inevitable, pointless suffering.'

'Thank God,' said Dr Moar, 'for that at least. She deserved that much if anybody ever did.'

But Fate is seldom totally straightforward in granting its favours. Characteristically, Miss Weldon's thoughts in reaching for the phone had not been for herself. She had been anxious to pass on some information. Two days after her lunch-time sherry party her brother and his wife had stayed with her. On the same morning they had set off back for Pembrokeshire her corgi Emma had savaged their Welsh collie.

Forgotten, the incident had come back to her as the police car had gone by her open window. But she had died with her lips sealed, leaving to Fate a later word.

CHAPTER TWELVE

The rain had fallen ceaselessly throughout the night. As morning came its violence abated and, as if attuning itself to the new mood of Abbottsfield, it fell in steady, depressing drizzle. Over-run by cars, the village green was degenerating into a quagmire.

Up all night, Mike Mallett had got the word round well. Nearly two hundred volunteer guns had been recruited. Local farmers, landowners, council officials, and huntsmen, they had either already gone on into the village hall or dispersed themselves in small and sheltered groups about the green, the length of the main street. Around them, the women far outnumbering the men, were stood the villagers. Despite the rain they held their ground observing each newcomer, every movement of the constant flow of police around Morant's mobile H.Q. Although they talked away among themselves their voices were low-pitched and subdued. They gave a sense of silent onlookers. Two things were left unsaid. No-one was crass enough to mention the conspicuous absence of all dogs from the grey scene. Nobody was so insensitive as to point out that this was the biggest thing to have hit Abbotsfield in living memory. There was no person present who did not know one of the bereaved and a simple decency refused to be excited by the show of force, the traffic jams outside the village, the overflow loudspeakers above the village hall's front porch.

It was not quite so with the Press, the media boys and girls. Ever since a junior clerk at Southampton General had earned his latest fiver with a quick call to a local stringer, the Press had quickly become aware rabies had broken out somewhere in Hampshire. Since six a.m. the BBC had been broadcasting a warning and appeal for help drawn up by

Morant, so that by nine-thirty the journalists and camera cars were thick upon the ground. The reporters elbowing their way about in a self-conscious way were the sole people to bring a note of animation to the dampened scene. It was a false note of sensationalism almost everywhere rebuffed.

Shortly before ten a mechanical beat of wings was heard coming from far away. And at once Morant was seen leaving the police H.Q. Nobody could have guessed from his appearance that this was a man who had spent a sleepless and a full-stretched night. As he stepped towards the centre of the green the villagers could feel a burst of local pride. The man trying to stretch his legs and match Morant's long stride was P.C. Reid. Meanwhile with clacking insistence through the rain the beat had been growing louder by the second. Abruptly, much lower and nearer than most had realised a Westland Whirlwind chopper shot into view from behind the range of autumn beeches at the green's far end. It rose a fraction, pirouetted in its own short-length and came easily to a hydraulically cushioned rest. With the rotors still whirling the side door slid back and two men were scrambling out on to the soaked grass. One seemed neat and nondescript. The other, even at a distance, seemed eminently the man to have made such a descent from so god-like a machine.

Hatless, he had fair hair parted and trained straight back. As straight was the classic nose dividing the symmetrical and wide-mouthed face. His broad shoulders were straight and upright. He was as tall as Morant with whom he was now shaking hands. They were a well-matched pair. But where Morant, you would have said, was a fighter, using native wit to rise up from the ranks, this man's appearance immediately conveyed the verve and cutting edge of the aristocrat. His weapon, surely, was the rapier. As the pilot finally cut his engines to reveal in the ensuing silence how intensely noisy they had been, Morant, Reid and the newcomers began to walk towards the village hall.

'You stupid bitch! What the fuck do you think you're doing!'

146

The woman's angry shout had come from the direction of the pub. A knotted circle of onlookers suddenly gathered. Morant was on to it like a shot, Reid a step behind. That there must be no panic was the thought speeding them both as they broke into the circle.

They saw several things. A spiralling length of exposed film was dangling from a BBC film camera and tripod to form a tangled heap upon the sodden grass. A cameraman in a green anorak was shrugging ruefully to a grinning sound-recordist. A teenage girl was weeping bitterly on a young woman's shoulder. A third woman, the same age but decked out elegantly in suede and silk was staring murderously at the second whom she seemed to take to be her country cousin.

'I'll sue you for that,' she was saying. 'Sue you from here to breakfast! What bloody right do you think—'

'All right, what's happening here then?' Morant had cut her short in mid-sentence.

The city-slicker wheeled around, recoiled one doubtful second and then was instant sweetness and charm.

'Oh, officer, thank goodness. Perhaps I can ask you to be kind enough to witness what's just taken place.'

'I can hardly witness what's already happened and I haven't seen,' Morant said evenly. 'Perhaps you'd be kind enough to let me have your version.'

Reid could just detect the irony.

'Certainly,' she said, 'I'd be glad to. My name is Renee Lees. As you can see I'm part of a BBC news team – no, don't do anything with that yet, Chuck, leave it there as evidence. We were in the middle of shooting a little interview when because of the noise from the helicopter we had to break off. We were watching the landing when that woman over there came racing up to our camera while our backs were turned and undid the door to our film magazine. You can see the result for yourself.'

'Thank you,' Morant said. He turned to Reid. 'Do you know these two young women?'

'We're quite capable of introducing ourselves,' the other woman broke in with. 'I'm Margaret Peacock. I teach in the primary school here. This is Jenny Swinton. You'll recognise the name, I hope.'

'Charlie Swinton's sister,' Reid muttered quickly.

'I suggest you ask Miss Lees there the exact nature of her "little interview".'

'It was merely an attempt to establish how long—'

'It was merely an attempt, you bitch, to ask this poor bereaved and bewildered girl the most wounding and personal questions about her little brother, dead less than one day! You had her beside herself with—'

'The public has a right to be informed of all facts.'

'Facts! Yes! Maybe. The bloody public, namely you and your bloody make a hot-shot-name-for-myself camera have no right at all to invade the private grief – exploit the private grief – of any individual!'

Maggie was crying now herself:

'I taught that little boy. He was sensitive and—'

'One moment, Miss!' Morant's voice was instant return from hysteria.

'You do admit you performed the action Miss Lees has just described?'

'Certainly! Of course!'

'I'm surprised you had the know-how,' Morant said mildly and surprisingly.

'I suppose she's got some tacky little Audio-Visual diploma!' Renee Lees hissed. Her sweetness ran on a tight rein.

'What's your background Miss?' Morant asked her.

'Oh, I read History at – what's that got to do with it?'

She looked daggers at the widely grinning cameraman.

'Look,' she said, 'she's publicly admitted it. What I'd now like to know is what exactly do you propose to do about it, officer?'

'That lies with you,' Morant said. 'If you would like to bring a civil action claiming damages you're quite at liberty to do so and it's unquestionably your privilege.'

'Thank you, officer. It's as I thought. And I've no doubt that I will. It was a hard morning's work gone for nothing.'

'Well, I've no doubt,' Morant said. 'Oh, while we're here – Reid make a record of these, will you, please – could I see your Release, please, Miss?'

'Release?'

'The legal permission signed by Miss Swinton's parents giving you the rights to interview her for the purposes of a public broadcast. Oh, and also your permit to film from a tripod. The permit, that is, from the rural district council.'

Miss Renee Lees whitened with rage.

'I don't believe it!' she said. 'You're on her side!'

'You mean you don't have the documents, Miss?'

'You know damn well I don't have them.'

'Ah, well . . . in that case I would strongly caution you against the advisability of involving yourself and your employers in any form of legal action that—'

'You sod! I'll report you to your Chief Constable!'

'I am the Chief Constable.' Morant said with a grand manner and a dead straight face. 'Also I would caution you against the use of abusive or obscene—'

'I'll still bloody well report you.'

'You can report me to Hendon, the Home Office or the House of Lords if it so pleases you!' Morant said. The ice had cracked to show the white hot temper he had banked beneath. 'When I became a copper I took an oath that I'd protect and serve the public. My job isn't to featherbed the media in exploiting them – yes, I take that point – any more than it is to see you spreading panic and alarm across the nation's goggle box. Got it? Turn over any more today on that coffee grinder and I'll see it's confiscated so quick you won't even have time to wet your knickers!'

He turned. His indignation had prevented a cheap laugh. Reid turning too, had thought of winking to the Maggie he was sure he would see smiling at a famous victory, but her face was still concerned and serious and her attention fixed again on Jenny Swinton.

The tall and handsome fair-haired man had been evidently an amused spectator to the entire incident. He smiled at Morant now.

'In my country, too,' he said, as they walked away. 'They

can be like vultures. Somehow I did not remember them being so like this in England.'

That was how the news came speedily across the bush telegraph that he was foreign, German or Swedish or something like that.

Built thanks to private donation and public subscription to mark the jubilee of Queen Victoria, Abbotsfield's village hall – The Royal Victoria Assembly Rooms properly spelt out – was an impressive building. Over the years it had become the focal point of the village's rich community life. It had served for every conceivable function from flower shows to public meetings to cubs' and brownie nights. But Reid thought, as he followed Morant past the cluster of villagers sheltering under the wrought-iron balcony-porch, and in up the narrow central aisle left open by the packed shoulder-to-shoulder crowd inside, it's never seen anything like this before. He found a place to stand by the Emergency Exit while the V.I.P.'s mounted the stage to join and whisperingly confer with those already there.

There had been a low level of conversation in the body of the hall, but it had died away in step with Morant's progress to the stage. There was a tense silence as he climbed the steps up to it. All faces were turned forward. Reid looked at them and was surprised that he knew less than half of them. Then he took in the ragged array of army-surplus combat jackets, old patched sports coats, heavy sweaters and he remembered that pride of place had been allocated to the guns. He'd seen to that himself. He felt annoyed. The tiny lapse of memory had served to bring to mind how deadbeat he felt. But how must Morant feel?

From his central chairman's position behind the long table on the platform the senior policeman was getting to his feet. He got straight down to business.

'Ladies and gentlemen,' he said, 'my name is Morant and I'm the Chief Constable of the county. By now, you will all know what this is about and why we're here. Rabies. We've got a job to do and we're shortly going to see that it gets done. I would like to say immediately that all of us up here are deeply beholden to you for the speed and willingness with which you've come forward to help us do it. It is a matter of life and death. Perhaps to you. Perhaps to those you love. . . . But, like all matters of life and death it will be an unpleasant job. Make no mistake. I don't intend to tell you otherwise. The purpose of this meeting is to bring home to each and every one of you how vital it is you co-operate fully and utterly with us whatever the immediate cost.'

He looked around the hall. His direct no-nonsense manner had them weighing every word.

'You don't need a policeman laying down the law to make you realise just what we're facing here. You need an expert. A vet. I'm going to hand you over now to just such a person. I'd like to introduce Dr Valerie Colburn from London and more particularly from the Ministry of Agriculture.'

He sat down as Dr Colburn stood up. There was no sug-gestion of applause from the body of the hall. Morant had set too business-like a tone. A few throats were cleared and then the trim and self-possessed new speaker had an audience once more totally attentive.

'Thank you,' she said to Morant. She turned to the hall. 'Ladies and gentlemen,' she said, 'it was kind of the Chief Constable to refer to me just now as an expert. In fact, I wish to say very little to you now other than to introduce a former colleague who is beyond any question far more qualified than I, to talk about the crisis here in Abbotsfield. Dr Erich Kesseler, on my far right, is beyond question one of the world's most knowledgeable veterinarians on the subject of rabies, one of the foremost experts in combating its spread. I cannot emphasise enough how fortunate we are to have him with us this morning. We tracked him down in France in the middle of last night. He is currently there liaising with French authorities at their Centre for Rabies Studies. Dr Kesseler is in the employment of the World Health Organisation on whose behalf he has worked exten-sively to fight and limit this disease not only in his native Germany but in the United States and India. It is a tribute to his status as a scientist that, at a time when the French have a massive fight against rabies on their hands, they should have called him in for consultation. If I may say so, it is a measure of his status as a human being that within hours of being alerted to our problem he should have made arrangements to cross the channel and be with us. He is going to talk to you now at some length. But he will preface his talk with a short piece of film. He has asked me to say this. The film shows somebody in the last extremities of rabies. It is very strong stuff. Could we therefore ask anybody who thinks they may not be quite up to facing it – particularly those, perhaps, who have close ties with anyone now thought to have contracted rabies – could we ask you to do the sensible thing and leave us for five minutes.'

She motioned to the rear of the hall. Reid saw a young man begin to wheel a 16 mm. projector on a trolley to the back of the central aisle. He had to pause a moment. Some twenty to thirty people, no more than half of them women, had taken Dr Colburn at her word. The significance of Mike Mallett being one of them was lost on nobody. As they filed out Kesseler himself was extending a collapsible free-standing screen in the middle of the stage. He seemed satisfied and nodded. For a moment each person in the hall was aware of himself, his neighbour to either hand, bracing and tensing against shock. Then the lights went out.

For a moment the screen was just black and then as the projector whirred a black that was somehow moving. Numbers jumped fuzzily into view and then were sharply focused. There was a second or two more of darkness and then without preamble the audience were looking from high up upon a man strapped in a bed.

His head was free and jerking uncontrollably in violent spasms from side to side. That seemed the horror of it. As the camera zoomed down and in to frame the thrashing head more tightly it became dreadfully clear this was no longer an individual. Disease had reduced this man to a sub-animal state of mindless spasms, of flesh galvanised by the arbitrary torture of its own embedded and mad muscles. Straining like a newly grassed salmon, the head lashed back and forth at an incredible rate. Perhaps that was merciful. It was only possible to gain an impression of the swollen, bloated lips, the spittle that flew from them. The camera moved closer still. People in the hall groaned and Reid, forcing himself to watch despite his hollow stomach, realised its black and white picture and absence of all sound made the elemental image more horrible. Now the threshing stopped. There was a moment of heart-stopping rest and then, the neck-cords rigid, the emaciated, spittle-covered face was straining upward. The closed lids opened on the eyes to show just whites. As people cried out in the darkness, the head snapped back and everyone could grasp that just as death had spared that poor victim further agony, so it had rescued them from the ordeal of any longer witnessing his torment.

The lights came on. Kesseler was already man-handling the collapsed screen off to one side. People were just drumming up the courage to turn and look their neighbours in the face as he returned to the platform's centre.

'Ladies and gentlemen,' he began, 'there—'

He got no further. With a despairing moan and then a reverberating crash, a gigantic figure had slumped head-long to the floor. Not quite unconscious, he continued moaning a girl's name. Bill Gadney had come to grasp at last that his daughter who had seemed fine in herself was threatened not by sickness but by death.

There were gasps, stifled screams, the scraping back of several chairs.

He had fallen quite close to Reid

'O.K. everybody, please stay in your seats,' Reid said. 'George, Pete, give us a hand here.'

With difficulty, and as rain beat in, the three men dragged the huge farm-worker out through the side door. He still groaned but offered no resistance. Kesseler had waited patiently. Now he began again.

'Not a very nice thing to have to watch,' he said. 'I regret very much having to shock you all like that. But it was, I think, necessary. Better than any words of mine it actually shows you what you are now up against. What you have to fear.'

His English was virtually perfect. There was the faint

suggestion of a guttural German accent and riding above that a stronger hint of American cadence. His authority was plain in any language.

'That poor devil happened to be Turkish,' he was saying. 'But I am not exaggerating or being alarmist if I say that he could have come these days from any of the countries that go to make up Europe. Germany, France, Spain. . . .'

He paused for effect.

'And now England,' he said. 'Rabies has crossed the Channel.'

'Dr Colburn was kind enough to thank me,' he continued, 'for coming here today. There were two reasons why I particularly wished to do so. One was that the spread of rabies that has marched steadily across Europe since the Second World War began pretty definitely in Western Poland, on the border with Germany. I thus feel a certain, er, *Angenessenheit*, er, appropriateness, er, surrounds my being here to try to help.

'The other reason is more personal. I originally intended to become a doctor – one who heals his fellow men. I did, in fact, qualify to practice medicine and for a few years did so. Then I stopped. The reason I stopped was, if you like, on account of my personal cowardice. I could not bear to see the children die. . . . I decided to become a vet as you would say and after qualifying – in England, by the way, at Cambridge – I began to concentrate on rabies. Many times, though, I have since asked myself: did I get my, er, priorities wrong just to suit my own convenience? Well, as you know, children are at risk now. It is something of a point of honour with me that I should join you here today.

'You have just seen the end-result of rabies. I do not want to dwell further on that. But I must, you will understand, outline for you the build-up of symptoms as the disease progresses. I am sure you will give me your undivided attention. First, the infection: rabies is usually contracted through a bite from a rabid animal or, more rarely, the lick from such an animal upon a skin abrasion. I will come back to this later. For the moment, it is enough to say that the virus has entered the body. Nothing will now seem to happen.

154

But in reality the virus is attacking the nervous system and literally climbing up the nerve fibres to the brain. No. Not a nice thought. How long this takes varies very much – the next stage can appear in anything from two weeks to six months or occasionally even longer. From what I have gathered so far, I think I am already quite safe in stating publicly that we are dealing here with a particularly virulent strain which may be setting a new lower limit to the period of consolidation by the virus in the body.

'The next stage is that the victim will become intensely depressed and uneasy. He will be restless and unable to settle down anywhere. He may well suffer a loss of appetite run a slight temperature and will talk in excitable terms. This disturbance will slide inevitably into the next stage – the one you are probably all aware of – a tremendous craving for water. This will soon advance to the most terrible and, er, the, er, *widersinnig*, er, yes, paradoxical stage: in his attempt to satisfy this raving thirst, the victim will experience a suffocating seizure. This will last some moments and will, of course, induce extreme panic. Hence, despite the thirst, will come an apparently insane, irrational fear of water. Finally, the muscles will experience the spasms you have seen. The patient will be seized by fits of maniacal fury. By now he will be tormented by a sticky secretion in his mouth – not his normal saliva by the way but something, er, more, er, . . . gluey. The thought of swallowing it will literally drive him mad. But – this is perhaps the most horrible thing of all – in these late stages he will experience long moments, islands, if you like, of calmness. He will know what is happening to him to the very end, I think you can understand now why the word "rabies" comes from a Latin word meaning "madness".

'So, if any of you have the slightest reason to believe . . .'

Once more he left the obvious unsaid. There was not one of his listeners who at this moment had succeeded in preventing themselves from feeling the most pressing thirst.

'Now. I have said that rabies is transmitted by physical contact – a bite, a lick. Most of you no doubt associate it with mad dogs foaming at the mouth and all that. That is all right as far as it goes but it does not go nearly far enough. Rabies is a disease to which all warm-blooded animals (including, of course, ourselves) are susceptible. Dogs, in fact, are less susceptible to the disease than such animals as cats, foxes, hamsters and cattle. In central and western Europe the red fox is currently the most important rabies vector. That is to say carrier. This explains why the disease has spread since the Second World War. At that time fox-hunting largely ceased. The fox population shot up and, short of territory, foxes began to take on new patterns of behaviour. They took to invading the suburbs of large cities, even the centres. At this moment, for example, there are rabid foxes in Chantilly virtually on the outskirts of Paris.

'Now, you can see that since rabies compels its victims to attack other forms of life it is only too easy for an ever-widening pool or circle of infected wild life to build up. This is where the importance of dogs and domestic cats makes itself felt. They, of course, can provide a natural bridge between this wild-life pool and ourselves. The image of a mad dog foaming at the mouth is perhaps after all not such a bad thing to be carrying in the head.

'I realise that I have shocked you with what I have said to you and what I have displayed, er, shown to you. I do not mean to be entirely a prophet of gloom, as you would say. This thing has its better – or not so bad – side too. Firstly, there is the fact that the disease has to be passed on physically. There has to be contact: usually a bite. Once people have been put on their guard, this makes it fairly easy to know when a potential victim has been infected. Now, once symptoms of the disease have shown themselves there is, to all practical intents and purposes, no cure. You die. Nothing can be done but make the dying a little less gruesome. But if the person bitten comes to us at once before the disease has had a chance to incubate, then injections can be given that will build up the body's resistance. You will live. Unfortunately, as I think many of you know, these injections are medically quite primitive. We are working on something better but at the moment it is necessary to receive some fourteen injections in the abdomen. They are painful and they often have nasty after-effects. But, as I say, you will live. That is the good thing, you see, there must be contact. The disease cannot creep up on you like a cold or measles, let us say. It is not an infection something you can . . .'

Incredibly he was lost for an English idiom.

'. . . pick up from thin air. Forewarned by the bite you can be forearmed against the disease.

'Secondly, although rabies has come to your beautiful island, it is not for the first time. There are precedents. It has happened before. At the end of last century after being here for goodness knows how long, the disease was stamped out by a policy of extermination and muzzling. Matters were helped by the fact that it had not spread to the wild life. Then, after the First World War it broke out again. Almost certainly a soldier returning home brought back to you a rabid pet. It took four years to do it, but finally the disease was once more wiped out from your country. You see, it can be done. It must be done. And as events have fallen out you are the ones to do it. You are the front-line troops in a new battle and, with luck, if the disease has not gone too far, it may be a brief battle.

'But it must be a bloody one. You must make it so. I know you people with guns are shortly going out to hunt for foxes, but remember what I said: all warm-blooded animals – squirrels, rats, stoats, weazels, badgers. . . . Anything with fur that moves. If you like to consider rabies as a visitation of Nature upon your countryside then you must be prepared to fight Nature with her own weapons. You must fight her tooth and claw! Anything less – you invite disaster.'

He was sitting down and perhaps because of the intensity of his closing words there was this time a ripple of applause. It promised to increase but at that very moment, Kesseler was back upon his feet. The clapping died away.

'I'm so sorry,' he announced, 'I had clean forgotten. It was arranged that I should introduce the gentleman who is to speak next to you and . . . I have to confess I cannot do so because I have absolutely forgotten his name.'

157

Somehow, with his handsome smile he had converted his confusion into a charming apology. Morant was starting to say something but the small neat man who had arrived with Kesseler in the helicopter was already on his feet and signalling he could take care of himself.

'It's Donaldson, Dr Kesseler,' he said, 'and, of course, ladies and gentlemen, James Donaldson.'

'Do please forgive me,' Dr Kesseler said.

Donaldson laughed easily.

'Really,' he said, 'after such a brilliant summary delivered in a foreign tongue – or was it, Doctor? I'm really not too sure – after that I think you can be very easily excused for letting slip out of mind the name of an obscure civil servant you met less than two hours ago in a noisy helicopter.'

He turned to face the slightly puzzled audience.

'I am,' he said, 'from the MAFF, the Ministry of Agriculture, Fisheries and Food. My job is to see the police get every kind of administrative co-operation – Parliament, Whitehall, Local Authority – they may need in containing and defeating this outbreak. It is also to spell out to you what measures are being taken locally and what is expected of you. If I may, I would like to take this opportunity of formally asking you to give all those in authority every assistance as may be required. By your presence here now you've already given much and I'm sure your continuing co-operation can be counted on. In return I can promise you one reassuring thing right away: perfectly adequate stocks of anti-rabies vaccine are available to meet any foreseeable contingency.

'More specifically, turning to the question of extermination, we shall be implementing a two-tier policy. Operation Tooth and Claw as perhaps we should now call it is, I know, substantially in your own hands, particularly those of' – he consulted a note – 'Mr Mallett. I shall say no more about it other than to let you know professional rodent exterminators are being called in right now to take care of the rats that I understand have been troubling you latterly. Similarly, as of tomorrow, army units will be in the area providing flame-throwers to clear ground and seeing to it that all earths and' – again the note – 'sets are gassed.

'The second tier of our programme will be, so to speak, on the Home Front. You must have concluded by now that the policy of extermination must be extended to the putting down of all dogs and cats in the village. This may sound harsh, even callous, but—'

'No!'

'You can't be serious!'

Two individual voices rang out and then Donaldson's attempt to continue was drowned in a great release of protest from the long pent-up audience. Reid, startled back from his fatigue to full awareness by the sheer volume of noise, began to realise that this nondescript man was the perfect example of 'the man from the Ministry'. Faceless, he would forever have the hatchet job to execute, forever be expected to clean up the unpopular messes created by others. He was turning to Morant now for help as the angry cries kept coming. There was virtually nobody present from that country village who did not have a much loved pet.

Morant was on his feet, his arms spread wide like a fervent preacher. Kesseler was standing too, concerned and anxious. Like a storm blowing itself out the noise began to die.

'He's quite right, you know.' From the back of the hall a firm authoritative voice had cut through the last few outcries. Heads turned as one. The speaker had been Dr Moar. Of middle-age, he faced the people whom for a dozen years he'd tended. He was liked and respected even more for his commonsense power to heal and comfort than for the ability to tie the best fly the length of the Test.

'Even though most of your animals will be quite healthy,' he said, 'we can't allow the off-chance that one pet who's rabid now will start the whole thing off again in a few weeks' time.'

He paused. People began to answer back but bringing his pipe up to his mouth Dr Moar was somehow able to cut them off.

'There's something I should let you all know,' he said.

'Sad and tragic news. I've just come from Southampton General. Miss Weldon died while on her way there late last night. She had contracted rabies from her corgis Emma and Jane. . . . Perhaps you would like to consider how often you've seen those dogs out and about these last few weeks.'

He finished. There had been more cries of grief and shock. Then, as the prim and slightly comic lady was remembered, saddened silence. Donaldson chose his moment well to counterpunch.

'Thank you, sir,' he said. 'I was just attempting to make the point that although harsh, our attitude was at least humane. We have arranged for teams to go from house to house. Your animals will be put to sleep quite painlessly.'

'What about muzzles?' someone shouted.

'Or serum? Vaccinations?' That had been Mary Burns.

'Vaccine. Simply not on,' Donaldson said. 'Enough, as I indicated, yes, for people who have been bitten. Not enough for blanket protection. Muzzling, in theory, "yes". For dogs. In practice there are insufficient numbers available and, frankly, even if there were, regarding this key central zone I would not be prepared to take the risk that one of you could either accidentally or, worse, deliberately, fail to comply with the order.'

There was the murmur of another outcry. He's a toughie, Reid thought.

'Do we have a choice?' Mary Burns was saying. 'I mean, is what you're proposing legal?'

Donaldson had obviously long anticipated that one.

'As yet, no,' he said. 'Nobody can force you to have your pets destroyed today. We do not quite live in that sort of country. However, I can assure you that within twenty-four hours we will have mandatory powers to tackle the crisis. I ask for your ungrudging co-operation today because time is of the essence. With ever hour the circle widens. Or would you prefer to sit through a second showing of our film?'

If such a thing as a collective shudder is ever to be seen among the English, Donaldson's last thrust provoked one. The muttering rose and died to silence.

'Very well,' he went on. 'I would like to say one last thing.

I don't wish to pre-empt Chief Constable Morant's role but on behalf of the Ministry of Agriculture I would like to make this pledge. At this time we do not know how rabies has returned to Britain. We should not, today, concern ourselves with that particular how or why. First things first. That question-mark, however, is almost certainly one for the police. I am prepared to go on record as saying that it is a certainty that rabies could never have crossed the Channel without human aid. That is, of course, a criminal offence. It is my promise that the criminal or criminals will be found and brought to justice.'

To silence, he sat down. There were angry and resentful glances at him from a score of faces. But he had carried his unpalatable point. His last attempt at arousing some more positive reaction had largely, failed. Yet here and there it had set people thinking.

Morant was on his feet again.

'Mr Mallett,' he said simply.

At some stage in the meeting, Mike Mallett had slipped back into the hall. He came forward now to brief his hunters. It was a slow advance, he looked drenched with fatigue, haggard with worry. His shoulders had the distracted stoop of a man who has just been told that both his children are in the intensive-care unit of a hospital and on the 'highly critical' list.

CHAPTER THIRTEEN

The rain had decided it would rain for ever. With a monotonous melancholy it fell unhurriedly from a sky like tarnished silver. For the long line of beaters it added the last touch of misery to this grim mockery of their normal sport.

Asked to concentrate his efforts on the sixty-five-acre wood known as Bleane Cover, Mike Mallett had done his homework well. At the far end thirty guns standing forward stoically received all that the heavens emptied over them. At the near end, were men Mike knew and trusted, placed at strategic intervals. Their instructions were brief and to the point: they were to maintain a steady advance in a straight line, each person keeping level with the one to his right and left to ensure this; three blasts on the horn to commence, two for all forward shooting to cease at once; no game birds to be shot at; other birds that might arise allowed but God preserve any man holding an empty gun the moment a fox broke cover.

The rain still fell when right on schedule, the helicopter, refuelled at Middle Wallop, clattered into sight. With conscious effort Mike Mallett braced his shoulders back.

'O.K.,' he said.

He sounded the three blasts.

Almost at once an isolated shot rang bleakly out from further up the line.

In the village the vets, who had all been inoculated against rabies, were about their thankless work. They left a trail of tears. Children were sent upstairs, out to the back, to look for sweeties in the jar, as the specially equipped vans drew up and the unsuspecting pets were hastily passed across the threshold to go to their doom.

One household offered a grim variation to the pattern. Mrs Maitland, an elderly widow living by herself, opened the door to them with shocked relief. Her face was like a Spanish Christ's. Blood glistened in a dozen bites and scratches. Just minutes before, her dear old cat had transformed himself into a spitting, snarling witch's familiar. Without warning he had leapt at his mistress's face as she had sadly bent to pour him one last drink. Milk had bespattered everything, the bottle been shivered to smithereens, as screaming, fearful for her eyes, she tried to beat him off.

Mrs Maitland was past further shocking. They shot the cat on the spot. An ambulance came at once to take her for a course of injections.

Still the rain fell. Slowly the line advanced. With unsettling irregularity, from double and single barrels, hammer and self-loaders, side-by-sides, over-and-unders and repeaters, the shots rang out. Poised high above the line in the hovering Whirlwind, Erich Kesseler strained to peer past the incessant hypnotic rhythm of the windscreen wipers on the running Plexiglass. At times the film of rain made his task impossible. But at times vision would clear and he could see something. He would press the button on the air-to-ground RT. Then at four intervals along the line the receivers would crackle.

'Fox breaking north-west on left wing.'

Arnold Swarbrick gave the vets their first refusal. A pensioner who lived by himself, he would not let them touch his mongrel dog. In growing old, Arnold had grown gentle to the point of being simple. Now he was like iron. Nothing they could say or do would persuade him to part with the pet he'd come to think of as his one friend. The vets went away. At about two-thirty in the afternoon they returned armed with the official order which had just come through from the Home Office. All his life Arnold had had a fear of forms. He never understood them. Now his ignorance and fright betrayed his last companion on this earth. He patted the friendly little dog who wagged his tail and went to sniff the men. Tears ran unchecked into the wrinkled hollows of the old man's cheeks and a high-pitched wail came from him as if from a child.

'Nanny!' he seemed to say. The hair on their necks stood on end. The nurse that they had thought to bring stepped forward with a tranquilliser.

It seemed to Mike Mallett that the rain had beaten him. He was past praying now. Two halves divided him. For one of them, what he now did was anathema. He had lived his life out among wild animals and birds, he had respect for his friend and foe. It was his job to get rid of the squirrels that damaged trees, the fox that prowled around his pheasant coverts, the rats that sucked the eggs from beneath a sitting partridge. But this extermination, this crude, relentless massacre was alien to his every instinct.

All day his other half had not allowed the image of his two children in white beds to fade out from his mind. That half had taken savage pleasure in each sharp, acrid report. Beyond all logic he thought that each creature's death redressed the balance and bought an improved chance his children would get better.

The helicopter grinding away above varied its pitch. He looked up through the veil of grey rain. As Kesseler waved the chopper abruptly zoomed into the gathering gloom. A crackle on the RT next to him confirmed it had gone to refuel. Eyes still on the grey dome of the sky, Mike Mallett yet again began to pray.

The trail of tears was drawing to a close. The vans of the three teams had covered their allotted zones and now only the 'C' team hadn't finished. Still subdued after their sad encounter with the heart-broken Arnold Swarbrick they drew a blank at a pleasant Georgian residence called Gunn House. No one was at home. They made a note that a later check would now be necessary. So Troy sleeping in the garden shed out of the rain had, for the time being, saved his skin.

That left them one last call. They drove some minutes

through the rain to a secluded cottage on the further out-skirts of the village. Their hearts sank as the door opened. The old man staring blankly at them might have been brother to the pensioner whose mind had tottered as they killed his dog. Richard Foulsham started to explain their purpose. But, though living so far out, the old man knew of it already. He silently handed them a greasy length of rope. It was the makeshift lead to a splay-legged springer spaniel, older and smellier than belief.

'All I've got,' the old man said tonelessly, ambiguously.

They muttered thanks but with blank eyes he shut the door on them. They led the dog back up the long path to-wards the van. Richard Foulsham was reaching in his pockets for the keys that would unlock the back when, as he heard two loud explosions, a searing sensation of red-hot splinters blasted across his back. He writhed in agony and gyrated round. Graham Edwards, the dog let loose, was kneeling on the ground. Beyond, from an upstairs window of the cottage, a rusty pair of gun barrels wavered beneath a puff of rising smoke. Edwards was scrambling to his feet. Shock compelled him to proclaim the obvious.

'The old fool's firing at us!' Both men took cover on the other side of the van while the dog sought shelter from the rain beneath.

'You all right?' Foulsham was asking.

'Hurts like stink.'

'Get in the cab and let's take a look.'

They clambered up out of the wet. It was a natural thing to do. The cab faced away from the cottage and was out of the line of fire. It was a natural action – and unfortunate.

The shot had not gone off unheard. P.C. Simpson was at the moment driving towards Abbotsfield with orders from his Stockbridge sergeant to stand in for the local constable. Morant had asked for this.

'You never know,' he said, 'we're headline news here now. Radio. TV. Get a flap like this on and you often find the small-time villains think it's tailor-made for them to try and get a bit clever.'

Now P.C. Simpson had heard a shot and seen two men,

apparently hurt, bundling awkwardly into a fifteen hundred-weight Ford Transit. He braked. Keeping a wary eye on them he walked cautiously towards them. He was a few feet from them when they heard his footfall and looked up.

'Look out! There's—'

They were too late. Another shot had blasted from the upstairs window. At a range of thirty-five yards, Simpson was hit in the head, chest and arms. He yelled just once in surprise as much as pain and mid-way between a fall and dive was flat upon the ground. He began to gasp hysterically, and, as shock diminished, with mounting noise.

Foulsham got down and crawled to help him. The policeman's hand was pressed tight to the left side of his face. Blood oozed stickily from between the fingers. Of the twenty-three pellets to strike him, one had pierced his eye. It was terror of losing it as much as raw pain that caused Simpson's high-pitched moans.

He had a sense of someone else, of help. His training, his own sense of pride forced him quite literally to grit his teeth.

'Car,' he said. 'Radio. Get on to channel two. Just down the road.'

Shortly Abbotsfield could once more hear the now all too familiar sound of sirens. After morphine had been administered and the casualties were helped away, the cottage was staked out by a dozen crouching, soaking policemen. Five of them were armed.

Sergeant Bennet began by the book. He reached for the loud-hailer.

'Mr Burrows, Mr Burrows,' his metallic voice brayed through the rain, 'as you can see, this is the police. We know you're in there. We know that you're upset. We know how you must feel. But you must come out now. Quietly. Without further trouble. You must give yourself up. You can see that further resistance is useless. I'm going to give you five minutes to think about it. When you've decided you want to come out, show us by throwing your gun down out of the window. Then come down to the door. We will do nothing for five minutes.'

Perhaps it was this strange noise that roused the old dog,

up to now ignored under the van. He rose to his feet and was making for the gate he now nudged open. As he tottered up the garden path several policemen could watch his progress. One of them was P.C. Bennet. Twenty, fresh from training at Hendon and from Folkestone, he had been overjoyed to get a posting in his uncle's station. Now, just two weeks later he saw the chance to make his mark. As the gunbarrels disappeared from the upstairs window, he launched himself towards the garden gate. He was at it, through it, when the cottage door began to open. He kept right on. He was halfway up the garden path before he lost his nerve. Had he not done so, had he kept charging forward, things might have gone differently for him. Instead, faltering, he received a whole ounce and a sixteenth of lead straight in the chest at a range of twelve feet. He dropped as the dog slipped inside. Before the door slammed a second shot had sent his stunned and rising colleagues scrabbling back for cover.

Silence fell. Then the faint moans of the young constable grew strong enough to carry and, as the barrels reappeared above, the uncle could begin to see the rain washing away the widening pool of blood.

He all but went berserk himself.

'The fool! The bloody fool!' he screamed at everyone and no-one. 'Why! Why did he bloody have to! For what! For bloody what!'

Startled by his own vehemence of speech he looked about him at the anxious glances of his men. He was himself again.

'Right, Morrison,' he said, 'you're the gab merchant. Get on the hailer and keep talking. I'm going round the back. Clark, Willis, come with me. The rest of you – nothing until I say so.'

The three moved off. They were in the overgrown and dripping garden when the next shot came. And the next. And nothing. The rain upon the leaves made the silence louder.

Clark looked at Bennet.

'It's an old trick,' he said.

'The boy's bleeding to death,' the uncle said half to himself.

He was off and running, and crashed through the back door without a further word.

Inside was deathly stillness. A half-eaten meal offered up a congealed egg yolk for inspection. Dust was everywhere. Dust; dirt, the smell of old people. The unmistakable smell of burnt smokeless powder. Clark and Willis had joined him.

'Let me get upstairs and then go to the boy,' he said.

Listening, pausing, he climbed the stairs. There were two doors on the tiny landing set at right angles. Both shut. He tried the left-hand one. It did not want to give. He tried the right. It gave and opened on to dust and, in a corner, trunks sixty years old. Nothing else. He put his shoulder to the left-hand door and heaved.

The remains of the old man were sitting upright in a chair. The gun was on the floor where it had fallen from his lifeless hands. He had sat down, put the muzzle of the gun into his mouth and pulled the trigger. Half of the top of the head was consequently missing. In spite of himself, Bennet looked up. He saw skin and hair, red blood, grey brains, stuck to the ceiling. As he shuddered, something detached itself and fell with a soft plop on to the arm of the chair.

The dog was dead behind the door. That was why it had been hard to open. He heard the front door click.

The sergeant raced downstairs and, through the door, out to the gathering gloom.

He had done that much before he realised he could hear no groans from his nephew. As Clark waved the ambulance to come straight to the gate, Willis was crouched above the saturated figure on the path. He looked up and shook his head. The rain seemed harder now.

The drive across Bleane Cover lasted until close to nightfall. Then, as the helicopter disappeared once more behind the curtain of the rain, the men were free at last to climb into the hastily drummed-up lorries, vans, Land Rovers and cars, sent to bring them back. They said little. They were cold, hungry and tired. Their long exposure to the grey weather had crept into their marrow, had brainwashed them. They were giddy and the earth reeled for them as the car ignitions caught.

They dropped Mike Mallett by the police H.Q. He still had the last chore of giving a report to Morant. Numb and drained, he clumped into the trailer. New faces lifted to regard him and he saw eyebrows being raised. For a moment he saw red: Morant was catching up on his shut-eye while he . . . He held himself in check and stated his business then learnt he'd done Morant considerable injustice: the Chief Constable should be back any minute. He'd been away an hour over at the village hall conducting a press conference. Mike said he'd wait and slumped into the chair they'd found. In the close warmth he started to nod off.

'Here, Bob, slip into the boozer for us. Buy us half a bottle of Scotch.'

'Who's paying for it?'

'I am, you burke.'

Mike never knew the name of the young policeman who was soon offering him the largest Scotch he'd ever downed. But he was back in some kind of coherent shape ten minutes later when Morant walked in. There was some kind of kerfuffle by a desk and Mike just glimpsed a bottle disappearing out of sight.

'Who the hell—' began Morant.

'He got it for me,' Mike Mallett said.

Morant looked at him, at his glass, back at the worried, defensive policeman.

'That's right,' Morant said, 'thirty hours straight and it's a new book of rules. Give us the bottle, son.'

As he took it there were suddenly two pound notes left lying on the desk.

'Sorry,' Morant said, 'I've just come from the gentlemen and ladies of the Press. You won't have seen this yet – we're plastered right across the evening headlines. One word in three-inch type – Rabies! Same treatment on TV.'

Angrily he slammed a drawer, slammed a clean glass down upon the desk. The Chief Constable poured himself a drink. His hand was steady and, as the measure rose, he was steady once again himself.

'I don't like it because they're playing it sensational,' he went on. 'Scaremongering. And human-interest. No facts. They'll scare the pants off people and have them raising false alarms from here to Aberdeen. God save us from the tabloids in the morning.'

'Maybe they're right to,' Mike Mallett found he had to say. Morant looked at him.

'Sorry,' he said a second time. 'It's going on a bit . . .' He drank and pulled an appreciative face. 'O.K., then, Mike,' he said, 'how did it go?'

'Two foxes, three weasels, a stoat, twenty-three squirrels, four crows, a magpie, two jays, nine pigeons, thirty-four rabbits.'

'Any more foxes?'

Mike shook his head.

'We only got the two,' he said.

'What about earths?'

'None in use. Bleane Cover's clean.'

'Good.' Morant nodded his understated congratulations. He allowed himself that quick, sharp grin.

'And no pheasants, partridges?' he added.

'Saw a mint. But no one shot.'

'So the boys did well by you there.'

'Yes. God knows when it'll ever get back to normal. If.'

'Come on,' Morant tried, 'foxes gone, you'll be quids in for years.'

Mallet just looked at him.

'Anything else?' he said.

'No.' Morant shook his head. 'You're off the hook. But just to let you know . . . I now have approval from White-hall for my mass kill on a twelve-mile radius. Just as I planned. The Army's being briefed right now. It's huge, of course, enormous. It's being broken down into five thousand acre pockets and those will be sub-divided on a unit basis within — hell, man, you're out on your feet. And so am I. You can get back in on the act later. Right now you're overdue a good night's sleep.'

This time Mallett was shaking his head.

'You are tired,' he said.

As near as he still had it in him, Morant blushed.

'Christ,' he said. 'How could I! We get too used to using people. You could use a car and driver, I expect.'

Mallett nodded.

'Roberts, take Charlie Four and drive Mr Mallett to Southampton for me. On the gong. The hospital. Stay with him.'

'Yes, sir.'

'Give me twenty minutes for a shower,' Mike said. Wearily he levered himself up.

The Dog and Fox was bursting at the seams. Half of the hunters were inside trying to drive the cold out of their bones. But there was little merriment. The mood was strange, subdued, a shadow of the normal relaxed heartiness. Service was slow, Wilf's rarely seen wife had genteely descended to supervise the bar where Maggie Peacock and Mary Burns had volunteered their services behind the counter. Little beer was drunk. Well before closing time the run on spirits had achieved a record profit for the pub.

It would have been all one to Wilf. He was in Southampton at the bedside of the regular barmaid.

At night the whole hospital seemed hushed. It seemed unreal. It seemed an island floated out of time, floated away from all the missed trains, cars that would not start, money problems, sights of pretty girls, grins from misbehaving kids, roars from crowds at the home end and all the petty nuisances and pleasures that are taken for granted. As Mike Mallet followed the squishing tread of the Staff Nurse down through the subdued light of the white ceiling-tiled, eau-de-nil walled corridor, he sensed this hush, this sense of extra effort to do the most ordinary things. He wondered why he'd thought of missing trains. He'd not been on a train in years. He must be in a state of shock.

The Staff Nurse stopped outside the door.

'I believe your wife is still in with her,' she said.

171

She opened the door and nodded.

'It's your husband, Mrs Mallett,' she said.

She opened the door wider and he found himself walking through it. His wife looked up from where she sat beside the solitary bed. The room was not very large. He heard the door close softly behind him and saw that there were great dark circles, chocolate and lilac, stained about his wife's red eyes. His daughter Tricia lay quite quietly on the bed and might have seemed asleep had he not learned from the staff Nurse, but five minutes since, that she was dead.

His wife did not get up. He went and stood by her and she stretched out her hand and he reached out and took it. He looked at his dead daughter. There was a tenseness, a rigidity about the jaw and neck that said, if you looked hard, this was not sleep.

'I should have thought,' his wife said out into the silence.

Or I, he thought. Animals are my trade. He did not say anything by way of comfort because such words had not been made. He knew that this dark bruise upon their hearts would cause them pain until the world ceased for them too. Blame was superfluous. Unthinking, in pure ignorance, they had not done something that needed to be done. That was all. And everything.

He did not speak. After a while he began to weep. A while later his wife spoke.

'They wouldn't let me be here at the end,' she said. 'I didn't mind. It wouldn't have been her by then.'

This time he had to think of something to say fast. For her sake or for his, he was not sure.

'Where's John?' was all that he could do.

'Next door,' she said. 'They keep them separate because they frighten one another.'

'I'd like to see him.' He had almost added the still unspeakable. He felt his wife gather her calm and strength.

She stood up and leaning forward, kissed the daughter whose short life she had not looked to see her own embrace.

'I'll come with you,' she said. 'They know you in the quiet times.'

Unescorted they went outside and then into the room next door.

Their son was not alone. Across from the door a nurse sat by the further wall. She signalled quickly that they should be quiet. It was perhaps for this reason that not until several seconds later did the parents see somebody else was present too. Opposite the foot of the bed stood the tall German, Erich Kesseler. Mike felt his wife stiffen with surprise and resentment. But immediately Kesseler had moved to them.

'Forgive me,' he whispered. 'I had no wish to intrude. The people here told me they had no objection to my observing. As a doctor. But you are parents. There is a difference between the personal and the scientific. I will go at once.'

'It's all right,' Mike Mallett said. 'I know who you are. It is your job. Stay if you want to.'

There was a moment of hesitation.

'Yes. It is my job. Thank you, yes. I will stay.'

Another pause.

'Your boy – he is putting up a fight.'

Kesseler moved away and Mike and Celia Mallett looked down on their son John. He was visibly wasted but for the moment lay in uneasy peace. He was not strapped down or in a strait-jacket. An oxygen cylinder ran to a tight-fitting device about his nose that left his mouth free. Drip-feed bottles of clear liquid hung upon a stand by the bed-head and there were plasters on his forearm that lay outside the single sheet that was his only cover. But, for the moment, there was no connection between the bottle and his thin, childish arm. The nurse got up and with a tissue wiped the glistening forehead.

As she sat down, a harsh, rasping, choking sound came from the boy's throat. No longer prostrate he began to jerk, to toss convulsively. The flexible chrome oxygen hose bucked wildly as it swung in crazy matching rhythm. Abruptly, as if stabbed deep in his stomach, the boy doubled his knees to his chest in a clenched spasm. He kicked them out full stretch, an extended, rigid hold and a long, piercing wail came from his straining lips. Mike felt his wife's nails cut into his palm. The more pain I can bear, he thought, the more I take away from him. If only that's how it could be, he thought. More tremors convulsed the little body. The sheet was kicked aside. He suddenly sank back, gasping. The nurse adjusted the cylinder and for perhaps a minute he lay in stillness that already looked like death. Sweat stood out once again upon skin that seemed to have shrunk helplessly to outline the skull and then, to mark his protest at the supreme injustice of his suffering, the boy let slip a line of tears from under his closed lids. They ran slantwise across the sunken, blue-grey cheeks.

Celia Mallett groaned as she cried too. Mike Mallett could no longer bear to look. He looked, instead, at Kesseler.

And Kesseler cried also. In the deep centre of his own scalding grief, Mike Mallett had room to wonder what demon of guilt, what angel of duty possessed the German and nailed him to the cross he had been made to bear. His cord jacket was stained a dozen times, the stubble on his face was heavy. Drained of colour his skin was stretched back tight across his bones. In that dim light he seemed close to an albino. Pressing himself back against the wall, his hands out at a distance from his sides, he looked himself a visitant, a helpless white Angel of Death.

Another wave began to bathe the boy in fire. Mike Mallett did not look. He felt his wife's nails in his palm and the tight-stretched unblinking gaze of Kesseler grew still harder. When the spasm stopped, it was Kesseler who moved out of a frozen pose and walked to the bed. The hand was so large, the head so small, for a freezing moment Mike thought the action was to be the ritual drawing down of lids upon eyes no longer seeing. He was premature. This time it was by the huge hand that the sweat was gently wiped away.

Kesseler walked round the bed to them.

'They have given you a room here?'

'Yes.'

'I should try to go to it now. It will be like this for a long time. They will come for you when . . . when there is news. I will stay for a while longer.'

'How long – how long before . . .' Mike could not say it.
'There is no telling.'
They moved to go away.
'He is a very brave little boy,' Kesseler said.

All hospitals are much the same. When Dr Kesseler came out into the corridor much later he was, for a short instant, literally not sure what country he was in or what language he had last been using. Sleep, I need sleep, he thought in German and like a great dog shook his head to fling off the clinging layers of exhaustion. He came back to the present and remembered. Southampton, he recalled, there's a hotel for me one block over and tomorrow there will be the first reports on samples of the wild life shot today. But when you are this tired, old friend, the only thing to do is to put one foot out in front of the other one step at a time.

He was halfway down the long and ghostly corridor when he was strangely accosted. A short fat balding man came out of a room. He carried a jacket on his arm and tears streamed from his wide-spaced eyes down his red-veined cheeks. Kesseler did not know him, but, compelled by grief, the man came to him as an intimate.

'She's gone,' he said. 'Gone.'

His anguish over-rode the comic, the grotesque.

'I asked her. For years I asked her,' he went on. 'She never would say "yes". I begged her time and time again. She wouldn't listen. She always said she'd never be responsible for breaking up another woman's marriage. I always thought I'd be the first to go. But she's gone first!'

Out of a sense of compassion Kesseler summoned his energy. He must talk to this man gently, normally.

'You are going home now?' he said.

Vaguely, uncertainly, the little fat man nodded.

'I will show you the way to the main exit,' Kesseler said.

As seemed most natural in that strange, submarine world he put his arm around the fat man's shoulders and they walked forward into the shiny, reflected stillness. So as to draw the weeping man out from his grief the German began to ask him simple questions.

He learned his name was Wilfred Hopper and that he owned a pub. A woman who had worked for him had died.

It had not crossed his mind that in England there might well be no night porter. He nearly found himself locked out. As it happened he was lucky. A policeman in motorcycle kit was waiting in the darkened lobby and could let him in.

'Didn't know where you were, sir,' he said as he handed Kesseler a written message.

'Is there a light?' Kesseler asked.

He read the message and muttered something that the policeman didn't catch. Christ, he looks done in, he thought.

'Excuse me. How do you pronounce this name?' Kesseler asked.

'Er ... Pembrokeshire,' the policeman replied. 'They said there'd be an answer.'

'You can tell them, my friend,' Kesseler said, 'that the good doctor is out on his feet and going off to bed and that he will be in Abbotsfield at noon tomorrow.'

'I'm not sure they'll be pleased with that, sir.'

'Then you may tell them it is quicker than Christ managed.'

He went upstairs. The message had brought news of seven alleged outbreaks of rabies across the British Isles. The one in the Welsh place had been confirmed.

CHAPTER FOURTEEN

Earlier that same evening P.C. Reid had helped the Chief
Constable of Hampshire finish off the now slightly legendary
half-bottle of Scotch. On the strength of this proof of
intimacy he dared to yawn as he put down his emptied
glass.

'O.K., I get the message,' Morant said drily. 'Bugger off
and go to sleep and don't wake up until you're sent for. And
thanks for a first-rate job.'

'What about yourself, sir? You've been going non-stop.'

'I've still got one good hour left in me. Or need to have.
There's this little matter of your replacement being an eye
short – and the Hampshire police a man short – Need a
lift?'

'No thanks, sir. It's not far. The rain's stopped. I'll walk
it and unwind.'

He only walked. It may have been the whisky but halfway to his house, Reid remembered there had been long,
long ago, like last evening, a message to call Mrs Denning.
He cursed. It was the last straw. But he needn't worry. It
could wait. It already had at least twice. Only it was the
sort of last straw that would tickle and prick at his conscience.

Twenty minutes later the phone at Morant's elbow rang.
He picked it up, clipped out his name and listened.

'Come on, Reid,' he said, 'can't it wait? You know what
state I'm in. I've just heard news from Wales that would
make your flesh creep.'

On the extension in the Dennings' bedroom, Reid broke
in on his chief.

'I think there's more to it than just a death,' he said. He
continued speaking for some several minutes.

Morant listened expressionlessly.

'O.K.,' he said abruptly. 'Stay there. I'll be with you in five minutes.'

It took him four. He and Reid and two other constables stood looking down on Paula Denning's body. The damp wind came on to their faces through the French window and almost masked the taste of sweet thick sourness in the room.

'Where did you call from?' Morant asked.

'Upstairs, sir. The extension.'

'You've touched nothing?'

'The left cheek, sir. It hasn't started to decompose out of rigor mortis yet, sir.'

Morant looked at Reid.

'Who told you that?' he said.

'It was in a book, sir.'

'She must have blown her brains out just after she made the call to you.'

'If it is suicide, sir.'

Morant looked at him again. This time there was the faint ghost of a smile.

'Too many books,' he said, 'spoil the copper. You say her husband's away on business?'

'Yes, sir. America, I think.'

'O.K., go on. Give it to me again and from the top.'

'I got the call. Called back. No reply. Come to think of it my wife said something about her sounding funny, but she put it down to the line. Anyway. Then this rabies thing hit and I pretty much forgot about it entirely until half an hour ago as I was walking home. So I thought I'd check.'

'You did?' Morant sounded incredulous.

'It is very close. I thought it would be routine. I rang the bell. No answer. No lights. But milk on the doorstep. Then the phone started to ring inside. It kept on for a long time and no-one answered. I got that funny feeling. I came round the house and saw the French window blown open in the wind. I came in. Found this. Then I put the light on – oh, I used a handkerchief – I saw the note and I saw these lumps of, well, phlegm, I suppose.

'So I thought of rabies. And then I thought if a person

shot herself on account of having rabies she'd have to know exactly what she'd been let in for. This was someone not like the others – someone who knew what it was all about. Then I remembered something.'

Reid paused. For the first time since his early encounter with Morant in his police house, a look of diffidence came to his face.

'I owe you an apology, I'm afraid, sir,' he said. 'It's something I should have thought of a lot earlier.'

'Well?'

'About three weeks ago, John Denning, her husband, reported a missing dog to me.'

Morant's head came up.

'I'd never actually seen it myself but I did hear the odd mention of it in the village. Apparently it was a stray that just turned up and they took it in. A biggish black mongrel.'

'How long had they had it?'

'A few weeks. Not long. They hadn't got around to getting a licence for it and I said they should. One thing struck me as a bit funny. You see, it wasn't actually a dog but a bitch. And bitches don't run off nearly so often as the males. They sit around and wait for it to come to them.'

'It just disappeared into thin air?'

'Yes, sir. Apparently. There is one last thing, sir. A bit before all this, in August, the Dennings were abroad . . . I mean, it's just a thought, sir. The other one, of course, is that old Ted, the tramp that died, lived only just down the lane.'

Morant was silent for several seconds.

'How long have you been here Reid?' he said at last.

'Six years, sir.'

'You like it here, then?'

'Yes, sir. Very much. Suits me down to the ground.'

'I thought so. Now let me say one thing. You don't have to go through that apology crap. You're one of the best coppers, uniform or plain-clothes it has been my pleasure to meet in a long time. When you whistled that big ox of a fellow, er, Gadney, out of the hall like that, you may well have prevented a mini-riot. Nobody can expect you to remember a dog you've never seen straight off, with all this going on.'

'Yes, sir. Thank you, sir. You were actually a bit wrong about him, how he'd react when the penny dropped.'

'Don't push your luck because I said something nice. The last we heard his kid was still alive. He's got to go through that yet. All right, listen. This is what we'll do. Quilley!'

'Sir!'

'Put through a call to Southampton Murder. We'll leave them to do the basic forensics and right bloody welcome they are too. When you've done that, stay here until they come. Reid, who does Denning work for?'

Reid told him the company.

'Right. McEvoy, first thing tomorrow call Detective-Superintendent Morrow. Tell him I'm asleep and tell him what's happened. Ask him to get Denning's firm to give us a trace on him and ask him to check with Customs if they had any dealings with a Denning during August–early September. They go by car, Reid?'

'Yes, sir.'

'Know which port?'

'No, sir.'

'O.K. Check the registration, McEvoy. It may help. Now, for the second time tonight, Reid, go home and go to sleep. I won't say this missing dog is the key to all of this – we still haven't had sight or smell of that other terrier. But I'm sure as hell going to find out one way or the other. Oh, and Reid.'

'Yes, sir?'

'If on the way home you find we're being invaded by greater-toed Martians with bug-eye lasers – keep it to yourself.'

The failure of the police to establish the whereabouts of Chip, the second of Ted's two dogs, could hardly be considered surprising. Indeed over at Midhurst, Terry and Dominic Wrinch, having been faced with the same problem, had already given up. The terrier had been something of a handful before it disappeared.

The disappearence was due to the manner in which two other brothers partly scraped a living. Francis and Colin Lloyd were petty villains. They had a record of probation, Borstal and gaol, as long as their four arms put together. One of their lines was a real doddle. Near where they lived was a Kennels which occasionally supplied a Government Research Establishment with dogs. Though keeping a low profile on its needs, the Government laboratory had certain sources from whom it regularly topped up its continually dwindling stock of animals. A Mr Blessington, in fact, had charge of this important scientific area. His grade was Higher Clerical Officer and, by now, he had had many increments. He knew the Kennels quite well as a reputable concern and assumed their dogs came from a bona fide source, although, naturally, other than their price, he asked few questions. The Lloyds knew nothing of this, they only knew the Kennels would pay them for a stray dog. They made a point of driving their old Commer van out of the Midhurst area before they started making use of their cord, sacks and clubs at the expense of dogs and the ensuingly bereft owners. In the case of the Jack Russell, though, it was a question of so obviously a stray it wasn't true. They made an exception to their local rule. Coincidentally they made a delivery to the Kennels with Chip the same night that Tricia Mallett and Florrie Beeston died.

There are no easy, comforting patterns. Chip, soon of course to undergo radiation treatment in the interests of medical research, was a picture of health. Neither of the Lloyds was bitten.

Another dog had, for a while as yet, fared with more luck. Troy, bored with the garden shed and hungry, had returned to the house. The kitchen door was shut. The french windows were ajar but he had not liked what he had scented there. He had whined and whimpered for a while. No one had come. Boredom and hunger had roused him to his feet. In the dark, led by some trace of memory, he had gone padding off to Mullen's Barn.

CHAPTER FIFTEEN

He was in a flat landscape. The light was lurid. The sky was a great grey wheel from dark horizon to horizon. The sea was somewhere. He was in the fens. Something was buried by the sea and he must run. Something back there, a shape, was chasing him. He had forgotten what it was but he knew that it was terrible. He must run. He must run through these wet, reedy fens that sucked at his feet and slowed him down. The thing behind was flopping, splashing after him. There was no hiding space under the wide sky. Without turning his head he could see the black shape flopping after him. A blob still but a bigger blob. He knew now what it was. It was the dog. The great black dog. The black dog of revenge. He could see it now. It was no longer a blob. He could see it as a shape to recognise because it gained so fast. Faster. He must run faster. But he could not. The water was up to his knees, his feet were sticking deeper in the clinging mud. The dog was gaining in enormous leaps and bounds. It had followed him from nowhere to run him down in this Godforsaken land. It was sable-black, with eyes as yellow as a cat's. Its mouth and tongue were blood-red like a wolf in a story-book. The dog was as big as a pony and he could feel it getting closer. His feet were moving now but he was moving on the spot. Steam rose from the dog. It was like a nightmare only this was real. The dog was right behind him, he could hear and feel its breath. He could not see it now. He turned his head. In the flat country under the wide sky, the dog was gathered for its spring. He tried to scream but no scream came. He turned his head. Oh God! Risen in close-shot straight before him was the grinning, rat-chewed, decomposed half-face with blackened scales of blood where eye-balls should have been. He screamed.

Someone was shaking him. He stilled his wildly thrashing head, opened his eyes. He stared into a face and shuddered because its eyes were on a slant. For a moment he believed he was in bed in Pusan and with the girl they'd bought him.

'You have bad dream, I think, sir. A nightmare, I think. I am sorry waking you but it is better. Would you like me to get you something, sir?'

Then he remembered where he was and knew where he was to be worse than any nightmare.

'Thank you,' he said. 'Scotch. I'll have a large Scotch.'

The hostess bowed and smiled, gave him a cellophane-wrapped tissue. She minced away down the aisle. He dabbed at himself. His hair was plastered to his skull with sweat.

His name was John Denning and he was aboard a JAL night flight bound from Tokyo to London via Anchorage, Alaska. Anchorage! It was there, ten times magnified, the nightmare had resumed.

It had been bad, very bad, going out. Carroll, with his professional Irishman act, had been Celtic salt in the running sore of his doubts and fears. But that had helped. He had gone into conference, not naked but armed with an indifference to the outcome that had made him quite invincible. Whether they made the damned things in the States or in Switzerland, in England or in Ireland had no significance beside the matter of life and death he carried at his heart. Whose tobacco at what price, his own job, were meaningless alongside the grim spectre that had once been Ted Rimmer. He had worn that indifference on his sleeve. The paste-on fraternity boy smiles, the hail-buddy-well-met handshakes and the shifting, insecure eyes of his American counterparts had found no common ground in his sullen refusal to play in their professionally amiable ball-game. They had been intimidated at first, then routed. When Paula's phone call had sent sweet relief coursing through his veins, he'd indulged that feeling of relief by showing the contempt he'd always felt for these shaky rug pedlars. The result had been astonishing. In all his experience he'd known nothing like it. He had wiped the floor with Carroll. Gaining momentum he'd gone from victory on to victory. When, with obvious scheming, somebody back home (Petersen, it had to be) had tried to keep him away from base by dreaming up the trip to their Australian and Far East sources, he had simply let himself ride with it.

Then it had been a blurred procession. Salads and steaks, Barossa Valley and teriyaki and altering his watch so often as he flew in and out of zones that jet-lag had not had time to strike. Until the last couple of days. Then, as he was quitting Seoul, home had taken its turn as a visible, up-coming landmark on his route and his thoughts could once more turn to England, home and beauty. He had made his peace with Paula: that was now set fair. For a while, cruising from the moment he left Alabama, fêted, his euphoria rising with each stop, he had left in a locked compartment all thoughts of Abbotsfield. In the meantime, he had other things to worry about – his laundry, taxis to arrange and would his missing case come in on the next flight. And diversions. He had made his peace with Paula but a balance could be silently adjusted. Twice, in Tokyo and in Pusan he made impersonal but pleasant use of ladies whose English counterparts (less skilled, no doubt) he would have thought beneath him to approach.

It had been quite . . . functional. No harm in it. Nobody hurt. Now, as proximity beckoned, he unlocked the compartment and took thoughts of the village out of moth-balls. It would be nice, you know, to get back after all this racketing around.

He had religiously sent Paula postcards. Phoning was more difficult. There was the displacement of their time zones. There were the language problems with the operators. But he telexed back to base. And as his kaleidoscope of a schedule drew towards its close, he phoned twice, and both times it rang on and on. Ah well. It would have been nice to catch up on the news, have word of Troy and to have been met at Heathrow. But tomorrow he would be in Tokyo and boarding a flight home and able to do all the catching up he wanted. He would get in some shooting too.

At Anchorage there was a refuelling stop of an hour and a quarter. Confined to the two-acre warmth of the provincial out-of-town terminal he had drunk coffee, stretched his legs between the Hertz and Avis desks and, hovering aloof in a tired no-man's land detachment, watched the people wander to and fro. His steps had led him to a news stand and to the realisation they had copies of the overseas edition of the *Telegraph*.

It is funny how the mind works and can direct the eye. The first word to rise up at him from the front page was 'Abbotsfield' – buried in the text. The bold headline 'Rabies' registered only a micro-second later. Then nothing registered. He stood there, the paper shaking in his hand, while his mind tried to reject what it had read. It failed. The facts would not be denied. The deaths. The anticipated deaths. The wholesale extermination. The fears of further spreading. He collapsed into his seat back on the plane, oblivious of how he'd got there. As they took off new thoughts surfaced from the depthless hell he had created for himself. Killed in the purge, Troy would now be dead. And Paula! Perhaps the reason that the phone had gone unanswered. . . . On impulse, he had swallowed pills. The engines had droned on and he had slept And dreamed.

The hostess had tripped back. She reached across the two empty seats and handed him his Scotch. He drank. He felt it burn but knew no taste. She watched him for a brief moment and then went. Paula, Paula! Surely she would be alive! She hadn't been bitten. Not by Asp. If you hadn't been bitten, you couldn't get it. That was right, wasn't it? Yes. But perhaps there were exceptions. Perhaps she had been bitten. By Chop or Chip. Mike Mallett had taken the dogs in. His daughter was now on the danger list. . . . Oh, perhaps the phone had kept on ringing because Paula had had the sense to take Troy right away from the area. No! That would be the same crime all over again. Might be. Perhaps he could have the captain radio ahead and . . . then they would all know. But they must all know now in any case. If Paula hadn't told them he must go straight to the police. It would break Rupert's heart. Troy dead and his own daughter responsible. Oh God, it would break his heart in the real sense!

He began to cry. Slewing round to put his head against the headrest he let the sobs come from him loudly and unchecked. The maelstrom of disordered thoughts and warring impulses began to recede, began to be dissolved and lost in the hot, sticky tears that gave a kind of physical comfort as they dried upon his cheeks. After a long time he had cried himself out and the sun that they were hurtling towards was rising. He straightened, turned his head. Sitting on the seat next to the aisle was the hostess. She was looking at him. It seemed she had been there for a long time. She smiled sadly.

'Better now,' she said. 'I go get you new drink. On house.'

She went. He realised that across two different cultures and thousands of miles some basic quality of sympathy, of being nice, had kept its concerned watch on him. The international plastic of a jet had not destroyed the girl's kindness. For her sake, as she returned, he successfully fought down the softer tears her gesture prompted him to shed.

At Abbotsfield, the same sun that brought its grey dawn to John had already risen on a second wave of carnage. This time the Army were in the vanguard. Given the target area and the terrain it was now asked to sweep, no other body could have furnished sufficient manpower. The twelve-mile radius bit well into the New Forest. The scrub, the gorse, the close-set woods and copses constituted a tangled mass of logistical headaches with which only the sophisticated mass weaponry of the army could come to grips. There was much commonsense liaison with keepers and local men. Colonels to whom field sports were foreign had the sense to step aside while Captains and Lieutenants ran the show. But, fundamentally, as flame-throwers burnt at the damp undergrowth, as fresh cannisters of Cyclon-B were driven forward to earths and badger sets, rat holes, and rabbit warrens, it was the army's fire-power that made a massacre on such a scale possible.

On that same morning three men rose far later than the sun. Morant had gone to bed knowing that with the Army primed and on the job, his talents as a field commander could take second place to his experience as a cop. Over breakfast he thought about all that he had gathered from Reid in the tired hours of the night before. He still felt rough but no copper was worth his screw if he didn't get to feel this way once in a while. The second cup of coffee helped a lot. By the fourth he was reaching for the phone. The first call he put through was to his colleagues on the Murder Squad.

It was necessary for a nurse to wake up Mike and Celia Mallett. On instruction, she left it to the last minute that the hospital kitchen's busy schedule could allow. Then she brought them breakfast in bed as if they were admitted patients. There was no change in their son's condition. He had held his own. He had maintained enough resistance to ensure the coming day would be another one of torment to him. Mike Mallett knew that his work of the previous day had done much to halt the outbreak's spread but it seemed small comfort now. A feeling of resentment lodged in him. A man should have the right to be beside his wife the day their daughter dies. He knew where he would spend this day.

Woken by the travelling alarm he'd purchased in Miami, Dr Erich Kesseler was on the phone within minutes. He had a decision to make at once and needed facts. What he heard, in part, pleased him. Routine police work had established that the Weldon family now lying dangerously ill in Camarthen had recently been on a visit to a relation in Abbotsfield, Hampshire. The overwhelming certainty must be that their collie had contracted rabies there. Kesseler decided that it was better to stay close to the apparent source of both outbreaks. He began to discuss the hastily evolving plans for containing the disease within the Pembroke peninsula. As he gathered an impression of the terrain, his hint of morning optimism faded.

One man had risen early that same morning. Rupert Marsh had been sick with worry since the evening of the day before. The so-familiar views of his daughter's village had never seemed so totally unreal as when suspended in his drawing room upon the television. In his haste to turn the volume up he had spilt his pre-dinner sherry on his cardigan. He heard words he could not take in or credit. Then he did and thought of Troy. He had been on the phone at once. No answer. He had been looking for his shoes – he'd drive right over, see what was what – then Hilary had told him he must simmer down. Paula would call before long. Sooner if she needed help. Meanwhile there was grilled trout coming up and the Newsoms due for bridge. The news was terrible but a certain sense of due proportion would stop us all getting too excited. Changing partners, they played three rubbers. On all the pairings Rupert lost. Everyone was very understanding. He got up to telephone four times. Each time there was no answer.

Then before eight the next morning there was a knock. They kept no servants now, he must answer it himself. He heaved himself hastily up, grabbed his dressing gown. He went anxiously down the twisting, low-beamed stairs. It might be Paula. It was not. It was the police.

John thought he might be sick, that he might faint, that he might open his mouth and scream for ever. He did none of these things. He stood in the line behind the brown-skinned woman who was trying to buy travellers' cheques with some Far Eastern currency. The soles of his feet itched with impatience. No wonder this had been the short line. Everyone else had had the sense to get into the other. Maybe he still should. No, there were eight people in that one now. Three of them were oriental. All he wanted was change, for God's sake! The woman, for the third time, was having it explained to her she should sign here right now but there – no, there not there – when she endeavoured to cash the cheques. The clerk still hadn't reached for her calculator. It would be hours. It seemed to him he'd been through all this somewhere before. Or something like it. He remembered where. It had been in Calais, queueing incessantly to get cash for the deposit on the boat in which they'd taken Asp. This time a groan escaped him and the clerk looked up and tried to flash him her best apologetic smile. He did not see. He was thinking of a second chance. A chance to put things right. A chance to go back there and cast Asp in the sea with a stone about her neck. . . . There were no second chances.

He had survived the last hour into Heathrow in the knowledge he would in minutes be able to get to a phone. But well before the plane had started to descend he had been aware that amongst his international collection of small-change he lacked the English coins for a long-distance call. Well, he could reverse the charges. But, no, that would involve giving his name and, very possibly, the operator would be listening in. He had realised then that his mind was still not made up about going to the police. He must first of all talk to Paula. If Paula . . . The endless cycle of ifs and buts had started up again. He had been first off the plane and after a running walk along the endless ramps and all-glass corridors of Heathrow, he passed with minimal formality through passport control and customs. But now, this woman. At last she fumbled to one side. He presented the cheque he had already written to the girl asking her to give silver.

Furnished with the necessary coins he waited eight more minutes. At last the phone was free. He ducked into the bubble and almost dropped his clutch of change. He forced himself to dial the familiar number slowly and regularly. No mistakes. From the first ring at the other end it had the unmistakable tone of sounding through an empty house. She was in hospital for sure. Then the phone was picked up. 'Hello?' A man's voice and just that.

'. . . Oh, I'm sorry, I think I must have a wrong number.' But I dialled so slowly to be sure. Sod the GPO.

'What number did you want, sir?'

John told him.

'Yes, sir, you have the right number. Is this Mr Denning, by any chance?'

'Yes, it is. Who the hell are you?'

'This is Detective Constable Tillson of Hampshire CID.'

'Where's my wife?'

'I regret—'

'What's going on?'

'I'm afraid I have to inform you, Mr Denning, that your

wife has had an accident. She is now in Southampton Hospital.'

'What sort of an accident? How bad? How bad is it?'

'I'm afraid I can't exactly say, sir.'

'What do you mean – you can't say?'

'Where are you calling from, sir?'

'London Airport. What do you mean—'

'My instructions were, that I should request you to present yourself to Police Headquarters here at Abbotsfield as soon as possible.'

'Police Headquarters? What Police Headquarters?'

'We have a mobile unit set up for the emergency.'

'What emergency?'

'The rabies outbreak.'

'Oh, yes.'

'Oh, yes, you've been away.'

'Listen, officer, please. Can you please tell me what has happened to my wife?'

'I'm sorry, Mr Denning. I cannot tell you any more than I have. My advice to you is not to worry and to get back here as soon as you can. When do you think we could expect you?'

At the other end of the line, John Denning had already hung up.

The Master of Fox Hounds had stopped using his St James' voice to protest and now looked resignedly grim. The Huntsman was inconsolably in tears. The Clarendon, Hampshire's second oldest hunt, was on the point of losing its entire pack.

They were kennelled within a twelve-mile radius of Abbotsfield. Just possibly the professional care with which the hounds were supervised and their virtual segregation from less specialised animals might have won them a stay of execution. But on the way back from a walk-out some days before, a dog, apparently upset by a sore on his hind-quarters, had swiftly savaged his partner and the couple straight in front. The Huntsman had whipped them smartly in and the incident had passed. Then, subsequently, un-precedented fighting had broken out in three of the four lodges. There had been a quite unbelievable set-to a few days later in the draw-yard. The Huntsman had begun to fear the worst even before he found the original dog foaming at the mouth. In all forty-six couples were to be put down.

The vets came into the brick-walled, wire-fenced drawyard. They carried their humane killers in nondescript cases. They were solemn. As professional men they knew well enough what generations of controlled, selected breeding they were about to expunge. Major-General Wrigley spelt it out.

'Decades of care going out the window in one hour,' he said. 'You might as well send the records up in smoke, Tom, and remove the last bloody trace. Then nobody need ever know. My God, if I had the fool who started this in front of me!'

Out of deference to the Huntsman he broke off. Tom Reynolds had not progressed into anger yet from grief.

The vets began to move to the nearest lodge.

That evening the putting down of the Clarendon's pack was featured on the television news. There were many across the country who cheered.

The roundabout was coming at him too fast. John braked and thought what-the-hell who cares and then had skidded round it. The hired car handled like a pregnant cow. Another roundabout ahead. Bloody Basingstoke was full of them. And police. He'd better slow down a bit, he'd used up all his luck on the M3. It seemed funny being on this side of the road again. He kept on feeling he was going to meet something head on.

CHAPTER SIXTEEN

The Mobile got more like a sweat-box every hour, the duty officer thought to himself. He yawned, then, as he heard clumps upon the steps outside, lifted his head. The door was flung open and a tired-looking man in a grey suit asked for Jock Reid.

'Who's this Jock Reid?'

'Oh, for Christ's sake! He's the village bobby.'

'Oh, er—'

'Look, I'm John Denning. Can you tell me what's happened to my wife?'

'One moment, please,' the sergeant said. He reached out for the phone.

The Dog and Fox was closed due to bereavement. However it was still open to the police. Wilf had been past caring when they'd asked him to allow them a working run of the kitchens and toilets and – they'd see him right – the bar. It was there that John was asked to wait.

He went to have a wash. He half expected one of the silent constables lounging near to him would keep him company, but neither did. He had five minutes to himself. He looked into the mirror over the washstand and saw five days would still have been too short. He looked as bad as he had feared. And as he felt. On hair, limp collar, askew tie, the grime and dust were meanly visible. The sweat of fear seemed visible as well. The slick executive was gone. He should put a better face on it than this. The staring eyes in the drawn face were those of any common criminal put photographically on file. . . . In water refusing to run hot he did the best he could. He still felt awful. His hands were shaking as he tried to dry them on the awkward roller-towel.

His knees were weak, his legs and stomach hollow. It wasn't just the worry. It was the jet-lag from the overnight Atlantic hop. . . . It was the knowledge that right now he had to make his mind up to confess.

He went back into the lounge bar. His shadows had disappeared. Two different men stood up. One was Jock Reid. The other was also in uniform. A uniform with lots of silver. Jock, significantly, did not smile or nod. He was leaving it to the other man to speak.

'Mr Denning?' this one said.

'Yes.'

'How do you do. I'm Chief Constable Morant.'

John said nothing.

'You already know Constable Reid.'

'Hello, Mr Denning,' Jock Reid said. He spoke in a constrained, embarrassed fashion. John found he was lost for words.

'We are grateful to you for getting down here so quickly,' Morant said. 'Have you had a chance to go home yet, by the way?'

'No. I was told to report straight to the police.'

'Ah.' He turned away a moment, took two steps as he considered.

'My wife's dead, isn't she?' John said. It was only just a question. He had a sense his face was quite dead-pan.

Morant turned and looked at him.

'How did you know that?' he said.

'How do I know that when you've instructed all your goons not to let on, do you mean? Especially that mealy mouthed sod answering my phone?'

He had not planned this vehemence. It had just slipped out in the face of the chief constable's unruffled calm.

'The officer answering the phone was carrying out my instructions.'

'In withholding information?'

'Yes.'

'Why? To spare me distress?'

'In part. Yes.'

'And otherwise? The other parts?'

Morant made no reply. John brought himself back to it. 'Well?' he said at last.

'Well what?' said Morant.

'Is my wife dead?' He could not help but shout.

'Oh. I'm sorry. I gathered you had heard she was. Yes, I'm afraid she is. I'm very sorry, Mr Denning.'

John walked to the bay window and stared out on the green. It looked very different from when he last remembered it. Now a functional dark-blue trailer blocked part of the view. Tyre tracks were scored criss-cross fashion on the soiled and slippery grass and bare mud patches had appeared around the edges. And Paula was dead. Paula and the child. For the first time he thought about the life that had been taken away, taken from him and from itself, even in the giving. The desert of his feelings had one tiny point of comprehensible focus and he was suddenly shaking through his body with a tearless rage. Paula! If only! That sod, that swine, Halliwell! If only!

He turned, outwardly calm.

'Would it be all right, you think,' he said, 'if I had a drink?'

'I don't see why not,' Morant said. 'Reid, perhaps—'

'I'll help myself,' he said.

He went to behind the bar, found a glass, poured himself a very large Armagnac. Morant timed it well. He waited till the glass was half-way to his lips.

'The pub is closed today,' he said, 'because Mrs Beeston died. Of rabies.'

The spirit ran over John's fingers as his hand shook. He put down the glass untouched.

'How many?' he said.

'Let's see. The children. Charles Swinton, Patricia Mallett. Two so far in Wales. Mrs Beeston from here, we've mentioned. Miss Weldon. You knew her? Ah, yes in a place this size everyone knows everybody else. We can't quite include Raymond Burrows, I suppose, and P.C. Bennet, although personally I think we should. And, oh yes, I was forgetting. Another child. The reason for my absence when you arrived was I had just heard the news of Marion

Gadney's death. There are three more who'll shortly be dead too. John Mallet, Robert—'

'All right! That's enough! You missed out Paula Denning!'

He tossed the spirit back. Someone had chiselled that roll-call of the dead upon a marble surface remote within his mind. Cold logic told him that these were names to haunt him to the grave, to bring the great black dog of his nightmare back time upon time. But for the moment he acknowledged the future prospects of unceasing remorse with detachment. He was hideously guilty, yes. Shortly he must begin the endless confrontation with that fact. But for the moment this was anaesthetised by the contemptuous anger that he felt towards this supercilious bastard's cheap and nasty try at shocking him. It was like being back in Maryland. The mean copper's trick was just as crude as some of the ham-tongued efforts there to needle and wrong-foot him. All right – so he would make a free and frank confession while he had disgust to sharpen his mind and lend him a last dignity. He was opening his mouth as Morant spoke.

'The reason, Mr Denning, I omitted your wife's name is that the circumstances of her death were somewhat different from the others. Mr Denning – I have the painful duty of informing you that your wife died by her own hand.'

The black dog broke forth from the whiteness and sank its teeth into his heart. As the bar, the tables and the chairs shimmered like a mirage to his dazzled sight he saw Paula smiling up at him from where she lay stretched on the cushions of the punt. It was their honeymoon and she was in a pale green cotton dress that blended with the willows. There was soft and lapping water and a softness in his heart.

'How?' he heard himself saying.

'She took her life at home, Mr Denning. She used your revolver. Mr Denning, the autopsy confirmed—'

'Autopsy!' A stark image of the violation made him retch.

'Naturally. The autopsy confirmed what was immediately largely obvious. Your wife would have died anyway. She was in the terminal stages of rabies . . .'

'But – are you . . . sure. It wasn't . . . an accident . . . ?'

'There can be no possible doubt. A bullet was fired into her temple from point-blank range. I don't wish to cause you undue distress, Mr Denning, but you must see what begins to puzzle us is why Mrs Denning made no traceable effort to seek medical help for her condition. Why she apparently seemed aware she . . . well, shall we say aware that in committing suicide she had nothing to lose. Do you think you might possibly be able to throw any light on this aspect of the death?'

Rupert, John was thinking, Rupert, Hilary. Their daughter had put a gun to her head and pulled the trigger. He moved to the phone behind the bar, yanked it towards himself.

'Mr Denning, may I ask who you intend calling?'

'No you may not.'

'Mr Denning, anything you say now, may be used in evidence at your wife's inquest and you are, of course, entitled to legal representation at this—'

'For Christ's sake, man! I intend calling my father-in-law! My late wife's father! Let's worry about solicitors and all the bloody rest of it later.'

'Mr Denning.'

He began to dial. If they tried to stop him he would hit them.

'Mr Denning. The reason I asked if you had been home is that Mr Marsh is there waiting for you now. In your absence we took the initiative of informing him about your – his daughter's death and he answered certain routine questions for us. He asked whether he might go to your house to await your arrival and we saw no objection.'

'How nice of you,' John said. His heart skipped a beat. That had been one of Paula's expressions. He started to walk towards the door.

'Mr Denning, may I ask where you think you are going?'

'I think I'm going home.'

'Mr Denning, I would appreciate it if you would bear with me.'

'Home! I'm going home! I'll be there—'

'Mr Denning, were you until recently the owner of a large black mongrel dog?'

'Yes,' John said. 'Did Paula – did my wife leave a note?'

'Yes, Mr Denning, she did. This dog – I understand from P.C.—'

'May I see it please?'

'I beg your pardon?'

'May I see the letter?'

'I'm afraid that's not possible, Mr Denning, at the present moment.'

'It's not – why not?'

'The letter is currently at Southampton Central Police Station.'

'By what bloody right?'

'By the right of—'

'Was it addressed to me?'

'Yes.'

'Then it was a personal letter. To me. My property. You had no right whatsoever to—'

'Don't be so bloody bound up in yourself! Of course I had a right! I had the right of any policeman| investigating a violent death! I had the right of any policeman trying to track down the out and out criminal lunatic responsible for bringing this God-awful thing over here. Responsible, that is, for the innocent deaths of men, women—'

'All right! All right!'

'And children!'

The two men faced each other like spent boxers breathing before renewed assault.

'Children, Mr Denning,' Morant said quietly. 'Children.' There was that fact. And no escaping it.

'That was my right. My need is to trace the source.'

'Are you charging me with an offence?' John said.

Morant was still. For perhaps five heart-beats his eyelids remained closed. He opened them.

'I'm sorry I shouted, Mr Denning,' he said. 'With some understatement we can perhaps both agree it is an emotional, er, situation. No, at present I am not making any charge. I would merely ask of you that, as simply and directly as you can, you answer certain questions I would like to put to you.'

'I would like to see that letter,' John said.

'As I explained, that isn't possible right now.'

'It is my wife's suicide note.'

'It's in Southampton.'

At first John spoke in an even voice.

'Listen,' he said. 'I have just returned from visiting six countries in eight days. I have hurried straight here after flying the Atlantic overnight – that is to say after a night spent without sleep and a paper with the headline news of rabies loose in Abbotsfield screaming at me from my lap. My insides feel like they've been taken out and scoured and I've had to drive here in a muck sweat because of your half-arsed bureaucratic instructions to some cretin on the phone. That same drive concluded in the news that my wife committed suicide. Now, how would you feel in my place?'

'I don't know, Mr Denning. I'm not in your place. How you feel is not my business.'

'I give you warning: if you wish to keep me here one moment longer without charging me, it will have to be by force.'

'I really—'

'Right now my one wish is to go home and see my father-in-law. Allow me to do that and I, in turn, give you my solemn promise that I will be at Southampton Police Station at any reasonable hour you care to nominate and that, there, having been allowed to read my wife's last words to me, I will volunteer a statement that, I think I can assure you, will answer each and every question you may have in mind.'

For that short time Morant closed his eyes again. As he was opening them a sergeant entered to them. He hovered uncertainly.

'What is it, man?' Morant snapped.

The sergeant approached close to him and muttered a quick message. Morant nodded and threw John a look. The sergeant went.

'Mr Denning,' Morant said, 'I can promise you that for

every night you've gone without sleep there are a dozen people in this village who've gone two.'

He paused. He's unsure what to do, John thought, he's trying to make up his mind. Morant stared hard at him, unblinking now.

'All right,' he said. 'I take you at your word, Mr Denning. Ten o'clock tomorrow morning.'

John nodded.

'I'll be there,' he said. 'I can go?'

'Yes. Oh, Mr Denning, I don't think that one way or another you'll do anything foolish, so, of course there's no need for me to counsel you otherwise. It's not really a question of crime and punishment, is it, Mr Denning? It's a question of personal honour, is it not? Of being able to live . . . well, I suppose I don't really need to spell that out either, do I, Mr Denning?'

'If you call me Mr Denning one more time I'll scream.'

'Can we offer you a lift, sir?'

'No, the walk will do me good.'

Unsteadily, John continued to the door. The only thing clear in his mind was that he must see Rupert first. Rupert must learn the final shame and shock from his own lips. That way the brutality of the news just might be softened. That way, though there could be no absolution, there might be some understanding.

Three steps beyond the threshold of the pub John halted. There was a new reason to make his senses reel. A car he recognised was parked hard by the Police H.Q. A yellow Scimitar. He knew the driver too, although both he and Peter Halliwell stared at each other without recognition. John did not know the policeman sitting next to him.

The boy's body arched into an upward-straining bow. For perhaps five seconds the spasm held him, then it pretended to relent. The tiny frame crashed back upon the bed with a violence not credible from such fleshless skin and bone. It found no respite. Only a variation in attack. The hands, of themselves, it seemed, beat a frenetic tattoo upon the sheet. It gathered to a flurry of crescendo and then froze. Pity of a kind was at last vouchsafed. With a burbling, rasping at his throat, the little boy subsided into a sweat-covered stillness.

Mike Mallett looked down on his son. The clenched fists at his sides showed knuckles helplessly white.

'It didn't last so long that time,' he said.

Erich Kesseler said nothing.

'That's good, isn't it? It must be good,' Mike Mallett said.

The tall German winced. Celia Mallett was not there. She had taken some pills and gone to get some sleep.

'This apparent remission – it is often this way before the end,' Kesseler said.

CHAPTER SEVENTEEN

John Denning crossed the road and paused at his front gate. He looked upon the house that he now solely owned. It seemed as reassuringly gracious as ever. A safe place. Nothing could happen here. He wondered how many times opening the gate, turning into the driveway, he had been greeted by that thought, been welcomed by that confident impression.

He pushed the gate aside. As he did so, the front door opened and Rupert Marsh stood there. He must have been listening out for him. John looked at him and from the look of tortured pity on the face of an old man knew the house lied. Something had happened here and there were no second chances.

Passing the well-clipped laurel he continued up the path. Rupert stood motionless watching him approach. At his side he held John's shotgun. On his face was a terrible uncertainty, a fearful questioning. It was a face that had changed overnight from a sense of jovial well-being to sunken despair.

'I've been with the police,' John said. 'I know.'

Without speaking Rupert nodded. He stood aside and John entered his own house.

'You've got no cases,' Rupert said. He shut the door.

'No, they're following on,' John said.

'Are you all right?' Rupert asked.

'Yes.'

They were standing awkwardly in the hall. The blue and white umbrella stand and the sporting prints were still there.

'You could probably do with a drink,' Rupert said.

'A cup of tea more than anything. I'm parched.'

'Travel-weary,' Rupert said.

They went into the kitchen. John received a visual jolt. He had forgotten the new Italian furniture. It seemed all wrong. Plastic and chrome were quite wrong for this room, this house. Irrelevantly, he wondered what had got into Paula. He must . . .

Rupert put the gun upon the table next to a white dish. 'I'll do it,' he said. He crossed the room to fill the kettle. He gestured at the gun.

'Thought I'd clean it,' he said. 'Something to do. Didn't need it, of course, but I was feeling a bit down.'

A choked-off sob half escaped him. He turned his back. John went to him and put a hand on his stooped shoulder.

'Sorry,' Rupert said in the muffled voice that follows weeping. 'Didn't mean to. So tired, though. Here, the kettle's boiling.'

They drank some tea. There was an orange in the dish. The orange on the white looked nice.

'Where did it happen?' John said after a while.

'The study. There's no need to go in there.'

'I have to,' John said. 'Have you seen the letter Paula left?'

'No. They said it was addressed to you.'

John got up and left the kitchen.

The study, at first glance, was as he'd always known it, quiet, ordered and restful. The subdued colours, the dark glow of good wood spoke once again of peace. The rows of books suggested this was a still place in which whatever the present storms outside the wise thoughts of the past might be distilled and enjoyed. He'd never done them justice, really, of course, the books. His stamp things were still there. Perhaps he would be allowed to keep them up. He still had his first album. It went back, how long now . . . gosh, twenty-seven years. He'd had his first gun when he was fourteen.

His eye fell on the cabinet and on the jagged star punched in the glass. Funny, he thought, she knew where the key is— She – he began to conceive something of the state his wife had been in during her last hours. He wondered where exactly . . . There were several strange grease marks scattered about the carpet, dried and sunk in. That might be the police with their equipment, their insensitive flat feet treading in muck. He stared down at the pedestal desk. A dark stain, surprisingly small, disfigured the green leather surface. She died in character, he thought, directly, without nonsense, like a man. Such a small stain. Abruptly he could not bear the room, its memories, the knowledge of what had happened there. He could never sit in it again. He hadn't had the thought before but now he did. He'd sell the house. He'd do it while in prison. Closing the door upon the study and upon his way of life, he went back to the kitchen.

Rupert raised his head and John was irresistibly reminded of an always faithful dog grown worn and old.

'Troy is dead I suppose,' he said.

Rupert nodded sadly.

'They put down so many,' he said.

'Forgive me, I should have asked before: how is Hilary?' Rupert cleared his throat.

'Subdued,' he said. 'Under sedation. I called the quack in and he called up Hester. She'll stay with us and run the show for the next day or two.'

'I haven't said how grateful I am you took the pains to come and wait for me here. It meant a lot to me to see you at the door.'

As he said this John realised it was true.

'Oh, it was nothing,' Rupert said. 'Nobody knew where you were. Your company were all at sixes and sevens. Couldn't have you coming home to an empty house not knowing – when will your luggage be here?'

'Hmm? Oh, tomorrow, sometime.'

'Better pack another case, then.'

'Why?'

'You can't stay here tonight. Not ... now. You're coming home with us for a few days.'

John walked to the window. The pane of glass that he'd put in was thicker, more opaque than its fellows. There was a flaw in it that made the garden ripple as you moved your head. He stared out at the rose-bed. He turned round. He must face him as he spoke.

'Rupert,' he said, 'there's something I have to tell you. After I have, you probably won't wish to have me as a guest under your roof.'

Rupert looked surprised and uncomfortable. He waited without speaking.

'It's a long story,' John said. He began to walk the kitchen end to end. Gently, as unsensationally as he could, he told the old man almost everything. Of Asp – and all that followed Asp – he gave a full and frank account. Only from respect for Paula, concern for the listening father, did he sometimes skip or minimise. He kept the sex right out of it. As he talked on, he had a strong sense of confession; of unburdening his guilt upon the probity and wisdom of a better man. He had meant to minimise the other's pain. He found as well the age-old lightening of his spirit in recounting a dark secret held too long. The strain went from him as he spoke.

'You have every right,' he finished, 'to despise me and to hate me as the person responsible for your daughter's death. The deaths of . . .'

Unable to voice the thought out loud, he gestured.

'You have the right to be ashamed of knowing me,' he said. 'I'd best stay here, tonight.'

He fell silent. Rupert had listened to him without comment. The eyes that had followed him back and forth had glistened but his face had been drained of expression. Now, just once, he sighed. He sat as if, like the Gorgon's head, the prospect of such hideous knowledge had turned him to old stone. He sat, John realised, as judge, jury and priest. When finally he spoke, his voice was low but firm.

'I presume your being here now means the police don't know of this as yet,' he said.

'They know. They haven't heard it from me as you just did, but they know. I was on the point of telling them an hour ago and then I found out you were here. I suddenly knew I had to tell you first. The thought of you picking it up second-hand, from papers, from the police themselves . . .'

He pulled a face.

'Besides,' he said, 'I didn't like their manner. The cheap tricks. The head man there wouldn't—'

'Morant?'

'Yes. He wouldn't let me see Paula's letter. He said it was at Southampton. I'm sure it wasn't. I more or less walked out.'

'It probably is,' Rupert said slowly. 'That's where he saw me. He's got a devil of a job to do.'

'I'm due to see him there at ten tomorrow morning.'

'Ah. . . . You'll tell him what you've just told me?'

'Yes, I've told him that I'll make a statement, what else can I do?'

Again, Rupert sighed. He levered himself slowly from his chair and carried the two dirtied cups over to the sink.

'I could have been a good father to boys,' he said. 'I suppose I've got what I deserved, starting at that age.'

'You weren't so old.'

'No? Well, some said so. A bit long in the tooth for nappies and bouncing babies on the knee, so it was said. I always thought it was not having boys that made it difficult. You can do more with them, can't you, really, if you're a man . . . I won't insult you by saying that it's not all quite frighteningly horrible. I suppose almost the most dreadful aspect of the whole ghastly thing is its ordinariness. From such a seemingly harmless beginning – such an end. It's almost like a motorist who doesn't renew his road fund licence and then finds out that somehow that's the reason he mowed down a bus queue of pedestrians.'

'It's not that easy,' John said. 'I should have thought.'

'No. I suppose not. Cause and effect the more direct. I don't want to minimise what's happened. Or your part in it. But, John – I don't think it should be exaggerated either. God alone knows, you've told a grim tale. But I admired two things about the telling. One: you didn't whine. You didn't go down on your hands and knees begging forgiveness. We both know that's irrelevant from me. We've known each other too long and too well. You are what you are. It's your own forgiveness you must seek. The other thing: your use of the word "I" . . . I know better, John. I knew my daughter . . . I knew my daughter because, more than anyone, I have to be held responsible for her growing up so spoilt. No! Don't argue. She was. Both you and I let her push us both around far far too much. Oh, she was witty, charming . . . there was no real harm in it. Ye gods! . . . I'm an accessory of sorts, myself, John. I have to be included among the guilty, too.'

'That's ridiculous.'

'No. It's true. Even though you haven't said so in so many words I know as well as I know my name's Marsh, that Paula was the driving force behind this whole catastrophe. She'd have been soppy enough to fall for a dog like that. She'd have seen getting it back into this country as a most delicious bit of fun. I can hear her saying it: "one in the eye for all those silly little men in stuffed shirts and peaked caps". And, having set her mind on such a thing, Paula would have been determined enough to see that you, if you don't mind my saying so, and that poor Halliwell fellow, would do exactly what was necessary to pull it off.'

How can he be so astute on one level, so blind on the other, John thought.

'So what are you saying?' he said.

Rupert turned and faced him.

'You asked me what else you could do. Well, I can't tell you what you should or shouldn't tell the police tomorrow. You know what I mean when I say that in a case like this no customary punishment begins to be adequate. And yet, in your case, I suspect, almost any punishment might be morally too much.'

'I can't accept that,' John said. 'I wasn't an innocent bystander to begin with. And there were clear signs later I chose to ignore.'

'Did you know the bitch had rabies?'

'Yes. In my heart of hearts.'

'And that is where your real punishment will always be. Is now, I'm sure.'

'Oh yes. It's so conveniently portable that way.'

'Granted that. You might consider just how relevant some token years in prison really are.'

'Rupert—'

'And certainly I absolutely forbid you to rush to martyr-dom because of some half-baked notion – honour though it

does you – that in sacrificing your self you can somehow protect Paula's name and thereby protect Hilary and me. Your
basic crime is that of having "loved not wisely but too well".'

'Rupert – unless my memory is playing tricks there's
something about there that says: "nothing extenuate". It
doesn't sound like you, you know, to hear you hint perhaps
I should. You of all people.'

Rupert Marsh walked to the table. He put his hands upon
the thin back of a chair and, head bowed, leaned his weight
upon his arms. John had been marvelling how calmly he
had borne the blow that the truth behind his daughter's
death must have been. There had even been an element of
verve with which, so accurately, he had deduced his
daughter's rôle. But now he saw the delayed impact of
those blows. Rupert was suddenly a slumping man whose
clothes were all a size too large. The resilience had faded,
the brave front gone, and with a frightening suddenness the
old man, hollow and shut off from the future and from hope,
was permanently returned. For him to contemplate the
future now was to foresee his death. He turned to John and
might have read his thoughts.

'You're quite right, of course,' he said. 'You must forgive
a foolish fond old man. You're not just my son-in-law – you
know that. You are my friend. The son I never had. I'm
certain that you fear the thought of prison less than I dread
the prospect of . . . being robbed of your presence while
I . . . and being robbed too of a grandchild . . . oh, like you
I don't believe in God. I won't see Paula again. If I die
while you're away . . . so, forgive me, if from selfishness I
yielded just a little to temptation.'

He dropped his head and did not finish. His hand moved
to the shotgun and he lifted it. His shoulders straightened.

'No way to treat a Purdey,' he said with an effort, and his
usual briskness. 'Best put it back where it belongs.'

John moved and took it from him.

'I'll do it,' he said. That final act of courage as Rupert
braced himself had touched him even more than the superfluous apology. His own pain seemed washed away by the
compassion he felt for this old man, his friend. If any reason

still remained for looking Morant straight in the eye and categorically denying . . .

'You said I hadn't and you admired me for it,' John said. 'But now I do. I'm the one to ask forgiveness. For you – there's nothing to forgive. It's just . . . look, while we're in a mood for half-forgotten fragments of quotations there's something in the Bible I once heard that's really rather beautiful. I don't remember it at all well but it's something about a man feeling able to enter into his own house justified. It says it all really, doesn't it? Perhaps these past few years – the gin and tonics, the tearing my hair out to sell a few more gross of cigarettes – well, perhaps I haven't always been so justified. You always have, sir.'

He smiled at Rupert and felt privileged.

'I'll just pack a few things,' he said.

* * * * *

. . . I have much to be ashamed of and I feel that I am being punished justly. I hope you will understand. I cannot bear the thought of the awful suffering and final indignities. I wrote above of a 'grim irony'. The appropriateness of all that's happened lately is enough to make me think there is a God. Of some sort. Perhaps you can pray for me. I give you my last and, I swear, my best word that if such things are possible, I will love you always. Goodbye my darling.

Paula

'May I keep this?' John asked. The swines had in any case only given him a fuzzy photostat.

'Certainly,' Morant said.

John folded the shiny paper into half, folding it again. He found he had to do this with great care and neatness. By concentrating on bringing the edges of the paper exactly level with each other he was better able to blink back his tears. He was damned if he was going to break down in front of those three see-all-evil monkeys. He slipped the paper into his breast pocket. Almost overpoweringly he felt the need to walk up to a window and look out from inside upon the sky and clouds and trees and fields. But in this institutional shoe-box of a room there were no windows. There were four walls covered in a pale blue-green emulsion dirtied with the stains of years of wear and tear. There was an oiliness to the light like being under greenish water. Jarringly set dead centre was a plain, drawerless table, bolted to the floor. A thousand cigarette butts had burned down to sear its top. Well, a table has no feelings, John thought.

Behind the table, watching him without a blink, there sat three men. One was Morant. The other two were not in uniform and sat to either side of him. One was a Detective-This and one a Detective-That. John had already confused the two and forgotten their names. Tweedle-dum and Tweedle-dee. Both had the hard eyes, the coarse pores and heavy features of men who had spent their lives inspecting the world's soiled underwear. They stared unrelentingly. He could feel, could almost see, the waves of hate, disgust, contempt they sent crashing about him. Routine intimidation, he wondered, or in his case was there special edge and malice. Hate for a killer of children: contempt for the non-pro. Morant stared too. He had an open file in front of him.

'Well,' he said, 'you promised us a statement.'

The words hung in the thick air as if it were viscous.

'Yes,' John said. He cleared his throat. Dully, he gave them the account he had already given Rupert. They listened without interruption, took no notes. After what seemed a long time, he heard his own voice stop and the silence come back to the room. It was a silence that went on and on.

'Why didn't you tell me this yesterday?' Morant said.

'You annoyed me.'

'You were obstructing a police officer in the execution of his duty by withholding vital information.'

'You should have let me see the letter.'

'Also, you wanted to talk to your father-in-law before you made the statement we've just heard.'

John made no reply. He looked down at his watch. Five past ten. They'd played no games making him sweat outside.

'Mr Denning, would you agree that what you have just

admitted having done is a criminal action of the most serious nature?'

'Yes. In its origins – in human terms – I think it's very understandable. In its consequences it's quite appalling.'

'Like planting a bomb in a crowded pub?' the man on the right said.

'No. There was no malice aforethought.'

'But you agree the consequences were all the same appalling?' Morant said.

'I've just said that.'

'Yes. Strange, then, isn't it that no less than three individuals should all claim prime responsibility for what's happened.'

John blinked.

Morant pushed across to him a second photostat. Again he recognised Paula's handwriting, but this time the copy was even fuzzier than the first.

'We found fragments of a letter in the wastepaper basket by the desk at which your wife was found,' Morant said. 'We pieced them together.'

'To whom it may concern . . .' It was the incomplete letter in which Paula had begun to claim sole responsibility for bringing rabies into England. John read it slowly twice.

'Now, Mr Denning,' Morant said, 'in view of what you've told us, why would your wife say that?'

'To protect me. She knew she was going to die. She could say anything.'

'Then why tear it up? Why not finish it?'

'Perhaps she realised that if she confessed I must be implicated. Good God, man! She had rabies! You don't believe she was totally coherent, do you?'

'Perhaps she tore it up knowing we would find the pieces, Mr Denning. Perhaps she hoped thereby to make her confession more credible. Perhaps it's a sort of double bluff.'

'Mr Denning,' the man on the right said, 'would it be possible you might lie to us?'

'Why on earth should I? About something like this?'

'To protect your wife.'

'She's dead,' John said huskily.

'Her name. Her reputation.'

'No,' said John. 'It's not possible.'

The silence came back. The detective on the left had started to smoke. The air got thicker.

'Mr Denning,' the one on the right said, 'we know from Customs you came back alone.'

'Of course I did. I've told you how that was. I had to get the car back – obviously.'

'Yes. So – physically, as it were – you didn't bring the dog back with you? It didn't come back in the car?'

'No! I've told you all that! I knew in advance it was coming back in the boat.'

It was still the man on the right.

'Mr Denning, did you know your wife was pregnant?'

'What's that got to do with it?'

'Did you know your wife was pregnant?'

'Yes. Of course.'

'Who by?'

John made no answer.

'I asked you who by, Mr Denning.'

John stared back at the man.

'Perhaps I should tell you,' he said, 'I have an arrangement with my father-in-law. If he hasn't heard from me by phone by twelve o'clock, he will ask my solicitor to present himself here with instructions to act on my behalf. In the circumstances, I will defer answering that question until such time as he is present.'

'Mr Denning,' Morant said. 'You are aware that a p.m., a post-mortem was carried out on your wife's body. In the routine course of that we sought and obtained access to her medical records – from her GP, from Winchester Hospital and so on.' His voice had assumed an exaggerated patience. 'We know from those records that, er, you and your wife were unable to have children because, on account of the fact that—'

'Because I'm supposed to be sterile,' John said.

'Supposed? You are, Mr Denning.'

'I changed. I got lucky. It was the French climate and the wonderful food.'

'Well,' said the man on the right, 'believe that, you can believe anything. We can always conduct tests.'

'Over my dead body.'

The man smiled.

'All right, I know. That can be arranged.'

As if irritated, the man on the left blew smoke out noisily.

'Did you know your wife was having an affair with Peter Halliwell?' the one on the right asked.

John felt himself stiffen; knew he had given them their answer.

'I'll defer that question too,' he said for the sake of formality.

'Thank you,' the right one said with heavy irony. 'Perhaps there's no need now.'

'What do you make of this?' Morant said.

He handed across a copy of a third letter. This one was brief and to the point and old-style Paula.

Dear Peter,
    You are a prize shit.

Paula.

'The Peter, of course, is Peter Halliwell,' the right-hand man said. 'Your wife showed remarkable prowess with a pen just before she—'

'Shut up!' John said. 'You can't help looking a sod. You don't have to behave like one.'

The man sniffed, looked at his spread fingers as he flushed with anger.

'Well?' Morant said.

'Well, what?'

'What do you make of it?'

John shrugged.

'Peter was an old friend of mine. Paula and he never quite hit it off. Perhaps—'

'Hit it off, Mr Denning? Or had it off?'

John was out of his chair moving towards Tweedle-dee. Somehow Tweedle-dum was around the table and pushing him back down again. He couldn't on a Bible have sworn he'd been actually struck, but the experience was not without sharp pain. He returned Tweedle-dee's professional needler's stare.

'Why ask me something like that,' he said. 'Everyone knows the police are in the Guinness Book of Records for the occupation with the highest divorce rate. How many wives have you been through – one way and another? How many of your fellow boys in blue have been through yours?'

'You shouldn't have said that,' the man said. His flush had returned.

'Or you,' John said. 'I don't answer any questions after that.'

Morant might just as well not have heard a word of this.

'I mentioned three confessions,' he said. 'What interests me is why Peter Halliwell should also be claiming prime responsibility for bringing the rabid dog to England.'

John's head started to come up. Once more he had telegraphed his reaction. But he was stunned.

'Asp was a bitch,' he said mechanically.

'Ah yes. Mr Halliwell does make that point. His story only agrees with yours as far as the meeting in the Channel outside Calais. According to him at that time no dog was involved – just certain bottles of wine and spirit. While on his boat, he says, your wife expressed a wish to go directly back to England with him and not spend another night' – he consulted the file – 'another night messing about running on the spot waiting for the ferry the next day. You, he says, agreed to this and went off. He claims, though, it was in fact a subterfuge for your wife and him to be together and that once they were she said she was in no hurry at all to return home. He claims that instead they sailed south for a while and then went illegally ashore near Hardelot. He says they got very drunk there and that it was then they chanced upon this stray dog. Bitch. He says that thinking it at the time the most tremendous joke your wife became fixed on the idea of bringing it back and – I quote – "sticking the thoroughbred dog-nut with this all-time mongrel monstrosity".'

'Then how—'

'One moment. He says that on your return home you

were told by your wife that she had found the animal on the doorstep and, in short, that it was an English stray. He says that you knew no more than that. He further claims that intimacy between himself and your wife took place several times on this occasion and had occurred at infrequent intervals in the past. This, he says, is what she was referring to when talking about being "ashamed" and so forth in her letter to you. On learning that she was pregnant, though, he says, your wife telephoned him and said she wanted to break off the affair. She said, he claims, that her object in having sex with him was simply that – to become pregnant. There was, if you like, nothing personal in it. She got drunk in Hardelot, he says she said, to make it easier.

'Apparently, though, she called a second time. And this time she was in great distress. The bitch was showing rabid tendencies. One Tuesday, in the morning, while you were at work, he went over to your house and using your own gun, shot the animal dead.'

'You see, Mr Denning, it could be said you've been rather pre-empted.'

John's head had been spinning, that Peter Halliwell should suddenly succumb to *noblesse oblige* and play at Captain Oates was something totally unlooked for, not to be believed. What he'd claimed was almost plausible. There was even justice of a sort wrapped up in it. But he saw a chance to blow the rigmarole sky-high.

'Well,' John said, 'if all that's the case, no doubt Mr Halliwell has been able to tell you exactly where the animal was buried.'

Morant nodded.

'He did,' he said.

'He did!'

'In your back garden. In a rose-bed. We dug it up first thing this morning. What's left of it is being examined by forensic as we talk.'

'But . . . but you don't believe him!'

Morant looked at John.

'No,, he said, 'not necessarily.'

'Where is he now?'

'In this building.'

'Can I see him?'

'No, Mr Denning, I'm afraid that won't be possible.'

It was five-thirty in the afternoon. Feeling exhausted and numb with bewilderment, John sat in the front passenger seat of Rupert Marsh's Rover. Rupert was behind the wheel. The car was parked a stone's throw from the police station where John had spent the entire day having his story checked, questioned, checked once again. He had stuck to it throughout. Finally, in the claustrophobic, airless room and the elongated presence of the senior partner from O'Donnell, O'Donnell, Pressey and O'Donnell, he had laboriously gone over it yet again for the benefit of a police stenographer.

Giles O'Donnell was the third occupant of the stationary car. His heron-like figure was craned forward from the rear seats. In the shoe-box room, witnessing John's statement, he had given the impression of standing on one leg, in readiness to strike like lightning and impale the ambiguous or detrimental phrase. In fact, alerted to John's wish to make a statement that admitted guilt, he had made very little comment Even now, comment had to be extracted from him.

'I don't begin to understand,' John said. 'Why have they let me go when they're holding him?'

'It's interesting – but I'm afraid we'd best not draw too much comfort from the situation. They're merely being cautious in your case. Consider it from their viewpoint. They have two conflicting testimonies. One thing is common to both. The dog was brought into the country on a yacht, sailed by Peter Halliwell. That is a criminal offence – a clear-cut one that they can charge him with. All that you claim to have done, he at this moment strongly refutes. Now, from what you tell me I strongly suspect, in fact I know, that they believe your story to be the basic truth. But what precise charge do they bring against you? This is the most widely publicised area. I'm not telling you anything new when I say that there will be people in this country –

and newspapers too – screaming for your blood. The police want to get their sums right. Manslaughter – on how many counts? – or just accessory before and after the fact of smuggling an animal into this country? It's important. If they indulge in over-kill in charging you initially, they could be made to appear very foolish at your trial. At this moment, they have no witness who's prepared to corroborate your story. The one person alive who could, flatly denies it. They have a problem. I've no doubt the wires to the DPP's office are humming at this moment.'

'But to let me go.'

'Excuse me, but they haven't let you go. They've released you while asking you to hold yourself ready for further questioning. They know you're not going to run away.'

'They can check with the owner of the boatyard.'

'I'm sure they will. We can go into that later.'

O'Donnell broke off. He had heard the staccato clack of approaching high heels. From around the red-bricked corner and then over to the car came the neat figure of Joan Pressey. John was still able to make two wry mental comments on the scene. It had not been an ill wind for everyone. However horrendous the consequences for many, O'Donnell, O'Donnell, Pressey and O'Donnell would not emerge diminished. And, even here, Peter still veered towards the female. Joan Pressey slid into the car. She anticipated all questions.

'He's sticking adamantly to his version,' she said. 'He's signed a statement.'

'Curiouser and curiouser,' Giles O'Donnell said.

'Did he have any word for me?' John asked.

'Yes. We couldn't talk properly, of course, but he said two things. He said he was genuinely deeply sorry Paula had died. He said the last time they had met it was by accident and on the spur of the moment he played a mean trick on her.'

'Oh.'

'He didn't say what. And he had what he called a special message for you. He said it was like the Lancing match all over again.'

'Does that mean anything?' Giles O'Donnell said quickly.
'Yes,' said John. 'It means he wants to do a Sydney Carton.'

The Lancing match! Unlike Paula, John held the BMW down to a speed acceptably close to the limit. But, in following the same, last route to Abbotsfield she'd driven, he too relied upon the autopilot of his instinct. His eyes were unconsciously on the road. His mind was twenty years away seeing a graceful line of poplars and their shadows reaching out across the yellow-green of a school cricket field. It had been for the third wicket. One hundred and thirty-three runs. He had been in front from the start, the sheet-anchor opener nudging and deflecting his way to an already respectable score by the time Peter joined him. Peter had looked so tanned. As he took guard he had smiled at John, then glided from his crease to crack his first ball for a cover-piercing four. His key signature. He had swashbuckled the bowling to all points of the field. With tea and an inevitable declaration one over away, he had almost overtaken John's score. But John's score stood at ninety-seven. And Peter had the bowling. For two balls, unaccountably, he failed to score. Off the third he called John for an impossibly short single and, self-sacrificed, was run out by a mile. He'd smiled as he walked out. He'd given John the bowling and John had cut the last ball of the innings for the four that gave him his first century with one to spare. The first and, as it proved, his only century. He had been a king as he walked in to tea. There would be no tomorrows that would not be like today and he'd be lord of warm, eternal summers . . .

It was too much. Unable to bear the sadness of remembered hope mocked by events, John came back to the road. He turned the radio on.

. . . nearly two cents below the previous record low of ten days ago.

Rabies has been officially confirmed in a third area of the British Isles. After outbreaks that are still being fought in Hampshire and Pembrokeshire, the Midhurst area in Sussex is the latest to be affected. Two people are now known to have died of the disease and a death cordon of a twelve mile radius has been drawn around the town. All warm-blooded animals within this cordon, an area of some four hundred and fifty square miles, are to be exterminated. The precise origin of this latest outbreak has not so far been established. It is known that visiting relatives were unwittingly responsible for creating a rabies link between the original, Hampshire, appearance of the disease and the Pembroke occurrence.

Meanwhile the police are continuing their investigations on the theory that human agents were responsible for bringing the disease to our shores. A man is at present helping them with their enquiries in Southampton.

In Peking today Chinese Government sources are quoted . . .

He switched it off. In – what – thirty-six hours it would be his name and he would have top billing. Hmph! He was living on borrowed time. He should live it up. Gather his roses. Drink himself silly. But where? With whom? Not at the Dog and Fox. That had his chalk mark on its door and now there was a third place. If there could be three, there could be thirty-three. His hands on the wheel were trembling. That was too cruel. Paula had talked of 'grim irony'. And rightly. Sink to this level of ill-fortune and every occasion seemed to rise up in some way to inform against you. Pregnant with irony. Pregnant . . .

He changed down needlessly to change the rhythm of his thoughts. Rupert had begged him not to return to Gunn House for the night. He had agreed. But there were things he had to pick up while he still had opportunity. In his agitation the night before he had packed such a rag-bag of stuff he'd left out half the essentials: a belt, clean socks, the adaptor for his razor. And, gruesome though it might seem, there were all the papers on Paula's insurance, the house. If he was going to sell it Rupert and Giles might as well pursue that for him while he was . . . inside. The visit he was making now to his home was probably the last chance he'd have to look upon it as the owner. Tomorrow the sky would fall. And poor Hilary and Rupert would be crucified each time they heard a radio.

The thin boy in the hospital bed lay motionless. His skin had yellowed. It seemed to have shrunk and been pulled taut upon his jutting cheek-bones. For all his stillness you would not have said he looked at peace. The man stared sightless at the wall, the woman's eyes were closed in fitful sleep. A second man standing at the bed's foot stared down intently on the child.

The boy opened his eyes. The standing man drew in his breath.

'Mum,' the boy said. It was still hoarse but it was louder.

'Yes. Yes, John,' the woman stammered.

'Can I have a drink, Mum? I'm thirsty.'

The startled woman seemed to grow rigid with fright. She turned to the tall blond man at the foot of the bed. He was holding himself very still as if afraid to break a spell. The sitting man reached out and grasped the woman's nearer hand. He too seemed to be holding his breath. The tall man nodded at the woman.

Shaking, rattling the jug against the glass, Celia Mallett poured a drink. She bent over his wasted form and bracing him up on her arm, put the glass up to his mouth. With painful difficulty he sipped and swallowed a minute drop of water.

'My throat don't half hurt,' he whispered.

Nobody spoke. He took another drink.

'Where am I?' he said.

'In . . . in hospital,' his mother said. 'You've – you've not been well.'

'Oh,' he said. His head fell back. His mother lowered him on to the pillow.

'Mum,' he said, 'I'm hungry.'

His mother was crying but he could see her try to smile.

'What do you fancy, love?' she said.

'Fish fingers,' he said. 'Am I still ill or am I all right again?'

His mother looked at a big man he had not seen before. He must be the doctor. The big man nodded. It was funny. He knew that girls were meant to cry but it was funny to see his Dad and a big man like this one crying like his Mum.

CHAPTER EIGHTEEN

He left the car parked in the road outside. By night the house seemed less serene. The dark silhouette spoke less of permanence and stability, more of the conjuring of history's ghosts – the masked gentleman of the road, the hanging. . . . Well, this was nonsense from a fevered brain. He turned the key in the lock, flipped on the light switch in the hall. The house was deathly quiet and from instinctive deference he turned consciously to close the front door with a minimum of noise. He was midway through the motion when it struck him something was wrong. He wheeled around and the door banged anyway. It took him several seconds to put his finger precisely on what had disturbed him. The blue and white umbrella stand, the sporting prints! They were missing! On top of all else, the house had been burgled!

He gave a groan that midway through had almost converted to a laugh. It was not the last straw, merely, in its relative triviality, a drop in the ocean. He was insured.

He walked on in. He put the light on in the living-room. With its customary indifference the colour television glassily returned his stare. Nothing seemed disturbed. The liquor, the silver-framed photograph of his mother, the Gabriel Sleath teapot were all present and correct in their proper place. No. Not everything. The Durs Egg pistol was missing from the wall. Now he realised that he was listening hard. Had been for some time. And yet the house was soundless. It was the silence that flared in his ears and set his pulse beating uncomfortably fast. It was the silence telling him that at this moment he was watched by a thousand eyes.

Oh, of course! Rupert, while awaiting his return had

moved the pistol and the prints! He'd been cleaning the Purdey. The old field sports' addict in him had no doubt whiled away the time.

God! In the doorway to his study, John stood rigid with disbelief. A savage welter of debris littered the entire room, sprawling across his desk and down upon the open carpet like a trail of vomit. His gun cabinet had been hurled to the floor. Across it sprawled what was left of his Purdey. Its stock had been severed at the hand and its barrels hammered flat. The antique pistol lay near it similarly twisted and crushed. His rods lay snapped like twigs. Cartridges had been opened and the powder, the shot, sprinkled crazily about the room. There, amid their own shattered glass, ripped from the smashed frames and torn across, were the prints. And books. Ripped apart page by page what had been the beloved nucleus of his library was everywhere laid waste in a white-leafed sprawl. He knelt to confirm his fear. Yes – these were pages from his first edition Surtees and there, mocking him now, his own 'Ex Libris' sign upon a forlorn inside cover.

Perhaps that was the spur that galled him into corrosive anger. A sense of desecration, of dirty vandalising hands on his possessions, unthinkingly destroying the beauty, the expertise of craftsmen filled him with so malignant a bitterness it sickened him. Bloody yobbo bastards! Shut out by their own laziness from anything worthwhile they could find no higher pleasure than this mindless destruction. He lifted the phone for the police. He had dialled two digits before he saw it had been ripped from the wall. It was as, cursing, he replaced the receiver that he saw the great pallid ghost outside the window and for a moment felt that his heart had stopped. He had recoiled instinctively behind the desk before he realised the pale shadow was Bill Gadney and he could relax.

Strangely the French window was unlocked. Bill Gadney opened it from outside and came in.

'Phew! Bill – you should have knocked. You frightened me half to death,' John said. 'Look what some bastard's gone and done.'

'My father hath chastised you with whips, but I will chastise you with scorpions,' Bill Gadney said.

His great moon face was cast slightly to one side. His eyes took in a view private and all his own. A car went by in the far distance and in the ensuing silence, quiet as the grave, ice formed at the core of John's spine. This was not a teenager's spree but vengeance to the death. A glance at those eyes made it clear that the giant of a labourer had been driven down into madness by his grief.

'I will repay, saith the Lord,' he said.

A hand, huge as a ham, was raised, stretched forward.

John took a pace back. He was fighting to stave off the sense of nightmare trance that rooted him to the spot. Combat would be unequal. All of his guns were smashed. Gadney advanced one huge stride.

'All right, Bill,' a sharp voice said.

John pivoted around. Standing in a doorway were two others whom he recognised, Maggie Peacock and Mary Burns.

'Thank—' John began. Something in the way they stood made the benediction die upon his lips. He whirled to look at Gadney. The arm had dropped. He had otherwise not moved. Maggie had. She had moved into the centre of the room. She stood amid the formless ruin and looked upon John with a glowering malevolence that seemed the next thing and the last thing to a smile. In a moment of cold certainty he knew the desecration was symbolic. And he knew what of and why.

'You did all this,' he said quite simply.

She nodded.

'Everything to do with killing we could find here,' she said. 'To do with the massacring of innocents. Guns that shed blood. Books glorifying it. Telling you how to do it. Pictures celebrating it. If it flies through the air – no matter how beautiful – kill it. If it moves on the surface of the earth – kill it. If it swims in the waters – kill it.'

He shut his eyes. Wrought up to such a pitch she would be deaf to the arguments of culling, balance and control he had used so often against these impassioned wrong-headed rantings.

'His type,' Mary Burns was sneering. 'Privileged. Born and bred with silver spoons. Never known what it is to have to fight, to struggle. No idea of what it's like to worry yourself sick wondering where your next meal might come from. What it's like to have to struggle to exist. No wonder he's got no respect for life. When you're rich, life's cheap. Property's all he's got it in him to care about. Acquiring, getting more. And keep the council houses out if they mean the value of your home is going to drop. If they spoil the view. If they mean losing a bit of ground you can use for killing animals on. Keep them out. Let people eat cake and go homeless.'

'No respect for life,' Maggie Peacock said. 'Animal or human.'

She looked at him like an unforgiving snake.

'We know what you did,' she said. 'Ted told us that black bitch of yours attacked his dogs. He told us it had a funny look. He told us you ordered it about in French. You don't deny it do you? Mr Denning, pillar of our propertied society?'

John took a deep breath.

'Listen, please,' he said. 'I don't deny it. No.'

With a kind of vicious satisfaction, Mary Burns hissed.

'And I didn't deny it to the police today,' he said. 'I told them exactly how I and my wife – my wife who died because she contracted rabies like so many others – I told them how, unwittingly, we brought a dog, yes, you're right, illegally back with us to this country from the continent.'

'Then why are you walking around free?' Maggie Peacock said.

'Apparently they're deciding what to charge me with. It's complicated.'

'Privilege protecting privilege,' Mary Burns said.

'No. It's not like that.'

'What charges?' Maggie Peacock said. 'Illegal importation of an animal. Fined five hundred pounds and three months in jail! Two years suspended sentence! Naughty boy – don't do it again. Or they get tough. Manslaughter. Five years. Out in three with full remission! Tell me, Mr

224

Denning, would you consider three years adequate atonement for the death of innocent children? What is, Mr Denning? Ten years? Fifteen? How do you atone for the death of an innocent child. It's a question you should have considered.'

She was suddenly screaming.

'I was the one who found Ted Rimmer and I still can't go to sleep!'

He could not say he shared with her the memory of that carrion face, the eyeless sockets. But, as the leering death's head rose up now, he shuddered. It had always vowed revenge. The black encrusted holes told him to put small faith in his confession.

'We worked it out. But you were away,' she said. 'Then the police got you and we thought we'd missed our chance.'

Chance. With that word his mouth went dry and his knees dissolved into an insubstantial marrow. He slumped backward against the desk for support. Loud in his ears his pulse was pounding at his breathless chest. She had not worn a black cap but the word made unequivocally clear what was the sentence they judged should be executed on him.

'We were going to set fire to your house, your property,' she was saying. 'As a gesture. Now there's no need. This is better. All right, Bill.'

He rallied for a last stand.

'Wait,' he said, 'the police. Call them – ask them if I've made a statement. The extension. There's an extension—'

Gadney was lumbering towards him.

'The children,' Mary Burns said in a low voice.

Bill Gadney brushed aside his upraised arm. The huge hands were about his neck, the thumbs like iron wedges pressing at his throat's soft centre.

He thought Maggie Peacock was screaming again.

'Old Ted, my friend,' she perhaps said. 'The children! The sweet, innocent, noisy, helpless children! How do you atone for that?'

The hands had tightened. They were past making him feel sick. The blood was pounding at his ears, behind his eyes now. The room swam. The moon-face bulged before him. He knew that he was going to die and he tried to die with dignity. But as iron hands contracted about his lungs and there was no passage through his bursting throat a swelling panic engulfed him. Through the pain he was aware his arms had passed from his control. Like an unjointed puppet's, like the wings of a dying moth, they flapped helplessly at his side in ludicrous, feeble spasms.

It was his last conscious impression as he sank into a sea of rasping blackness.

His throat ached as if stuffed with razor blades. From deep down wherever he was, he knew that to open his eyes would multiply the force of the dark pendulum crashing back and forth inside his skull. He was on a hard floor being jolted cruelly. Arbitrarily. There was no warning. No rhythm. No pattern in direction. He tried to move his arms that they might take the shock. They would not budge. They might as well have been tied. He would wake up from the nightmare soon.

'He's coming round,' an echo said.

Despite the threat of pain he opened his eyes to see the echo. In the dark he slowly made out two women's faces looking down on him. He remembered everything and whimpered. As whatever vehicle they were travelling in, rocked savagely from side to side, he was jolted hard against some metal and hurled spinning back down the bottomless black well.

Hands beat at his cheeks. They sent giddying waves of nausea rocking across his brain. He must stop the hands. With an effort that caused him to groan he opened his eyes and looked into the face of Mary Burns. He made to push it away and found his hands were tied behind his back.

'Get him up,' she said.

Bill Gadney was above him. He was dragged and lifted through an opening and on to his untied feet. Without warning, in a way that scorched his throat, he was throwing up down the side of a Volkswagen bus. He brought his head up as he gasped for air, and a fierce arm spun him round.

The earth went spinning by. It slowed. He was in a forest, among trees. It was night. There was a man. There was a building. The earth slowed to a halt and he saw Maggie Peacock standing right before him. In her hand she held a knife. Because it was a kitchen knife the horror was complete.

She advanced towards him and sucking his stomach in, he braced himself. But she made no thrust. Instead, seizing his shirt — his jacket and tie were already gone — she began to cut it off him. His vest was cut away. Bare-torsoed he stood like a prisoner awaiting torture as she backed away. The fierce malevolence glinted once more in her eyes.

'Hold his shoulders,' she said.

Gadney had them in the vice of his two hands as she advanced.

'The shoes,' she said.

She and Mary Burns tore them and his socks from off his feet. She stood erect. He tottered slightly as the stony ground thrust at his feet. He felt her pull the cold blade of the knife breathtakingly flat against his belly. Her arm sawed. In loud tearing rents they ripped his trousers away from him. And his underpants. Hands tied behind his back he stood naked before them.

He swallowed past the rawness of his throat. His eyes were on the knife. He wished his balls might both dissolve away, his penis shrivel further down to nothing. Those two and their feelings about men. It wasn't hard to follow how they thought. Children had died. He who had robbed them of life must be robbed of the power to engender more. This was their concept of atonement. This what their insistence on the symbolic had brought them to. And useless for him to scream out their gesture would be empty. They would not believe him as he shrieked they were about to geld a sterile man. Moonlight glinted on the knife. He felt his blood congeal even as the sweat broke from him in the cold air. He tried to step away but Gadney had him fast for ever. He looked from one woman to the other.

Maggie Peacock gestured with the knife.

'Bring him inside,' she said.

Jolted from behind, his feet lacerated, he was force-marched into the roofless ruin of a cottage like a sheep to shambles. There was little wind but such as there was made a strange, low moaning noise about the stones. A match scrabbled and flared. A hurricane lamp was lit. Yes. There was a ruin of a table. It could no doubt serve.

Mary Burns turned to him.

'Maggie couldn't face going back to Mullen's Barn to get the books,' she said. 'I went instead. There were still lots of dead rats. I found something of yours too. I shouldn't have taken it really, I suppose.'

Maggie stooped swiftly and he flinched, sucking himself away from her. But she had bent down to the floor. She looked up at him.

'You'd better have it back,' she said.

Her arm swung back and up and she had opened a trap door. The cottage had a cellar. The moaning of the wind grew louder as dank and fetid air rose up cold about his body, his face, making him gag. A strange, scuffled, whimpering made itself heard. As he realised that it was not the wind that moaned but something down there alive in the cellar, Maggie Peacock nodded. He had half-gleaned the final truth as a huge executioner's hand shoved him, feet first, hands tied, a condemned man, through the trap. He crashed down into blackness. From his bare heels, agony jarred up his shins and through him as, without arms for balance, he smashed sideways into a stone wall and on down to a stone floor. The grey rectangle of half-light overhead weaved mistily back and forth. He all but passed out a third time. But a biting pain in his left knee nagged at his consciousness and now the grey square held a fiery centre. He blinked and screwed his eyes up and forced it into focus. It was the hurricane lamp, lowered some two feet downward from a cord. By its light he saw the spacious, filthy cellar in which he was trapped and saw the panting, whimpering thing with which he shared imprisonment.

No longer golden cream, the coat was matted and besmirched with mire. The ribs stood out as if it were a hell hound sent forth from Revelations. The eyes were wildly alight with the torment of implanted madness. They rolled to show their whites. It was no hound of hell. It was not the great black dog of nightmare. But real and of this world. He knew it at a glance. This was what rabies had wrought of Troy. It was of hell. Hysterically he screamed and kicking with his legs drove himself backward tight into a corner. He tried to stand, forcing his back scrapingly up against the joining walls. The ceiling was no higher than four feet. His stomach creased he could do no more than crouch. He was screaming now beyond control, without coherence he screamed until blood came into his tortured throat.

The whimpers had changed to a dreadful, unearthly bark. The eyes blazed forth as once more they knew vision. On legs that buckled, almost gave, the dog got to its feet. As it lurched forward into the circle of light he could clearly see the gluey, blood-streaked whiteness all about the muzzle.

He wished to, but he could not, faint.

The attitude of the British to the presence of rabies in their midst had fluctuated. With the first announcement of its arrival across their television screens the people had oohed and ahed. The news that six children had been bitten by a rabid dog was a human-interest story that the tabloids had sunk their own teeth into, shaken and worried and not let loose for several days. There had been photos of the 'parents who wait'. There had been in-depth interviews conducted throughout in words of one syllable. Opportunist Members of Parliament had asked questions in the House and used the occasion as they fulminated against laxity of regulations to bolster marginal majorities. With no less haste the Central Office of Information made a trio of 'Watch Out for Rabies' commercials that contrived to look as greyly faked as they were under-budgeted.

But it was a nine-day wonder. The nation had more pressing and intriguing concerns. Liverpool, sensationally, had opened the new football season with only three points from their five games. Finland had held England to a draw. As the pound levelled out at 1.50 against the dollar, the Chancellor had announced an interim autumn budget and it was expected that the Road Fund licensing fee would escalate to sixty pounds. Petrol was now one pound a gallon and milk cost twenty pence a pint. Following the failure of the Government to hold the line on the rate of inflation, the unions had put in a claim for a unilateral thirteen per cent rise in wages. They threatened a General Strike within ten days. The NUS had already declared a strike. With unemployment topping the two million mark, students the length and breadth of the country were staging sit-ins at universities and centres of higher education. Their demand was for a guarantee of employment on the completion of their studies.

The hurricane lamp was abruptly withdrawn. Blackness effaced the grey square as the trap slammed home. All light was denied him. The cold darkness was complete. Now he could only hear the approaching animal.

The announcement of another rabies outbreak down in Pembroke left the rest of the country cold. The deaths in Abbotsfield had introduced the law of diminishing returns. It was like another killing in Belfast, another oil-rig diver lost in the North Sea. You shook your head once and wondered what the film was on TV tonight.

Entombed in the total dark, he had been bitten a dozen times. As the trap closed him off for ever from the face of the earth, he had tried to shift position. He had inched along the wall. But the snuffling, growling thing had scented him. Blind, he could hear it lurching close. He stopped his own movement and attempted silence. The dog was silent too. Nothing. He was torn between the primitive desire screaming inside him to lash out with his feet and fend the beast off and the certain knowledge that to do so would invite immediate attack upon his naked flesh. Close, very close, the dog was panting once again. In the cold, echoing cell he could not tell from which direction the sound came. The panting continued as nothing else occurred. Minutes went by. The beast seemed to be circling. He could hear its nails scratch on the stone. The ultimate obscenity of being bitten, of being injected with a poison that would so vilely kill him, began to prey upon his waiting, helpless mind. Dark, total dark. His hands tied. At any second. Now. Or now. Listen . . .

He could stand no more. To get it over with he screamed and struck out with a foot. The dog barked and sprang. Troy bit him many times as they rolled over.

As far as was ever known it was the almost simultaneous discovery of rabies' victims in Midhurst, Lambourne and York that sparked off the national hysteria. Arbitrarily, it seemed, apathy turned to panic and 'Rabies!' once again become a one-word headline able to boost any paper's circulation. Perhaps it was because a popular racehorse, a winner of the Eclipse and Abernant Stakes was among the many summarily put down, that public imagination was now captured and stampeded. Perhaps it was the seven-figure sum claimed from Lloyds by the bloodstock syndicates that impressed the man in the street. The panic measure to suspend racing added to the feeling of disaster and the English, traditionally animal-lovers to a man, woman and child, chose to change their spots.

Across the country, vets' waiting-rooms were crowded beyond precedent. The pounds for animals to be put to sleep were overflowing. The adorable doggie in the window that had proved, full-grown, such a drain on the house-keeping, such a bore to take for walks night after night, could now be honourably destroyed. The kitten that little Chrissie must have at the age of eight but which at the age of an already defiled thirteen she never noticed, could now be got shot of to give a harrassed mother a bit of extra peace. Rabbits, hamsters, guinea pigs – the entire spectrum of childish pets were now sacrificed.

Not all pets were as fortunate. The canals and rivers of the country began to offer up a number of bloated carcasses. Each morning drivers on the motorways would jolt over un-recognisable patches of bloodied fur and bone. Wandering dogs left two hundred miles from their homes by weekend motorists became a routine worry for the police of many counties. The RSPCA took advertisements throughout the national press and their revenue from donations doubled.

There were, of course, many genuine animal-lovers whose last thought would have been to use the rabies scare as an excuse to put down an adored pet. And the resolution of the undecided was strengthened on the side of kindness, when the authorities announced a small distribution of preventive vaccine had been made available to vets throughout the country. Rabies could be made to go away. Now everything would be all right.

Only it wasn't. Queues a half-mile long formed around centres from Land's End to John O'Groats. Older folk said it was like the war. Except there was no mateyness. As owners came to snap at each other with more viciousness than the bored, bewildered pets they tiringly held, willingness to lend a helping hand was in scant evidence. And, within hours, the vaccine was exhausted. There were announcements about fresh importations from abroad. And, as in any war, there were rumours.

It was just like the NHS and the private beds, mate. I got a friend was telling me, if you can bleeding pay for it, then you've got no bleeding worries. Know what I mean? . . . None of them Cruft's dogs were going to go wanting their little top-dog jabs or those top-peoples' cats fed on boiled fish by MP's wives and duchesses in pearls. You could get it on the side still, course you could. If you knew where to go.

It was surprising how many credulous owners let charlatan practitioners dose their pets with solutions of sugar and water, chalk and oil, lipstick and powder and paint, only to see them die in agony. The problems of the vets were further compounded by break-ins to their premises carried out by both self-helping black marketeers and by desperate owners of Napoleon and Monty, Marmaduke and Soot. It did not give the police much of a let-up either.

John Denning's car was found abandoned in a Portsmouth car park. His name was released to the press and his photograph appeared in all the papers and on television. The reason he was being sought was not kept secret but most widely emphasised. The Isle of Wight and the two largest Channel Islands were among the areas minutely covered by the authorities' carefully conducted search. He was seen in Falmouth, Enfield, Preston, Glasgow and Cork.

Chief Constable Morant was put under the severest pressure to resign. In the absence of full knowledge of John Denning's whereabouts he stubbornly refused.

Suicide, of course, was considered by many to be the stronger possibility.

The dog had left him alone now for so long, that he could not tell how long it had been. From the sound it must be dying. Soon he himself would die of cold. He had lost feeling in his feet. His teeth were chattering with a force he was quite powerless to prevent.

With a sudden crash the trap door was thrown back. Light smashed into his face, pierced through his eyes into his brain. When he could raise his head again he saw them looking at him like the caged animal he was.

'Yes,' he croaked, 'many times.'

Their heads disappeared, re-arranged themselves. A shotgun's twin barrels were advanced down through the opening. They wavered, sought and pointed at the dog. With an echoing reverberation that deafened him, the gun was fired. The dog kicked but hit only in its belly began to stagger howling to its feet. A second blast deafened him again and, better aimed, tore into the befouled skull. Without a further twitch the dog that had promised so fair dropped beyond the reach of further pain or degradation. The acrid smell of powder just exploded drifted down to join the stench in the cellar.

'Please,' John tried to shout, 'shoot me too.'

The shotgun was withdrawn. The trap door stayed open. Without warning Gadney was levering his enormous bulk down; stooping because of the low ceiling, he looked like a giant from a Grimm fairy story. He reached back upward to the light. He lowered down a sleeping bag and then, slowly, two buckets filled with liquids. Steam came from one.

'Soup and water,' he said. 'We must look after our patient.'

Pulling a clasp-knife from his pocket he advanced on John. He turned him about. One hand on his throat, he cut John's bound hands free. John turned to face him.

'Please,' he said again, 'shoot me.'

'My little daughter lieth at the point of death,' Gadney said. 'She died and suffered all. An eye for an eye. So must you. It were better for him that a millstone were hanged about his neck, and he cast into the sea, than that he should offend one of these little ones.'

He thrust John to the floor and pulled himself up through the trap door. It closed with a thud and darkness rushed upon him once again.

As people queued to have their pets destroyed, rabies, for a while, became curiously chic. The term became endemic in the speeches of politicians, leader writers and television pundits. Overnight all phenomena from the declining pound to the state of football were analysed in images of disease. Statesmen dubbed the speeches of opponents 'rabid' and were themselves accused of 'mad dog' attitudes.

Naturally there were many commentators upon and participants in the national scene, who chose to make direct reference to the reinstated crisis. A former Cabinet Minister, now sitting in a sniping back-bench capacity for a Midlands constituency made enemies and won supporters by openly suggesting that rabies had been imported by illegal Asian immigrants to sully the quality of British life. Simultaneously there were those of the militant left who claimed to see in the deployment of army units to limit the disease, a further escalation of the guerrilla-warfare training of British troops for possible use later against a popular uprising.

Meanwhile the need to divide the country into rabies-free and rabies-control areas was seized upon by Scottish, Welsh and Cornish devolutionists. Many committed and, in some cases, professional environmentalists were heard agonising aloud over the massive imbalance being inflicted upon the natural order of things. Others more sanguine, argued the pockets of wholesale slaughter were merely the slightest variation on exactly that same natural order of things and that, experimentally speaking, they must bear the closest follow-up scrutiny. There were those that said the missing John Denning should be flayed alive in public. Others maintained even if it were his fault it wasn't like robbing a bank.

Light denied he had lost all sense of time. But it did not seem to have taken long. The need to drink was over-powering now and constant. He groped towards the bucket. He would ration himself this time and only sip. The level seemed further down than he had thought. He raised the bucket but his throat locked as he tried to swallow so he put the bucket down. On all fours he lapped straight from it like a dog. He wondered if they would return with more to eke out his suffering. He wondered if he should cast the sleeping bag aside and freeze to death – it might be quicker.

Nobody believed the rat was genuinely rabid. Indeed, it was killed and proved not to be. Everybody knew that the dockers were using their claim for 'rabies money' when working overseas ships as a lever against the Government. Twice now the announcement of a flat-rate basic pay increase had been postponed while negotiations with the TUC continued.

The Government scotched all possibility of 'rabies money'. Tilbury went out on strike and, as ships queued up along the Thames, so did the rest of the London docks. Produce rotted in warehouses and holds and then, as vessels were diverted or turned for home, the rest of the country's ports came out in sympathy. There were shortages as food prices rocketed. In the commodities market there were clear-cut examples of profiteering by witholding. Export orders were cancelled before the ink was dry. The pound plummeted to 1.40122 against the dollar as the balance of payments figures were brutally undermined.

The vote of confidence could have only one result for the

minority Government. Eleven days after the 'Rabies Strike' began, they resigned.

It was like having something in your eye all over. It was like waking in the night with the most terrible cramp – agony to move and agony not to. But this was cramp that held all of the body in its squeezing, contracting grip. It was like being strapped to a primitive electric chair in which death was not instantaneous.

It was many years since a General Election had been fought in the country with so many divisive factions. Issues ceased to exist as the totalitarian left and the totalitarian right marched and counter-marched. The uncommitted ceased to exist. Right-wing vigilante armies mushroomed to defend life and property. The newly launched Party of Marxist Unification claimed that such bodies were cells of a Fascist Army masterminded by retired Army officers and City interests. Certainly the PMU's Hyde Park rally was wrecked by organised and well-trained strong-arm methods while the out-numbered police stood helplessly by.

But it was at the TUC-sponsored meeting at Olympia – the meeting where it was demanded that henceforth, irrespective of party, Congress should supply two members of any British Cabinet – that the first of the political assassinations occurred.

The great black dog had caught him. Aghast, he had fled from it across the grey fen country, beneath the wide wheel of the sky. In vain. Its hot breath was on his back, its jaws gaped wide. It had lifted him up and was shaking him to and fro like a rag doll. It shook him so hard, so fast, he could not breathe. His heart was exploding. It would burst. From within his heart would burst. . . .

The next time the trap door was opened, John Denning did not see the square of grey. From the bruises and the cuts upon his face and the broken nails on his torn hands, those above could see that, in the final throes of disease, he had flung himself repeatedly upon the walls of stone.

CHAPTER NINETEEN

People might still smile a greeting, but Abbotsfield had become a place no longer familiar with the sound of casual laughter. The wounds were too fresh. As life bravely returned towards the everyday, the voices in the village store were pitched a little lower and people consciously thought up in advance things that they might say to Mrs Park. The Dog and Fox, shut and shuttered pending its sale, epitomised the subdued mood. There were yellow patches on the green where the police had set up their headquarters.

For Jock Reid it was a thanked-for return to routine. Almost. He was still required to make frequent inspections of Gunn House. John Denning might return. Vandals might try to take advantage while he didn't.

This particular evening the Reids were settling down to supper later than usual. They were in a sombre mood. That evening Abbotsfield had paid its last formal acknowledgment to the recent past. In a tiny Norman church a service had been held to commemorate the lives of those who had died from the disease brought into their midst. A fresh grave for each of the church's eight centuries now lay beneath the yews and cypresses. The children of the village school were pledged to tend them. This, above all else, had brought fresh tears for Maureen Reid to shed. Not feeling up to cooking properly, she had fallen back that evening on the convenience of tinned steak and kidney pie.

It was quite tasty, though, all the same and she could see the look of tired exasperation across Jock's face when, as if planned deliberately, the front door went and someone came into the outer office.

'No peace for the wicked,' he mumbled. He swallowed an extra large bite to tide him over his absence from the table.

It was not quite sufficient. Standing waiting for him were Maggie Peacock, Mary Burns and Bill Gadney.

Jock smiled a general welcome.

'Hello, you lot,' he said. 'What can I do for you?'

'In the morning it flourisheth and groweth up; in the evening it is cut down and withereth,' Bill Gadney said.

A funny look was in his bulging eyes.

'Jock,' Mary said, 'we've got something to tell you.'

Rupert Marsh had gone through the past three weeks as if in a world of shadows. People had come and gone and asked him questions. Probably he answered them; told them something. They had gone away. He had probably eaten. He knew that he slept because ever earlier, every dawn, he woke again to the taste of ashes.

A residue of hope remained as he went through the motions. There was still no news of John. But waiting for news was so nerve-wracking that he chose to bank down almost all belief he'd ever hear good tidings again. His son-in-law, his friend, had died or (was it the worse?) had welshed.

And yet. Three times he had driven to Gunn House. Why, in a world of shadows, was hard to say. To see that everything was all right and as it should be? That was to mingle vinegar with gall. In the hope a light might once again show through a window and a prodigal be returned? A heart so heavy could not entertain so bright an expectation. Still, for the fourth time now, passing a Volkswagen bus, he drew near to the house.

A little awkwardly, carrying too much weight, he got out from the Rover. He paused at the front gate and, as he did so, hope flared like a leaping flame within that heart. A light had flickered somewhere at the back of the dark house. John had— No, it was gone. It had been a reflection. Another of fate's tricks. It had been a reflection from a car or from a street light. But no car had gone by. There was no street lamp near.

A flame! A flame! It was a burning flame! Suddenly he was trying to run forward but his knees were so sore, his ankles so puffed that he could do no better than flounder forward. It took forever to turn the corner, turn the second to the back. And with each moment the fire was taking hold. It was the study. It was inside the house and in the study. He lurched ahead and pressed his nose against the glass of the French window.

A great beard of flame leapt upwards in the room. Its brightness made everything clearly visible. It made visible the obscene parody of a Guy Fawkes bonfire housed within. A grinning dummy set in a chair was at the centre of the burning pile of broken furniture. Through the smoke and the twisting orange flames there came and went the image of a naked man, the hideously distorted features of John Denning. Great black blisters were bubbling forth upon his flesh. There was the smell of roasting pork. His hair, satanically, was alight.

Rupert Marsh went to scream. He only choked. A child locked out, he hammered out of instinct at the glass. The door gave way and as he fell a seizure skewered him straight through the heart. Eyes open, his body paralysed, he lay across the threshold and saw the flames come nearer.

The police, alerted by Jock Reid, were there before the fire-brigade. They found several awestruck villagers and a stark black outline of a house filled with roaring flame. The fire-brigade arrived. There was nothing they could do. For a long time the heat kept them at bay. Hours later as the dawn came they found indications of not one but two charred bodies amongst the smouldering ash.

The fire was naturally reported on the radio that morning. The same bulletins announced that due to the unstinting work of many organisations it was now felt that the further threat of rabies spreading had been removed. The disease had been contained. Except in a twelve-mile radius of specific points of original outbreak, all emergency regulations would shortly be lifted.

EPILOGUE

In commonsense fashion, the Government Research Establishment at Midhurst just beyond the twelve-mile radius outside Abbotsfield, had carried on with their normal work. Controls upon the animals offered up for vivisection were, it went without saying, total. Records were maintained in triplicate on standard forms. Above all, it was unthinkable that several long-running, on-going experiments should be rudely cut across by panic measures.

The gag went among the staff that it might be a dog's life in the Establishment but it was a dog's death out.

One of the animals currently blessed with a rapidly terminating stay of execution was a Jack Russell terrier. He went now by the number LK 8762. Once he had answered to the name Chip but he now answered to nobody. Under observation it was noted that the radio-isotope bombardment offered only token resistance against the leukaemia that devoured and wasted Chip's system. To the healthy, the inmates of all death camps are apt to look alike. With the possible exception of old Ted nobody from Abbotsfield would have been able to recognise the remnants of left-over life, and the dead, of course, bear no witness.

The scientist-technician most immediately concerned with administering LK 8762's therapy and monitoring the rate and progress of his death was Lilian Shaw. She was twenty-eight, unmarried and had taken a First in Zoology at St Andrews University eight years ago, and a Masters at London two years later. One Monday early in October, she slumped across her bench in a dead faint. Colleagues helped her to a bed in the Establishment's small medical quarters and shortly after she revived. The incident largely passed.

The sole aspect to linger (and that only on a gossip level) was the interesting insight into Lilian's subconscious revealed by her fervid mutterings in coming round. The same thing happened on the Thursday. The next Tuesday she collapsed while walking down the corridor to lunch. She took rather longer to revive this time and when she did so, Dr Raley, the Director of the Establishment, was sitting at her bedside.

'Oh,' she said. 'I've done it again.'

Dr Raley smiled.

'I'm afraid so,' he said. 'How do you feel now?'

'Not too bad,' Lilian said. 'Could I have a drink?'

'Of course,' Raley said. He got her a glass of water.

'You know,' he said, 'three times in a row has me worrying a bit about you. You know, wearing my paternalistic, head of a happy family hat. Something's not quite right.'

Lilian smiled and then looked anxious.

'It's a bit worrying, actually,' she said. 'Before it happens – just before it happens – I get this feeling I'm, well, losing control. Mental control. It almost seems I want, there's something in me wanting, to, well, freak out, I suppose you'd say.'

'Oh?' Raley said.

She badly needs a man, poor thing, was what he thought. She could be quite pretty, really, if she tried.

As if in confirmation of his theory, Lilian slightly blushed.

'Can you be a little more specific?' Raley said.

'I seem to get what I suppose a clinical psychologist would call morbid thoughts. I mean they're not thoughts at all really – just images. Violent images. In fact, of course, one knows that such things are perfectly normal. It's just—'

'Indeed.'

'—that having them at eleven o'clock in the morning is, well, a bit bizarre.'

Raley considered a few moments. He didn't wish to seem to pry. He shifted his direction.

'Forgive the descent into melodrama,' he said, 'but, we've all been reading the newspapers these past few days. Have you by any chance been bitten by one of the dogs?'

Shaking her head, Lilian cut him short.

'Absolutely not,' she said. 'Don't worry. We're all alive to that here.'

'Sorry,' Raley said. 'Just checking. Hmmn . . .'

Greying, gold-rim bespectacled, he had the well-dressed anonymity of a scientist whose promise had long since run to waste among the dry sands of administration.

'Look,' he said at last, 'I'm most inclined to take the obvious view. Your work here – I don't have to tell you – is first class. Absolutely conscientious. Perhaps even too conscientious. Perhaps you've been overdoing it a bit. Heaven knows, we all do sooner or later. . . . Now, let's be pragmatic. Today's Tuesday. Why don't you take the rest of the week off? No sick-leave nonsense, form-filling. Just stay home, rest, relax. If you feel like it, go off for a day or two. See a show. Whatever. A couple of bottles of Beaujolais probably wouldn't come amiss. If you continue to have these spells, well, of course, phone your doctor, phone us. We can obviously get you in the fast lane if it's something that needs, er . . . that sort of approach. But my reasonably educated guess is you'll come back on Monday next as right as rain.'

Lilian smiled and thanked him. She said that, yes, she would like to take him up on that. Things had been a bit hectic lately. She went home that afternoon. She did not telephone during the course of the week. On the Monday she returned to work. She said she felt as right as rain.

The stock room on the second floor was not in perfect order. As he surveyed the rows of bottles and flasks, Brian Gilman knew the confusion was mainly down to him. So what, he thought. As a lab technician at the top end of a low-scale grade it wasn't worth his while to work his balls right off. If he were to keep up the payments on his Lotus and his hi-fi it was about time he began to think about a move. And the other, of course. That cost. With slight, fair good-looks, Brian was something of a ladies' man. Those warm-up drinks, the steak house noshes after a petrol-sucking burn-up were casting a lengthening financial shadow over the various beds that followed. All right ... start with the obvious. The flat and round bottoms needed sorting out.

Getting a slight headache from the constant reaching up, bending down, he had been at work about ten minutes when the door opened and Lilian Shaw came in.

'Hello,' he said. 'How are they treating you?'

She had smiled and then he'd had to react a bit sharpish like as he all but knocked a 300 cl on to the floor. By the time he had it safely in its hole, Lilian was next to him.

'Brian,' she said in a strange way, 'you're the only one.'

She opened her white lab coat and he was amazed and impressed to see that she was wearing nothing underneath.

'Brian,' she said.

She took his hand and placed it on her. Christ, she had big ones. He'd never really noticed it on her. It must be all that porridge. Christ!

She had pulled him to her and was kissing with an inexpert passion. He felt the old old feeling. It was risky, a bit, but this was an offer he couldn't refuse. He'd never had a virgin standing up. Blimey! Over her shoulder he had seen she hadn't even locked the door.

'I'll lock the door,' he said.

As he came back he couldn't resist it.

'Why, Miss Shaw, you're beautiful,' he said.

'Brian, take your clothes off too,' she said.

For a sheep as a lamb. He was pretty well hung anyway. He pulled her to him.

She was a bit broad in the beam. For some tottering moments he had difficulty coping with her weight. Then he got it properly away. No virgin after all. Pity. Must be a story there. Christ! She was riding him like he was a favourite for the Grand National. Christ! Listen to her panting! He'd never known a woman come so fast. It made him ... he began to feel the thickening sweetness gathering beneath his spine. The rising, electric, drawing, surge was spreading upward in a fire of concentration.

'Yes! Oh yes!' she was beginning.

'Yes! Now!' he said. 'Yes!'

He felt a leaping agony tear at his chest. Blood bubbled

in his throat. His last sight upon this earth was of a woman's leering face. A red silence engulfed him.

His head snapped across her shoulder. Blood trickled from the surprised mouth. Lilian Shaw who had a first in zoology from St Andrew's University tugged at the scalpel that, with some precision, she had thrust beside Brian Gilman's shoulder-blade and on into his heart. She disengaged herself from his fresh corpse. Smiling, she began to wipe herself. After a while she took the scalpel once again in hand.

The cat that Norman Statham and Alex Trott were dissecting would once have made more noise in entering the lab. The two men never heard her. Lilian looked at their two bending backs. The lab coat that she wore was crisp and newly white. The look upon her face was one of irredeemable insanity. With a slight gurgle, she launched herself.

Alex Trott received a scalpel in the occipital lobe. He was dead before he slumped across his splayed-out handiwork. Hearing his slight cough, Norman Statham turned his head and turned it straight into a scalpel. A shape, a shrilly screaming shape, was slashing at his face with expertise. He screamed as blood ran down into his eyes and raised his hands in pitiable defence. A finger was half severed and then a blow knifed at his stomach's pit. He was a screaming child, the trolls had come for him and he had dropped his hands. The surgical steel sliced through his lips. Then nothing. As shock held off the pain another merciful five seconds, the shape was choking, clawing at its own throat in a paroxysm of coughing.

The pain began. The technicians and staff crowding through the door found a man staggering at them who in a joke had been doused with red paint. His oozing hands were to his face. His screams seemed very convincing. The man collapsed into their arms and showed a face ribboned in pulsing scarlet. Behind him was a man with a thing in the back of his head and on the floor, writhing in a foam-mouthed fit, Lilian Shaw. Even as they tried to take in the grotesque scene she groaned horrifically and rolled the whites of her eyes up in a locked exclusion of her pupils. She lay quite still.

Raley arrived as they began the task of staunching Statham's bleeding. Perhaps because his educated guess had been a touch wide of the mark he too blacked out. His number two, Aidan Bedford, retained his consciousness. He ordered Lilian tied up and with the rubber hoses from the bunsen burners they managed something tolerably secure about her wrists and ankles. They tried to work fast lest she revive on them. All the same there was one slight delay.

As they rolled her over to get at her arm, a bloodied plastic bag rolled from the pocket of her coat. Its contents were predictably those that a female sexual maniac might be expected to show morbid interest in. Nobody present was able – or cared to – identify the piece and some twenty frenzied minutes were spent searching until the remains of Brian Gilman were discovered. In the meantime, although shaking like a leaf, Aidan Bedford commendably returned to the task of securing the amputator's wrists. Understandably enough he was all fingers and thumbs, but with help, he managed to get the job done.

As he was collecting a sample of her sputum from her lips, Lilian Shaw came to.

'Gosh,' she said. 'Where am I? Hey, what's going on? Why am I tied? What's all this red stuff?'

Lilian Shaw was moved to the University College Hospital of Tropical Diseases. She had been sent on from Guildford in a desperate attempt on the part of the authorities to identify and analyse her sickness. Her periods of lucidity became increasingly shorter and less frequent. It was necessary for her to be confined to a strait-jacket. Dr Raley returned to the Research Establishment from her demented bedside to find Aidan Bedford tense with pale alarm.

'I'd like you to look at something, Henry,' he said.

Raley had never felt less like carrying out his duty in his professional career but he was considerably ashamed that he had fainted at the height of the previous day's crisis. Shame brought him to his feet and over to the electron microscope. In silence, the scientist and administrator in him slowly reasserting itself over the shaken man, he studied what he saw for some minutes.

'What is it?' he said at last.

Bedford shook his head.

'Tell me what you'd say it was?' he asked.

Raley considered.

'Well,' he said, 'it's not my field. And we've heard so much about it that maybe the thought was already floating in my head. But those characteristic bullet shapes, the projections on the sides. I'd start to say it could be a rabies virus. Only—'

'Those elongated fins or tails. They're not typical.'

'Right. If it is rabies, it's an unusual type.'

'A mutant type of rabies virus. Exactly what I wondered,' said Bedford.

He paused.

'The specimen came from Lilian's saliva,' he said.

As the silence in the room grew louder, the two men looked at each other in wild speculation. At bottom there was no love lost between them and neither cared too much to commit himself.

'Lilian assured me she'd received no bite,' said Raley quietly.

'I know,' Bedford said. 'Bit of a puzzle, all things considered.'

'I'd better phone this through to the University College Hospital,' Raley said. 'They will have to run a proper check. Just so we're covered anyway.'

That same evening Chip died, putting an end to his unvoiced suffering.

Six days later an official Department of Health limousine drew up outside the Midhurst Research Establishment. And within thirty minutes Dr Raley was shouting at the top of his voice.

'It's unthinkable!' he said. 'You cannot close us down! Some of our experiments are geared to five-year surveys and beyond!'

'It is, of course, regrettable,' one of the smooth ones said, 'but the Minister has come to feel it is inevitable.'

'Been made to feel, you mean!' Raley stormed. He sensed he was fighting a losing battle and he attacked the nearest target. 'Why is this man here?' he said. He pointed. 'What right has he to poke his nose in?'

The tall German with the look of unutterable tiredness about his eyes, his wan and drawn cheeks, seemed to brace himself.

'It is your Department of Health's decision, not mine. I am here in my supervisory capacity as an employee of the World Health Organisation.'

'And your capacity as an acknowledged authority on rabies. You won't deny that in that capacity you have strongly advised the Government to take this monstrous and high-handed step?'

'Dr Raley, it is essential that we most minutely examine all animals within these walls for rabies symptoms.'

'You'll find nothing. I deny rabies can be found here.'

'Dr Raley, it was you yourself who first suggested the possibility.'

'I spoke of similarity of strain. That's all. We know beyond all shadow of doubt that Miss Shaw has not been bitten.'

'Neither have the three other members of your Institute who have collapsed; nor have the eight members of the general public from this area.'

'Precisely,' Raley said smoothly. 'Rabies is a contagious disease. Therefore it is ruled quite out of the question.'

The tall German shook his head. He did it with great slowness as if not for effect but because he fought a great resistance – fatigue, perhaps, or disbelief.

'The symptoms have been adequately monitored,' he said at last. 'It is rabies. A form of rabies. A hitherto—'

'It can't be,' Raley said. 'There has to be contact. You just can't pick it up out of thin air like the plague.'

The German was upon his feet: was smashing his fist down like a hammer on the desk.

'UNTIL NOW, YOU FOOL,' he bellowed, 'UNTIL NOW! You

247

don't see what has happened? Or is it that you refuse to see just what has happened?'

'I strongly resent your tone. We have done nothing here to—'

'Wrong! I will tell you what you have done here. I will stake my reputation on being able to anticipate what an official investigator will soon demonstrate beyond dispute.'

Nobody now had the nerve to interrupt his savage indignation.

'I predict,' he said in a voice suddenly distant with weariness, 'it will be found that sometime in the past you received into this institute an animal outwardly no different from all the scores of others but, in fact, already nourishing the rabies virus in its nervous system. Along with so many others, as is the trend of one side of your research, you will have subjected that animal to radioactivity, possibly for a long period. Several weeks, perhaps. We already know that there are at least several strains of the normal contagious variety. A new strain has been created. A mutant virus.' He paused. 'It is exactly as you said that it was not,' he said. 'This is a strain where there is no need of physical contact for the disease to spread. Think of that if you dare. There is no need of a bite or a lick. This strain is not contagious. It is infectious. A thousand times more deadly. It is something you can pick up. Out of the air. It is like the plague. You can get it. I can get it. Whole populations – of your country, of any country, of the world – can get it.'

Once again he paused. When he resumed his voice was lower and more deathly flat than at any time before.

'A black door has opened and pushed us across its threshold into hell.' There was a shuffling of feet, and glances. There were embarrassed coughs.

The German sank back into his chair. For a long time he seemed to stare out of the window as if into an endless tunnel.

'What have you done?' Erich Kesseler said at last.

Dr Raley knew that this was all of the most absolute and vital concern if he was to maintain his right to keep the Establishment open and all that he'd fought so long for.

He must concentrate. But for a moment he felt quite bewildered. This terrible sore throat made it so hard to think.

He became aware that on his left, his colleague Dr Bedford, was giggling uproariously. It did seem rather funny in a way.

Four days later, Lilian Shaw died. She was the first.